DEADLY PLEASURES

To celebrate the Crime Writers' Association Diamond Jubilee, a collection of original stories from distinguished members of the CWA.

An eclectic collection of short stories from the following members of the CWA:
SIMON BRETT; ANN CLEEVES; LIZA CODY; LINDSEY DAVIS; MARTIN EDWARDS; RUTH DUDLEY EDWARDS; CHRISTOPHER FOWLER; JOHN HARVEY – CWA SHORT STORY DAGGER WINNER 2014; DAVID HEWSON; ALISON JOSEPH; PETER LOVESEY; CLAIRE McGOWAN; MICHAEL RIDPATH; PETER ROBINSON; CATH STAINCLIFFE; ANDREW TAYLOR; CHARLES TODD; MARGARET YORKE.

DEADLY PLEASURES

A Crime Writers' Association Anthology

Edited by

Martin Edwards

Severn House Large Print
London & New York

This first large print edition published 2015
in Great Britain and the USA by
SEVERN HOUSE PUBLISHERS LTD of
19 Cedar Road, Sutton, Surrey, England, SM2 5DA.
First world regular print edition published 2013 by
Severn House Publishers Ltd., London and New York.

British Library Cataloguing in Publication Data

Deadly pleasures.
  1. Detective and mystery stories, English. 2. Large type
  books.
  I. Edwards, Martin, 1955- editor.
  823'.087208092-dc23

  ISBN-13: 9780727897473

Severn House Publishers support the Forest Stewardship Council™ [FSC™], the leading international forest certification organisation. All our titles that are printed on FSC certified paper carry the FSC logo.

Printed and bound in Great Britain by
T J International, Padstow, Cornwall.

CONTENTS

FOREWORD

I have always loved short stories, ever since I first discovered the genre in my teens, when I was studying French literature, and came across the brilliant and often shocking tales by Guy de Maupassant. I did not realize at the time, but he had carved a reputation as one of the fathers of the modern short story. It is years since I last read his work, but I can still remember them as vividly as if I had read them yesterday. All of them were beautifully written, exquisitely crafted, and left a lasting resonance.

That to me is one of the great powers of a good short story. The sting in the tail of the tale that stays with you long after you have finished. And some, like Maupassant's, remain with you, and prick you, for all of your life.

There has been discussion over the years about the word count that separates a short story from a novella, and a novella from a novel. Very curiously, this has changed in the thirty-two years (gulp!) that I have been a published author. Back in 1980, when, with almost delirious happiness I signed my first ever publishing contract – for my spy thriller, *Dead Letter Drop*, with the then publishing house, WH Allen – I noted that the contract specified my novel should be a minimum of fifty thousand words. But for at

7

least the past twenty years, my publishing contracts now specify a minimum of eighty thousand, and anything less is considered a novella. But how much less than that to be a short story?

According to the *Guinness Book of Records*, the shortest ever recorded correspondence was between Victor Hugo and his publisher. He had just submitted the first draft of his manuscript of *The Hunchback Of Notre Dame*, and his accompanying letter was one digit long: It was simply a question mark: '?'.

The reply he received, a week or so later, from his editor, was equally short and succinct: '!'.

The shortest known short story, consisting of just six words, is attributed to Ernest Hemingway, although the provenance has never been conclusively substantiated.

'For sale: Baby shoes. Never worn.'

It is brilliant, because, like all great short stories, and indeed all great writing, it fires the imagination of the reader. So many questions, and no answers, except the ones we invent.

This latest collection by CWA members is a wonderful assortment of fine, inventive writing, and extremely ably edited by Martin Edwards. Every story in this collection is a gem, every story will make you pause to reflect at the end. And I guarantee there are some here that we will all remember in thirty years' time. You are in for a treat, I promise you!

Peter James
CWA Chair
2011–2013

INTRODUCTION

This year sees the Crime Writers' Association reach its Diamond Jubilee, and this anthology celebrates that notable anniversary in a suitably murderous way. From humble beginnings, when John Creasey convened a meeting of fellow mystery writers, and a dozen people who attended at the National Liberal Club on Guy Fawkes' Night in 1953 agreed to form the Association, the CWA has grown in size and reputation, so much so that today, it numbers in its ranks many of the world's leading authors of popular fiction. And it's good to know that John's son Richard is now himself a member of the CWA.

The distinguished list of contributors to this anthology includes a host of award-winners. Many are writers whose novels have been turned into highly successful TV series, such as *DCI Banks*, *Vera*, *Blue Murder*, *Cribb*, *Resnick*, *Anna Lee*, *Fallen Angel* and *Shetland*, while David Hewson has reversed the process by writing novels based on the Danish TV series *The Killing*. The generosity of these very busy people, who have taken the time to write original stories for the book despite their countless other commitments, speaks volumes for the affection and loyalty that the CWA inspires.

As usual with CWA anthologies, I've been keen to include stories by a number of authors who have not previously contributed to the series. And they have come up with some wonderful stories, as well as offering readers a chance to catch up with several of their favourite characters. Fans of Bryant and May, Jack Kiley, Inspector Rutledge and Michael Ridpath's Icelandic books are in for a real treat. Those, like me, who mourn the long-time absence from the bookshelves of that terrific character Anna Lee will find a clue to her fate – or perhaps it is a red herring? – in Liza Cody's contribution. There is a story from a talented newcomer to the genre, Claire McGowan, and as well as that Rutledge mystery from one (or rather two!) of the CWA's overseas members, the American mother and son partnership who write together as Charles Todd.

John Harvey's story is a fascinating take on a highly topical and difficult criminal subject, while Lindsey Davis has written a story which is a sort of companion piece to her contribution to the CWA's Golden Jubilee anthology, *Mysterious Pleasures*. Peter Robinson's story began life in a different form, as a piece for performance by Peter, alongside the legendary Martin Carthy, at the Beverley Folk Festival last year. The collection as a whole demonstrates the wide and exciting range of modern crime writing. The book offers police detectives and private eyes, humour and history, poignancy and psychological suspense. And ... well, as you will see, there are plenty of tales of the unexpected.

My original plan for this anthology was that, in reflecting the vibrancy of the current crime fiction scene, and of the CWA, it should contain nothing but brand new stories. Whilst the book was in the course of preparation, however, the CWA lost one of its most senior and distinguished members, and a former Chair, Margaret Yorke. Margaret, who died late in 2012, was not only one of the most gifted modern practitioners of psychological suspense in a domestic, but distinctly uncosy, setting, but also a staunch supporter of the CWA. She was an accomplished short story writer and had contributed to CWA anthologies in the past, most recently at the time of our Golden Jubilee. I felt it would be a fitting tribute to include one of her stories, which had previously reached only a limited readership, and I am very glad that her family not only agreed, but took the trouble to read through Margaret's stories, and choose one which they felt was a suitable example of her gifts.

It scarcely seems credible that ten years have passed since I edited the CWA's Golden Jubilee anthology, *Mysterious Pleasures*. The title of this collection, shared with an excellent American magazine edited by George Easter, again reflects the pleasures that fictional crime can offer. And for me, as editor, being the first person to read the stories written by so many superb writers has proved especially enjoyable.

My thanks go to all the contributors, and to Margaret's family, for their kindness in helping to make this book possible. I'm also grateful to Edwin Buckhalter and his colleagues at Severn

11

House for their support for the project, and to Peter James for his foreword. The result is a collection which will, I feel sure, give countless readers pleasure.

Martin Edwards

THE FRAME

Simon Brett

Simon Brett is the author of crime series featuring the actor Charles Paris and Mrs Pargeter as well as the Fethering Mysteries. His stand-alone novels include *A Shock to the System*, which was filmed with Michael Caine. As a writer for radio, he has been responsible for *No Commitments* and *After Henry*, which transferred to television. He is a former chair of the CWA and current President of the Detection Club.

Time was running out for Jake Parlane. It had nearly run out many times before, but this was a situation he couldn't shoot his way out of. Fact was, he was getting old.

Old and respectable, mind. A respectable citizen of Ruthville, California. He'd heard it said that the United States of America was the 'Land of Opportunity' where anyone could re-invent themselves quicker than a rattlesnake's strike. And anything that was true of the United States was even more true in the Wild West.

He'd never blamed himself for the crimes committed in the early part of his life. With an upbringing like his, what else could a boy do?

Also it had been an escape from the bullying evangelism of his father. All he could remember from his childhood was hard work and biblical quotation. His parents had been part of an early wave of pioneers from the East, trying to make a better living in the newest 'Land of Opportunity'.

Jake had been only four when they hit the trail, so he had the haziest recollection of the journey. But from the few things his mother had been allowed to say, it had been tough. She was never allowed to complain, though. In her husband's eyes complaint amounted to criticism of the Almighty. Though it was he who had made the decision to go West, it was not his plan but God's they were following. And if God chose to bring hardship their way ... well, they must just put up with it.

God did bring a lot of hardship their way. Only in the disillusionment of his teens, when he ceased to believe in parental infallibility, did Jake realise how his father must have been duped about the quality of the land he'd bought. Nearby them were riverside ranches with lush pasture whose owners stacked up the cash, but to make a living from the Parlanes' few acres of dust and scrub was virtually impossible. The earth was too shallow to produce anything but stunted crops, the greenery too sparse to support the family's emaciated cattle. 'Subsistence farming' was too good a description of what went on at the Parlanes'. When he bought the property, Jake's father had been shaken down like a country hick in a city casino.

Not that he would ever accept that unalterable fact. For him crop failure after crop failure just meant that the family was not working hard enough to realise the plan that God had so generously devised for them. Setbacks only gave out one message: they had to work harder.

And that meant everyone. The day after they arrived on their plot four-year-old Jake was set to work on the endless task of picking stones out of the areas designated for cultivation. And the same fate of back-breaking toil awaited the sequence of brothers and sisters who sprang with such regularity from the womb of his exhausted mother. They all worked all the time.

Their day of rest was Sunday. And that was a rest only from physical labour. Jake's father, by continued Bible readings and prayers, turned the day into one long church service. But not in church. Though there was a mission a mere two miles away, the Parlane family never went there. The patriarch preferred his own version of Christianity to any existing form. And he preferred the company of his own family to seeing people he didn't know. No one ever came to visit the Parlane farm. It was only later in life that Jake realised his father had been completely mad.

It was ironical that, in the vast empty spaces of California, the dominant feeling of the teenage Jake was one of claustrophobia. He was locked as firmly into the routines dictated by his father as he ever would be in a prison cell. And it was in hopes of escaping his incarceration that, at the age of eighteen, he stole his first horse.

A horse represented freedom. From his home

he could see the buckaroos roaming unfettered, rounding up cattle on the distant plains. He watched the Wells Fargo stagecoaches, raising clouds of dust as they charged past the drooping locked gates of the Parlane farm. Everyone else was going somewhere. If he had a horse he could go somewhere too.

Of course Jake had no skills as a horse thief. No skills as a horse rider either. That was what was really pathetic about his theft. He tried plenty of times, but he never even managed to get up on the horse's back before the local sheriff was out calling at the Parlane farm.

And then all hell broke loose. Jake's father was not only furious that his son had been guilty of a crime; what seemed to irk him more was that this criminal behaviour had brought outsiders into their private compound. He disowned his son on the spot, telling Jake he'd never be welcome in the family home again (which was not without its irony, because he'd never felt welcome there in the first place).

Maybe with parental support at his trial Jake Parlane would not have got such a stiff sentence. Maybe not. Horses were what kept the local economy going back then and stealing one was regarded as a pretty serious crime. The owner of the horse Jake stole reckoned the five years the boy got handed down was too lenient.

Jails back then weren't fancy places. Men were there to be punished and a lot of the punishment came from other prisoners. Much of what happened during those five years Jake just blanked out. One thing for sure, though, prison was a brutalising experience. The experience that led to his life of crime. You came out of prison hating the world and wanting revenge on it. So he didn't feel guilty about any of what came after.

Jake Parlane sat back in his leather armchair and sipped at the fine bourbon in its cut-glass tumbler. The matching decanter stood on the table at his side, just where Aaron had left it. Jake looked across the veranda and beyond his garden to the neat little town of Ruthville, where the evening lights were beginning to come on. And he thought back to the past.

Back to the whisky they all drank then. God, it was rough. Didn't do to ask too much detail about how it was made. Not like this smooth, oh so smooth, bourbon that was as delicate as a breeze on a cornfield.

And he thought of Ruthville back then. It was a joke. Not just the place, the clumsy dusty assemblage of unfinished wooden huts, but the name, that was a joke. Ruthville. Named after Ruth, the broad-limbed – and broad-minded – Irish madam who supplied the girls in a shed that couldn't aspire to the title of a brothel. The place was named for her as a joke. The joke was forgotten, but as the town became respectable the name stuck. Jake Parlane chuckled. He wondered how the new pastor who'd just taken up his post in the gleaming just-completed Ruthville Episcopal Church would react if he knew where the name came from. (He also enjoyed the irony of the pastor not knowing the provenance of the

17

large contribution to the church building fund made by respectable parishioner Jake Parlane.)

Thinking of Ruth made Jake remember good times spent with her. And with some of her charges. Quite a lot of her charges. Back in the days when that kind of thing mattered.

His eyes homed back in on the frame. The ornate carved frame that stood on his fancy writing desk. The frame that had once contained the photographic image of Jake Junior.

And he thought again of the bullion secure in his cellar. And where he wanted it to go when he was no longer around.

Jake Parlane felt a pain in his gut. He took a long swallow of bourbon, and that numbed the griping. For a while. But he knew the time would come – and not too far away – when even whisky wouldn't kill the pain.

Yup, time was running out.

If Jake Parlane was going to see through the plan that had been forming in his mind for some months, soon he'd have to make a start.

He'd lost count of how many people he'd killed. Never kept a tally. He'd just done what was necessary for the job in hand. And if that involved someone dying ... well, everyone in his trade took the same risks. The next day Jake Parlane could be the one who got shot.

The Black Cross Gang. Most of them had served time in prison. Most had the same desire as Jake to be revenged on the world that had put them there. The polite world of small-minded men who thought about town planning and worried about keeping their neighbourhoods 'respectable'.

Funny that in later life Jake Parlane should have joined their ranks. The bullion he had stolen was worth more than he could ever spend. And, as shoot-out followed shoot-out, there were less of the Black Cross Gang claiming a share. When gang members died, it didn't worry Jake Parlane much. They were just gunslingers with whom he'd drunk rough whisky, shared danger, shared jokes – and sometimes women. But they were guys who knew the risks. Nothing to get sentimental about.

Jake Junior, though, that'd been different. He'd never been sentimental about the boy growing up, had no interest in him until he could hold his own with a six-shooter. And even then the boy was no damn use, too much of a dreamer. When he was allowed to join them, so far as his Paw was concerned, Jake Junior was just another member of the Black Cross Gang. And not one of the best members. Never going to match up to the exploits of his Paw.

And Jake Junior's death was kind of his own damn fault. The boy had been on reconnaissance duty, detailed to check out how the land lay at the River Crossing Bank. And he hadn't done a good job, dreaming as ever. Otherwise he'd have known that when the horse team had been attached by ropes to the window and pulled it away – along with half the wall – they'd find the bank full of the River Crossing sheriff's men with guns blazing.

The Black Cross Gang lost a lot of men that

day. Including Jake Junior. Served the little damn fool right.

But Jake Parlane had been surprised by how much the death affected him. Not right away, but kind of gradually. He let the boy's mother do all the weeping and wailing for the first few months. Her feebleness made him downright angry. She kept cradling that ornate wooden frame with the picture she'd had done of the boy by some huckster with a camera. Cradling it and weeping. Jake kept saying the kid would never have amounted to much, but that didn't stop her. Her constant tears got on his nerves. Finally, in a fit of fury he'd ripped the photograph out of the frame and torn it to shreds. That had, needless to say, prompted more weeping and wailing.

It was only after he'd destroyed the boy's image that he started to miss Jake Junior. Never told the boy's mother, of course. Jake Parlane had learned in prison how not to show pain. And, anyway, she died a few months later. Sentimental folks might have said her end was hastened by their son's death. But Jake Parlane didn't mix with sentimental folks, so he never heard them saying it.

Somehow doing the jobs the Black Cross Gang had always done didn't seem so satisfying with the boy gone. Not that Jake Junior had been the only one who'd been lost at River Crossing. The Black Cross Gang's numbers were down. Also, the lawmen were starting to show their first signs of efficiency. The banks and mail coaches were getting better security. Robbing them wasn't quite so much fun anymore.

One last job and maybe it'd be time for Jake Parlane to hang up his boots. Even to become a respectable burgher of the clean, expanding town of Ruthville. He'd always known he could buy respectability there. Pump enough money into a few civic projects, pay for the construction of the schoolhouse, contribute handsomely to the building fund for the Episcopal Church ... that'd do the trick. Reinventing oneself was still easy in the US of A. Most everyone in the West had a background to hide, and nothing hid it more efficiently than money.

One last job then. For many years Jake Parlane had been planning a raid on the Wells Fargo office in Santa Veronica. Now the moment had arrived to put his plans into action.

Then he'd change his life. Forget the Black Cross Gang. Forget Jake Junior's mother. Forget Jake Junior.

But even after he'd done the job he never threw away the wooden frame that had held his son's photograph.

When Jake Parlane started planning the Santa Veronica job, he knew it was going to be different. In the old days a bank raid hadn't needed much finesse. Only research you needed to do was have a gang member check the comings and goings of stagecoaches to the bank. Pretty soon your man got to recognise the ones that were delivering coins or bullion.

Way you got in was usually by pulling out a barred window – and often the whole wall – with the horse train. Just like they'd done at River

Crossing. Six horses in harness – sometimes stolen off Wells Fargo – but they didn't have a stagecoach to pull, just hooks attached to the window bars. Fix them up, and firing a few shots from your Colt near the horses' feet usually got them moving real fast. Not many windows could resist that kind of force. As a kind of private joke, members of the Black Cross Gang referred to the procedure as the 'Wells Fargo method'.

Jake Parlane was always present when they were doing a job, but he let Aaron take charge of the actual break-in. A former slave who'd survived the Civil War, Aaron was ageless and tough as ebony. He'd served his time in prison too and, though he'd been brutalised by the experience, he was fiercely loyal to Jake.

In the event you didn't have a team of horses to hand for the Wells Fargo method, you just chucked in a couple of lighted dynamite sticks. That usually brought the bank managers and tellers out in a state more than ready to hand over the keys to the strong room. Any who resisted got shot. Then the Black Cross Gang loaded up with the coins or bullion and hightailed back to their hideout.

But the Santa Veronica job was going to take more preparation than that. Wells Fargo were getting cannier all the time with their security. They had more men riding shotgun on their stagecoaches and they were making their buildings more robust. What had once been wooden structures were now stone and brick. It'd take more than a team of six horses to pull a window out of their new Santa Veronica office.

For the first time in his career Jake Parlane required the services of someone on the inside.

Finding the right guy didn't prove too difficult. Aaron was despatched to do a bit of scouting round the Santa Veronica saloons. Back then the landlords weren't too fussy about the colour of a man's skin. It was the colour of his money they worried about. And Aaron always seemed to have plenty of that.

So he lounged around the bars, almost unnoticed, steadily drinking rough whisky, his dark eyes beneath their hooded lids taking in everything. Occasionally he would engage some loose mouth in conversation. He always chose the drunks, who were less likely to remember the direction of his questions and more likely to be indiscreet in supplying him with information.

He discovered that the agent who ran the Santa Veronica Wells Fargo office was called Colonel Tuckett. He apparently said he'd been promoted to that rank in the Union Army during the Civil War, but local opinion doubted the claim. Rumour also maintained that he didn't attain the standard of incorruptibility required by Wells Fargo in their agents. Loans he organised through the company usually involved kickbacks for himself. Tuckett was also a strong supporter of Santa Veronica's saloons and brothels, where his transactions were rumoured not to involve money changing hands.

When Aaron reported his findings, Jake Parlane knew they'd got their man. All they needed to do was to sort out the deal with him. Aaron was despatched back to Santa Veronica to carry out the next stage of the plan.

It was easy. Aaron followed the oblivious Colonel Tuckett after he'd locked up the Wells Fargo office for the night. The agent didn't mount his horse but led it, suggesting he wasn't going far. Sure enough, the animal was tied up outside a saloon and, about an hour later, led to Santa Veronica's most popular brothel. Colonel Tuckett's business only detained him there half an hour, and he returned to his horse in the empty evening street to find himself confronted by a tall black man pointing a Colt in his face.

When Aaron suggested they ride out of town together, the agent was too scared to disagree. Nor did he make any demur when the former slave insisted on blindfolding him and leading his horse the last couple of miles to the Black Cross Gang hideout.

When the blindfold was removed Colonel Tuckett found himself facing Jake Parlane, behind a table on which were a bottle of rather good bourbon and two glasses. Coercion always remained a potential threat, but the gang leader thought he'd try the soft approach first.

And he found the Wells Fargo agent very amenable to his suggestions. Fright and greed proved to be a very successful combination. Colonel Tuckett seemed to be moved less by the implicit threat of violence against his person than by the prospect of creaming off a bit of the loot for himself.

He agreed readily to notify Jake when the next consignment of gold coins and bullion was due into the office. And he agreed to being tied up at his desk the night when the Black Cross Gang broke in.

'But that does raise a point, Jake.' He and Parlane were already on first name terms, Jake and Clinton. 'Breaking into the new office ain't going to be so easy. That place is built to last.'

'Dynamite?' his host suggested.

The agent wrinkled his face in wry disapproval. 'Seems a pity to destroy a new building.' He was clearly rather proud of his workplace.

'So what do you suggest?'

'Simplest thing would be – I unlock the front door and you come in.'

'Suits me.' Jake Parlane grinned. 'Might give you a bit of an explanation problem, though ... you know, to the high muckamucks at Wells Fargo.'

'Sure would ... if they think I'm the one who did it.'

Parlane was instantly alert. 'What you saying?'

'I'm saying I do it, someone else takes the rap.'

'You got someone in mind?'

'New junior clerk started in the office only a coupla months back. Name of Nathan Pooley. Head-in-the-air kinda kid. Lives in a world of his own.'

'The perfect fall-guy?'

'You said it.'

The details were quickly agreed. Two nights after the consignment arrived, Colonel Tuckett would work late, ensuring that he kept his junior clerk behind too on some invented emergency task. At ten o'clock, when all the good citizens of Santa Veronica would be getting ready for bed

25

and the bad citizens would be in the saloons, Tuckett would allow Nathan Pooley to go home, saying that he'd lock up. As soon as the boy was out of sight, the Black Cross Gang would enter the premises, tie up Colonel Tuckett, take his keys to the strong room and make off with the coins and bullion.

At this point in their planning Jake suggested that, in the cause of authenticity, his boys might also rough the agent up a bit, but Tuckett wasn't so keen.

Then, a couple of months after the raid, by which time any suspicions of the colonel – if there ever were any – should have died down, Jake Parlane would arrange for an ingot of the bullion to be delivered to a safe drop-off point. From where Colonel Tuckett would collect it at his leisure. And they'd be square.

The agent submitted willingly to having his blindfold reinstated and being led on his horse by Aaron to a spot from which he was free to ride back to Santa Veronica. Both he and Jake Parlane had the feeling that, not only had they made a good business arrangement, they'd also met a like-minded spirit.

Come the day of the job, everything went like clockwork. Colonel Tuckett found some spurious extra work to keep Nathan Pooley in the Wells Fargo office until ten o'clock, then duly released him to go home. The clerk checked that his boss really didn't intend to lock the door after him. (That was the normal practice; after office hours the building was kept locked at all times, even if there were still staff inside.) But Tuckett reassured his junior that he was about to leave and would lock up himself.

Then he just waited for the Black Cross Gang to arrive, which they did within half an hour. The colonel didn't get the full complement of villains inside the office, just Jake Parlane and Aaron. But there were others on the street watching, guns at the ready, in case anything went wrong. And also there was a covered wagon out there to take away the loot.

Even though he was not going to change his mind about retiring, Jake could see the appeal of this new style of crime. With the help of an inside man, the business was easy, even a bit formal, just like going to a bank to draw out money during office hours. Except, of course, he was withdrawing more money than the average customer.

Colonel Tuckett was very pleased to see them and eager to demonstrate that he had not been idle in anticipation of the raid. With pride he showed them one or two little refinements of his own that he had added to the plan. Most of these were designed to build up evidence of Nathan Pooley's guilt.

For example, in the waste bin by the junior clerk's desk Tuckett had planted a scrap of paper. It appeared to have been torn from a large sheet, but the remaining text read clearly: '...ORTH OF RIVER CROSSING AND WE'LL PAY YOU THE MONEY WE AGREED.' Then, above the words 'BLACK CROSS GANG', a cross had been scrawled.

'I can write my own name,' Jake Parlane

objected.

'Yeah, sure,' Colonel Tuckett apologised. 'Guess I got carried away a bit there.'

'Mind you,' Jake went on, 'I wouldn't have signed it on a note like that. Nice to keep a few secrets from the lawmen.'

'That's what I was thinking,' said the colonel hastily, though he'd only just thought of it.

To curry more favour from his new friend, he then showed off the bag of gold coins he'd secreted behind one of the drawers of Nathan Pooley's desk. Together with a copy of the strong room key that he'd had made.

'Looks like the perfect frame-up,' said Jake.

Colonel Tuckett smiled with pleasure. It was nice to get that kind of commendation from a professional.

'Right, let's load up the goods and get you tied up,' said Jake Parlane.

'Yes, but it won't be too tight, will it?' pleaded the Wells Fargo agent.

'Gotta look convincing,' said Jake, with a rather cruel little smile.

He let Aaron do the tying up. He knew the ex-slave's work would be convincing. Even down to the handkerchief stuffed in the man's mouth and the bandanna tied tightly to keep it in place. Colonel Tuckett's eyes looked terrified. Even more terrified when Aaron asked casually, 'Sure you don't want me to rough him up a bit, boss? So's it looks like the real thing?'

Jake was tempted for a moment, but he curbed the instinct. 'No, let him be.'

Then he went to open the strong room door

28

with the key hidden in Nathan Pooley's desk.

When they saw how many bags of gold coins and ingots of gold bullion there were, they sent out for more members of the Black Cross Gang to help load the covered wagon.

As they passed his office for the final time, Jake Parlane grinned at Tuckett and gave him a little wave. The colonel was in no position to give him a wave back.

The frame-up went as smoothly as the job itself. When a very uncomfortable Colonel Tuckett was released by his senior clerk who was first into the Wells Fargo office the following morning, he immediately pointed the finger of blame at Nathan Pooley. The accusation was repeated when Santa Veronica's sheriff arrived. Searches of the premises fairly soon found the planted evidence and before noon the junior clerk had been arrested on suspicion of collaborating with a criminal gang in the perpetration of a robbery. Bail was not mentioned – which didn't make a lot of difference, because the boy didn't know anyone rich enough to offer it. And Nathan Pooley was incarcerated in the county jail to await trial.

He didn't have to wait long. Rough justice was favoured round Santa Veronica, and speedy justice too. Within a week Nathan Pooley was up before judge and jury in the town's gleaming new courthouse. Jake Parlane thought about going to the trial. Nobody in Santa Veronica would recognise him as a member of the Black Cross Gang – they always masked their faces with scarves when they were working. And as for the 'WANTED DEAD OR ALIVE' notices, they were a joke. Jake had managed to leak into the River Crossing sheriff's office the information that the Black Cross Gang was led by a guy called Garton Crail. He'd even had smuggled in a photograph of an evil-looking desperado, whose mugshot now appeared on all the posters. So Jake Parlane could go wherever he wanted with impunity.

And the Santa Veronica Wells Fargo office had been his final job. There would be a kind of neatness in seeing it through to the end. So he did attend the courthouse for the trial.

What became clear from the start was that, in selecting Nathan Pooley as his sucker, Colonel Tuckett had done a great job. The boy was the archetypal dreamer, who seemed to move in a world detached from the real one. Like Jake Junior he was never going to make anything of himself, he'd never be anything more than a waste of provender. And he had no support in the courtroom. Apparently, on hearing Nathan had been charged with the crime, his father had disowned him.

Obviously that detail carried an air of familiarity for Jake Parlane. But the similarity of their experiences didn't make him feel any sentimentality or pity for the boy. It was an interesting coincidence, was all.

What was also interesting was how little effort Nathan Pooley put into defending himself. He seemed in a state of shock, unable to recollect details of what had happened on the night of the raid. His attitude to Colonel Tuckett was still that of a junior employee, deferential, unwilling to contradict anything said by his boss.

Which of course meant the court proceedings were pretty short. With a defendant apparently unwilling to defend himself and the abundance of planted evidence that had been found, the guilty verdict came as no surprise.

Nor, really, did the sentence. Sentencing in that time and in that place was an inexact science, pretty much at the discretion of the judge. Therefore dependent on prevailing political conditions, whether he'd woken up with a hangover, was suffering from dyspepsia or had just had a row with his wife.

As the American West struggled for respectability, there was a lot of pressure in aspiring towns like Santa Veronica to cut down the crime rate and to make examples of malefactors. Wells Fargo were particularly keen to improve their standards of reliability and safety for their clients' money. So scapegoats were needed. It was therefore no surprise to anyone when the judge sentenced Nathan Pooley to twenty years.

As with Jake Junior's death, it took quite a while before Jake Parlane thought any more about Nathan Pooley. According to plan, the Black Cross Gang was disbanded. All remaining loot was divvied up between the surviving members, with Jake as boss taking a very substantial lion's share. Some of this he invested in land and real estate. In particular he bought a handsome plot on the outskirts of Ruthville, on which he built a

31

fancy villa surrounded by verandas. Inside, it was equipped with all the latest newfangled inventions for gracious living. Just the kind of house his wife had longed to live in all her life. Though in fact she'd died before the first brick was laid.

Jake Parlane lived alone. Sure, he had cooks and maids and grooms, but none of them stayed overnight on the premises. Aaron slept in a room over the stables. He'd been offered a room in the main building, but turned it down. Compared to the places he'd bedded down for most of his life, the stables represented luxury. Besides, despite his emancipation, it still didn't seem right to him that a man and his servant should sleep under the same roof.

For a time there was speculation in Ruthville that Jake Parlane might marry again. Given his obvious wealth, he was not an unattractive prospect and there were a good few young ladies of Ruthville who set their caps at him. But nothing proceeded beyond civilities. He seemed to have lost interest in that kind of thing.

Jake Parlane enjoyed the irony of his respectability and he enjoyed his new life. Unexpectedly, he found pleasure speculating in real estate and construction, and he was good at it. Without risking any of the bullion hidden in the foundations of his villa, he made a lot of money. And – an incongruity that gave him especial delight – he banked it with Wells Fargo.

Life was fine and dandy. His evenings Jake spent in his leather armchair, drinking perhaps a little too much of the excellent bourbon he could now afford. And if it was too much, who cared? Not a great deal he had to get up for in the mornings, just keeping an eye on his latest construction project and letting his money accumulate. He could afford to stay in bed till the headache disappeared.

There was only one cloud on Jake Parlane's horizon, but it was a cloud that just kept getting bigger. He found he was becoming obsessed by the empty wooden frame on his writing desk.

'It's one last job, Aaron.'

The ageless black face showed little reaction. Just a slight wrinkling of the lines around his dark hooded eyes. Jake knew he had engaged the man's interest.

'Thought we done the last job at Santa Veronica, boss. Surely you ain't short of cash?'

'No, got more of the stuff than I know what to do with. That's kinda the problem. Why we need to do one last job.'

Aaron was silent, letting his employer outline the plan at his own pace.

'Fact is, I been thinking too much about Jake Junior. Maybe I never did all I shoulda done for the boy.'

'You couldn'ta stopped him being shot, boss. 'Less you'd forbidden him to come on the River Crossing raid. Boy sure wanted to come on that job. Wanted to prove hisself to you.'

'Hm.' Jake Parlane was thoughtful. 'Maybe so. But maybe it was because I put too much pressure on the boy that he wanted to prove himself.'

'Hey, what kinda talk's this, boss? You getting

33

soft in your old age?'

'I think maybe I am, Aaron.'

'Well, you just fill up your glass with bourbon and start drinking. That'll get you thinking better thoughts.'

'No, Aaron. I've made my mind up. I gotta see this thing through.'

The ex-slave shrugged. 'You the boss, boss.'

'It concerns that boy Nathan Pooley...'

The black face showed no surprise. No reaction of any kind, as he said, 'You tell me what you want me to do.'

Now that Jake Parlane was a pillar of Ruthville society, it wasn't appropriate for him to be too closely associated with the job, but he had complete confidence in leaving the arrangements to Aaron.

There weren't many of the Black Cross Gang still alive. A few had continued in the same business and got shot in the line of duty. Some had banked their cash and followed their boss down the path to respectability. But there were still three or four who were up for the job Aaron offered them. He told them there'd be no pay-out because there wouldn't be any loot, but he offered them fees. Their residual loyalty to Jake Parlane made them all say they'd do the job for free.

And the method they were going to use went right back to the early days of the Black Cross Gang.

The evening before the day that had been scheduled for the raid, Aaron sat up late with Jake Parlane. He watched him wincing at the griping pains in his stomach, pains that the bourbon could numb for decreasing lengths of time. The ex-slave felt concern for his boss, though no one would ever have guessed it from his expression.

'You double-checked everything, have you, Aaron?'

'Double-checked it good, boss. Bribed one of the prison guards, it was easy. He's given us the information we need.'

The prison he referred to was the one where Nathan Pooley was serving out his twenty years. A lot of Californian malefactors with long sentences were sent up to San Quentin or the more recently opened Folsom Prison, but the nearest penitentiary to Ruthville was a dilapidated wooden structure in Santa Veronica. Because the foundations had already been laid for a new modern replacement, very little effort was put into maintaining the old building. Which was ideal for Jake and Aaron's purposes. Ideal for the Wells Fargo method.

'And I bring him straight back here when we sprung him – right?'

'Right.' There was a silence. 'And do you want to know what happens then, Aaron?'

'Only if you want to tell me, boss.'

Jake Parlane grinned through his pain. 'Sure I'll tell you.' He pointed to the large new brass and rosewood camera on a tripod in the corner of the room. 'Soon as Nathan Pooley gets here, I take his picture. And when the photograph's developed, I put the damn thing in that frame over there.'

'The one that used to have the picture of Jake Junior in it?'

Jake nodded. There was the smallest of shakes from Aaron's head. He didn't understand his boss's reasoning, but he wasn't about to ask any more questions. What Jake Parlane did was up to him. And to Jake what he was doing made perfect sense. It was a way of setting the record straight. He'd always dismissed Jake Junior as a milksop, never taken the trouble to find out what was going on in the boy's cloudy brain. And there, languishing in prison was Nathan Pooley, an innocent who lived in the same kind of dream world as Jake Junior had. To Parlane's mind, what he was planning to do for the victim of Colonel Tuckett's frame-up would offer some kind of restitution – a resolution even.

'And when I've taken Nathan Pooley's photograph,' he went on, 'I serve him a good meal, best meal he'll have tasted for thirteen years. And I let him drink the best liquor he's tasted probably in his entire life. Then I show him to a bedroom where there's the softest mattress he's ever encountered, certainly a lot softer than the stinking palliasse he's been sleeping on in that prison.

'And the next morning, after he's had the best breakfast of his life' – Jake Parlane reached into the pocket of his vest and produced a large key on a gold chain – 'I open the strong room in the cellar and I show Nathan Pooley the bullion down there. And I tell him it's all his.

'Then you, Aaron, load the bullion on to the covered wagon, and you ride with him to the

36

Mexican border – you know, the place we always used to get through...' The black man nodded. 'And once you've seen him safely across the border, you come back here, and Nathan Pooley starts living his new life.'

One of Aaron's rare smiles crossed his face. 'You sure are, boss. You're getting soft in your old age.'

Everything worked like it should have done. The Wells Fargo method was as effective as ever, the team of horses ripping the window out of Santa Veronica's crumbling penitentiary. The prison guard's information proved to be correct – it was the window of the cell in which Nathan Pooley was incarcerated. And soon the boy, once again in the same state of shock he had been at his trial, was safely ensconced in the covered wagon.

Serendipitously, there had been other prisoners in his cell, so the operation became a mass breakout. And the prison guards and the Santa Veronica sheriff's men were so busy chasing the fugitives who'd escaped on foot that they didn't even notice the one who'd been driven away.

It was nearly dark when Aaron delivered Nathan Pooley to Jake Parlane's villa. The young man had said nothing on the journey, not questioned why he had been sprung, where he was being taken. Maybe thirteen years in prison had taken away his will, had inured him to the idea of having no control over anything that happened. Aaron was not surprised; he'd seen that happen to plenty of men when he'd been inside.

Nor did Nathan Pooley show much reaction

when they arrived at the house in Ruthville. He appeared not to recognise Jake Parlane – and there was no reason why he should have done. Jake had been just another face in a crowded courtroom thirteen years before. And the young man submitted meekly to having his photograph taken.

And once that had been done, Aaron reckoned it was time for him to go and bed down in the stables.

The scene that greeted him in Jake Parlane's drawing room the following morning was not a pretty one. Aaron had seen enough dead bodies in his time – indeed he'd been responsible for a lot of them – not to be squeamish, but this was something else. It was clear that, before he died, Jake Parlane had been cruelly tortured.

Needless to say, there was no sign of Nathan Pooley. Nor of the bullion from the strong room in the cellar. Nor, when the stables were checked out, of the covered wagon.

Aaron couldn't have said he was surprised. He knew – and he'd have thought Jake Parlane should have known too – that prison sure does brutalise a man.

THE PIRATE

Ann Cleeves

Ann Cleeves began her crime writing career with a series featuring George and Molly Palmer-Jones, and followed it with books about a cop from the North East, Inspector Ramsay. More recently, she has won acclaim for two more series, featuring Vera Stanhope and Jimmy Perez respectively, which have been adapted for television as *Vera* and *Shetland*.

The girl arrived into the island on the launch; she'd obviously just come into Scilly because she had luggage with her. I was sitting outside the Turk's Head to catch up with the news and see who was coming into St Agnes and she caught my eye immediately, striding up the jetty with the other tourists. She was wearing a leather three-cornered hat, battered and well-worn, and a red jacket. In my head I named her the pirate. She was straight-backed and fierce and I liked her at once. She reminded me of myself when I was a young woman, free and easy and at the art school in Falmouth. Now I'm sixty. I watch and I paint and I worry about dying. The drink or the smoking will kill me soon.

I saw the girl later from the front window of my studio. I grew up in this cottage and it came to me when my parents died. It has a view over Periglis, perhaps the best view in the island. I've been offered a fortune for the house, but what would I want with more money? My paintings sell well, and occasionally dealers come on the scrounge, prodding and flattering, and asking to buy direct, but I always send them away. My agent looks after that sort of thing. He rips me off but I can't be arsed to make a fuss. Life's too short. Each day here, with this view and the light over the lake and the sea beyond, is enough. That and the possibility that one day I'll make a perfect piece of art.

The girl walked past the lake with her rucksack on her back. No man. I liked that too. I've had lovers of course and was considered rather wild even in middle-age. There were no children. I still brood about that on the bad days when my work's not going well. I think I might have made a good mother. But for years I've been on my own and these days that's how I like it.

On an impulse I followed her and watched her put up a tent at the campsite at Troy Town. She was deft and competent and it was like seeing a ghost of my younger self at work. I didn't approach her and she didn't see me. I knew that I'd bump into her again. St Agnes is a small place and islanders and trippers all end up in the Turk's Head eventually.

She was there the following night. I was drinking my second rum and shrub and she came in, not cocky, as if she owned the place, but

40

confident as if she had a right to be there. She wasn't wearing the hat. A shame. It suited her. She bought a pint of bitter and sat next to me. Perhaps she knew who I was. People turn up occasionally, students and the stalkers of the art world, hoping that I'll do them a quick sketch on the back of an envelope. Islanders take pleasure in pointing me out because they know that I hate it.

'You're Maureen Dance,' she said. Her voice was West Country. Not Cornish. Devonian perhaps.

There didn't seem any point in answering.

'I've got some questions,' she said.

I didn't want to talk to her there with everyone staring. But I wanted to meet her again. Close to, I saw she had a strong face, dark eyebrows. The face of a pirate. I knew I'd like to paint her.

'Come to my house,' I said. 'Tomorrow night.'

She nodded and went to the bar. When I left, sure-footed up the path despite the dark, she was playing darts with a bunch of the boys who row in the gig team.

I thought of her all day. Of that distinctive face and the pirate hat. I imagined the painting that it would make and the story which the picture would tell. Of a woman easy in her own body, searching for answers. When she turned up at the cottage I was ready for her. There was charcoal and paper on the table and I sketched all the time that we talked.

The next morning the tent was gone and the campsite was clear. No rubbish. Just a patch of

41

flat grass to show that she'd been there at all. Again I had the strange sense that she was some sort of ghost, disappearing as soon as she'd arrived. I got on the phone to one of the boys who crews on the launch.

'The young woman who was camping at Troy Town, did she go out to St Mary's today?' From St Mary's you get the ferry or the plane to Penzance. It's the only way out of the island.

He hesitated for a moment. He's not the most observant of men.

'The girl with the hat. She's not here anymore.'

'Oh yes!' He's suggestible as well as a bit stupid. If anyone else asks he'll remember that he saw her, that he caught a glimpse of her leaving the island with the other visitors.

I recognised the hat as soon as I saw it on the day that she arrived. It had belonged to my favourite lover. He came to the islands when I was forty and he was my last chance of passion and a child. He spent a summer with me in the cottage, writing his poetry, helping out in the bulb fields. Occasionally he'd disappear back to the mainland and on his final visit to me he'd left his hat there. When he arrived in St Agnes without it I should have realised it was a sign.

That last night, I'd opened wine to celebrate his return. In the cottage near Periglis he took my hand and told me that he was leaving me. He had a woman on the mainland who was carrying his baby. Someone closer to his own age.

The bright young woman was his daughter. She should have been *my* daughter. She was here

42

with questions about the man who'd disappeared before her birth.

'I talked to his friends.' She saw that I was sketching her but she didn't seem to mind. 'They said he'd spent time here on St Agnes and that he'd always loved your work.' She looked up frowning. 'You know what happened to him, don't you?' And glancing up she saw the big oil that I'd painted of him. It hangs on the wall over my desk. Her mother had probably shown her photographs and she recognised him immediately.

Now she's lying in the sandy soil in my garden, buried next to her father. I couldn't take a chance, you see. She was intelligent and persistent and could start rumours and an investigation. She was a free spirit and for a while nobody will miss her and when they do they'll look for her on the mainland. Her rucksack, with the hat stuffed inside it, has been dropped into the water to be taken away by the strong neap tide. I couldn't let her live. There's too much to lose. There's this view and this light over the water. The chance that one day I'll create a perfect piece of art.

DAY OR NIGHT

Liza Cody

Liza Cody is a former editor of the CWA anthology, whose award-winning first novel, *Dupe*, introduced the private eye Anna Lee. A series of books featuring Anna resulted in a television adaptation starring Imogen Stubbs. More recently, Liza's novels have included the *Bucket Nut* trilogy, *Gimme More, Ballad Of A Dead Nobody* and *Miss Terry*.

I'm Shareen Manasseh. Sometimes I wish I had a plain name like Anna Lee which any fool can spell. Anna Lee is a good name – short, fits on a granite headstone in big gold letters. According to the date underneath she died two years ago. She's remembered – there were two fresh vases of daffodils and jonquils and a spray of yellow roses.

Rachel Silver said, 'I should have come before now. I feel terrible.' A slow tear rolled out from under her dark glasses and stuck quivering in the make-up on her left cheek. Her hands, in their beautiful suede gloves, fluttered. She seemed to be waiting for me to reassure her so I said, 'It isn't easy for you.'

'No. I don't come to the UK often. I was ill when she died – a basket case.' Again she waited for me.

'You'd been through a lot,' I supplied.

'No one gets it.' She sighed. 'When I first saw her ... Anna ... she was the first human being I'd actually *seen* ... they told me ... in nearly five months.'

I said, 'They told me that too.'

'He kept me in total darkness. Can you imagine that, Shareen? I thought I was blind. You've no idea how badly light hurts the eyes.'

Now her eyes were shielded by dark lenses. Her perfect hair was raked by a breath of early spring wind but it soon settled back into its smooth shape. She hunched her shoulders as if she were freezing. Why, I wondered, was she putting herself through this? It was like watching someone poke at an unhealed wound with a fork.

'I almost forgot.' She took a round white pebble out of her pocket. 'From Atlantic City,' she said and placed it on Anna's black granite stone.

I followed her example. Before leaving home I'd picked up a mundane grey pebble from the stock I keep for my grandmother's grave. Even in the matter of stones this woman made me feel like a pauper.

I said, 'Shall we get out of the cold?'

'It *is* pretty bleak,' she agreed, surveying the grassy ground with its network of narrow paths – a crematorium at one end and a chapel at the other. There were no lichen-covered stones, no Victorian angels or whimsical mausoleums. All the trees and dead people had been planted less

45

than a decade ago.

'Soulless,' I said without thinking.

She let out a sharp gasp and a brittle laugh.

We sat in her chauffeur-driven car with thick privacy glass between us and the driver. It embarrassed me. I wished my chief inspector had picked someone else to come to London for this assignment. I didn't know why it was a police job anyway. All he said was, 'You've heard of hush-hush? Well this is hush-hush-hush.'

Rachel Silver said, 'He kept me in the dark. I didn't know what time it was. He fed me through a letterbox in the door, shoving food through like I was a dog.'

The car had bulletproof glass, a bombproof chassis and a security driver. I'd been issued with a regulation Glock sidearm. But Ms Silver did not look like a woman who would ever feel safe.

'First he gave me a ham sandwich.' She shuddered. 'I said, "I can't eat this." He said, "You'll eat what I give you or you'll starve." I made up my mind to starve. But I'm weak.'

'That's not weakness. That's survival.' I felt she'd put me in the place of her therapist or someone whose responses she could rely on for comfort.

But she rejected the comfort. 'It was the thin end of the wedge. He said, "You've been here a week" and I said, "Okay," even when I was sure it was only a couple of days. And then it got so I wasn't sure. He'd shove a sandwich through the door and say, "Lunch," waking me up from a sleep so long I thought it must be breakfast. I'd say, "Is it day or night?" just so I could hear a human voice. He said, "It's what I say it is, stupid, dirty woman." And that was better than when he said nothing at all.'

Kept in the dark and lied to. A bit like what my last boyfriend did to me. He too was the kind of guy who could convince a woman that day was night. But he wasn't a terrorist so I had no reason to believe he was torturing me.

'He wouldn't let me wash,' Rachel Silver went on, her head bowed. She seemed to be giving a speech she'd returned to over and over again. Maybe her therapist said, 'Keep telling the story till it loses its power.' You'd think if that was going to work it would've worked after two years.

I was uncomfortable sitting so close to a woman who'd been brainwashed and tortured. But the chief inspector said, 'Do whatever it takes. The deputy commissioner in London doesn't want the Americans complaining we can't do a simple job right.'

I tried to change the subject. 'How did an English private detective get involved with this?'

'Anna Lee?' Rachel sounded as if she'd forgotten that she'd come all this way to visit her rescuer's grave. 'She was working in the States and I guess my dad had her on salary. He likes the British. Maybe Military Intelligence kinda seconded her because she was an outsider. I don't know. The operation's still classified. Even from me. They think I'm a security risk.'

'That's a bit unfair.'

'They think I was "turned". They still monitor

my calls in case *he* gets in touch. But he wasn't just one person. I think there were five of them but only one mattered. I had to call all of them "Friend". The real Friend escaped in the gunfire. They say he shot Anna Lee the next day. She was gunned down in the street, you know. It was like a regular LA gang drive-by, but they insist it was Friend because she was the only one who saw him and he was the only one who could possibly recognise *her*. He's still out there.'

She was beginning to sound like a tired little girl. I said, 'Do you want to go back to the hotel?'

'I'm exhausted.' She took off her dark glasses and I turned to look out of the window.

I knew, because it was in the notes I'd been given, that when she was rescued, Rachel had an eye infection so bad that she lost the sight of one of her eyes and eventually it was removed. I didn't want to see what was left.

I couldn't understand the resentment I felt – the toxic twin emotions of pity and impatience. 'Get over it,' I wanted to say. 'Your daddy's a senator. You're rich. You can afford all the therapy, all the security you'll ever need. What about the woman who got tangled up in US politics almost by mistake and lost her whole life? Is that what you rich important people do – hire someone to stand between you and the bullet that's meant just for you?' Because today it was me and my stupid little sidearm that I'd never actually used outside a firing range. We'd been chosen to stand between Rachel Silver and her own personal bullet.

I spent the night at her hotel in London because she wanted an escort to the airport the next day. Then she was gone.

After that, to my surprise, I was sent to a newly built office in South London to talk to a quiet man who called himself Mr Franklin. I was warned that he would want to see my case notes. He stood with his back to the window reading and turning pages. I sat on a hard chair embarrassed about my spelling and handwriting which I'm sometimes told is 'chaotic'. He didn't comment on either. Nor did he give me back my notebook.

All he said was, 'Thank you so much for your help on this one, Ms Manasseh. In the unlikely event that anyone should ever approach you about this matter I'd appreciate it if you'd report back instantly to Deputy Commissioner Mead in the Met – not anyone from your home station. Is that clear?'

He pushed some papers across the desk, and that's how I found out that the previous day's assignment was an Official Secret.

I don't know how it happened – I never said anything to *anyone* about my trip to London – but word spread all the way back to Bristol.

A few nights later I was in the Cat-Man-Do bar with a couple of women from work. Teresa said, 'We saw your ex last night, Shareen.'

'Al?'

'How many exes you got?' Jude said. 'You ain't *that* popular.'

'Yes, Al,' Teresa said. 'He said you were on Special Assignment to MI5 in London.'

I didn't know quiet Mr Franklin was MI5, so unless Al was bullshitting Teresa, he knew more than me.

I said, 'He's shitting you, Teresa. It's what he does.'

Jude said, 'He was with Norm and Kill-Bill from the armoury. They said you were issued a sidearm.'

How did they know that? The Glock was issued in London, not locally.

'It's a joke,' I said. 'I passed the basic course, that's all. *You're* both more qualified and experienced than I am.'

Teresa said, 'They told us it was 'cos you were babysitting that Jewish senator's daughter who was taken hostage by terrorists, remember? Because no one knows you in London.'

'Al said they always pick an "exotic" for a job like that,' Jude added.

'*Exotic*?'

'Don't get all huffy,' Teresa said. 'It doesn't mean you're more expendable.'

'Don't count on it,' Jude said with a malicious grin. She tipped the last of her pint down her throat. She still looked thirsty.

'Never mind her,' Teresa said, while Jude was at the bar getting the next round in. 'Al was talking about you and she hates that. You're supposed to be history.'

'I *am* history,' I said sadly.

'That's not how Al sounded last night.'

'Well, *he's* history,' I said even more sadly,

50

because he'd been gone for six weeks and I was lonely. It was dark in the bar, and 'Fix You' was playing on the sound system.

Al used to like me. Now he likes Jude. Or maybe it was exclusively about sex, and liking had nothing to do with it. I don't understand men at all.

Deputy Commissioner Mead told me that when Anna Lee freed Rachel Silver she ran into the underground bunker while a fire-fight was going on around her. He said that she had to dress Rachel in Kevlar and carry her out in her arms – not because Rachel was too weak to walk but because she didn't want to go.

As well as the eye infection, she was treated for multiple STDs. But according to the debriefing reports, she never once, even to this day, described a rape. Deputy Commissioner Mead doesn't understand *women* at all.

Sitting in the Cat-Man-Do bar, listening to 'Fix You' and waiting for Jude, who hates me, to bring more drinks, I knew I should leave, phone Mead and tell him that the Official Secret wasn't a secret – that my colleagues, the men and women I'd been trained to protect and rely on, were asking questions.

Jude came back with a pint for Teresa, a pint for herself and nothing for me.

'*Jude*!' Teresa protested, laughing.

'She get's stupid and slutty when she's rat-arsed,' Jude explained sweetly. 'That's what Al told me.'

'Al would never lie to *you*,' I said. 'You remind him too much of his mother.'

51

Jude threw knives with her eyes. Clearly she knew as well as I did what Al thinks of his mother.

'We used to be mates,' Teresa said. 'There's way more interesting stuff to talk about than some twat-faced bloke.'

'Like what?'

'Like what Shar was doing in London. Like, how does Rachel Silver look now? She used to be one of the Ten Best Dressed Women in Washington. Like were the terrorists really behind that private eye's murder or is it just another conspiracy theory?'

'Is she even dead?' Jude said. 'Kill-Bill says she's prob'ly in some witness protection programme somewhere. She's the only one who actually saw the leader. He was long gone by the time the military stormed the bunker.'

'They killed the other four,' Teresa said. 'Anna Whatsername can't be protected twenty-four-seven. Unless they fake her death and give her a new identity.'

'Don't look at me,' I said because they were both waiting for me to comment.

'You're involved.'

'I'm *so* not involved. Where on earth are you getting your gossip from?'

'Already told you,' Jude sighed impatiently. 'Al said you never listen.'

'Oh do shut up,' Teresa said, but added, 'Don't go, Shar. She's just trying to wind you up.'

'Failing,' I said. 'I'm bored.' And I left.

I should've rung Deputy Commissioner Mead. I

should've said, 'Teresa, Jude, Norm, Al and Kill-Bill know where I was last week. Everyone's speculating. No sir, I never said a word. I'm not trying to call attention to myself by implying I'm part of an international operation. Possibly the leak started in the armoury. Am I an exotic?'

I work with these men and women every day of the week. On duty, they watch my back and I watch theirs. Even Jude and Al. Rule number one – you don't rat on your mates. Never.

But a week later, at three-thirty in the morning, the phone rang. I wasn't even awake when I put the receiver to my ear.

A man's voice said, 'Shareen Manasseh? This is a friend.'

'Who?' I mumbled.

'A friend.' He sounded angry. 'We've got your number. We know your family. Believe that we can reach any of you any time we want. Your phones are monitored. We'll know if you contact anyone. Wait for our instructions.'

'Al?' I mumbled. But he rang off.

He wasn't Al, he rang on my landline, he sounded English – not like my idea of a terrorist, he...

I got up and dressed like a spook or a burglar, all in black. I left the flat, got in my car and drove randomly through Bristol streets for five minutes the way they taught us on the Security Driving course. I hardly needed to – it's easy to see if anyone's following you in a residential area at three-thirty in the morning. The streets were empty and dead.

What made me think the voice on the phone

was Al's? Maybe I'd been dreaming about him. Maybe it was because he used to ring at odd hours, sometimes pretending he was talking to a sex line. I miss him.

I drove out to the motorway and kept driving till I reached Leigh Delamere Services. Then I stopped and, from a payphone, called the number on the card the deputy commissioner had given me. It connected to voicemail. I left a message.

I went home and waited. And waited.

No one called or came so I drove to work at the usual time and spent the day in the usual way, rushed off my feet, dealing with urgent trivia and writing it up afterwards.

'Come for a drink?' Teresa said as we went off shift.

I didn't want to go home alone so I accepted even though Jude and Al were among the crowd going to the Cat-Man-Do.

But when I got to my car I found Mr Franklin waiting quietly in the shadows.

We drove to the underground car park behind the Watershed near the docks. He didn't speak until we were facing the water. Then he said, 'Tell me everything, Shareen – verbatim if you can.'

When I'd finished, he said, 'Is that all?'

I was offended.

He said, 'I know, he told you he was a friend and threatened you and your family in very few words – I mean, what else has been happening?'

I'd thought about this question all day and prepared an answer. I said, 'Everyone at my station and everyone at the armoury knows about me escorting Rachel Silver in London. Everyone's speculating.'

'Everyone? I'll need names.' He looked at me. I looked at him.

He sighed and said, 'Ms Silver is still emotionally attached to the leader of the cell who kidnapped her. She was half blinded and so messed up inside that she will never be able to have children, but she's still loyal to him.'

'She's frightened.'

'So are you. Rightly. But because she persists in a bad choice there are some very dangerous people still out there. One of whom you spoke to last night.'

'She didn't have a fair choice.'

'Agreed. But the choice about who you're loyal to should be reassessed in the light of new information. Mindless fidelity to a person, a group, a policy or a nation ... well, you, Shareen Manasseh, should know better than most what that can lead to.'

I was grateful to him for not naming the fascistic, extremist groups I might be afraid of. He gave me time to think.

In the end I said, 'Is this why you always choose "exotics"?'

'I beg your pardon?'

'Because we don't quite feel we belong? And so it's easier to persuade us that our friends aren't our friends?'

He looked me straight in the eye, holding contact till I looked away. His eyes were pale grey and his gaze was as frank and honest as Al's.

In the end I chose the family I'd left behind and I gave him the names he wanted. I gave up my friends.

As far as I know nothing at all happened to Teresa, Jude, Al, Norm or Kill-Bill. But I was transferred from Bristol to South London by the end of the month. I was given no choice.

I never heard another word from the so-called Friend. Why had I thought the caller was Al? It wasn't Al but it might have been a voice I'd heard recently. An English voice. Like quiet Mr Franklin's. So I began to wonder how 'friendly' *he* was. Could the threat have been made just to manipulate me – to expose a leak? Was Mr Franklin another man who could convince a woman that day was night? I wondered about this for quite a long time.

I never saw or heard from him again. And I still don't know who to be loyal to, unless it's to family – even though I left them behind long ago.

ZOUNDS!

Lindsey Davis

Lindsey Davis is a former civil servant whose first novel set in Ancient Rome, *The Silver Pigs*, introduced Marcus Didius Falco, and launched a highly successful career. She was the first winner of the CWA Ellis Peters Historical Dagger, and received the CWA Cartier Diamond Dagger for a crime-writing career of sustained achievement. She too has chaired the CWA.

'Zounds!' exclaimed Sir Mawdesley. 'You look as if you had seen a—'

He stopped. He was a gentleman, Sir Philip Sidney's friend. He accounted some words uncouth in company. Among his present companions it was polite to exclude 'ghost'.

The unlikely group who now spent time together – considerable time, indeed eternity – were Sir Mawdesley Mordaunt deceased, the under-rated Elizabethan poet; the late Major Penitence Rackstraw of the New Model Army; the White Lady, who was reputed (if she really existed) to be the tragic daughter of the Victorian industrialist Lord Mordaunt, a man ennobled for dubious reasons (aren't they all?); and the

57

Black Dog, a creature whose habits were utterly medieval.

Both Sir Mawdesley and the White Lady's supposed father, whom some called 'Mad Jack', were previous owners of Mordaunt Castle, that great stronghold of crusading knights which proudly towered over Mordaunt Street, in Middleswick. It had been rescued from bankruptcy by a businessman of impressive corruptibility, then turned into a money-spinning gem of the heritage industry, in which it is a sought-after privilege for historic buildings to be haunted, though perhaps not by the Black Dog.

Major Rackstraw acknowledged his companion with a slight squaring of the shoulders, a soldier's gesture. If he had not been dismally pale to start with, he would have looked so now, for something had indeed startled him. Shock had turned him into a subtly more substantial figure. As he materialised in his buff coat before Sir Mawdesley in the Postern Tower, his appearance was oddly colourful, his aura unnaturally warm.

'We are in extreme danger, sir!' he exclaimed, full of urgency. 'Traitors have a plot in hand.'

The White Lady manifested herself with an abrupt shimmer, manipulating smelling-salts for Rackstraw's use if he would accept; he did not. Although normally seen in desolate tears, she never let snuffling block her nose for excitement. 'You look distressed, Major!'

Her male companions exchanged nervous glances. One thing was known about the White Lady, if she ever existed: thwarted in love, she died of misery. Both Sir Mawdesley and the Major suspected she was looking for some new man to be miserable about. Neither wanted it to be him. Death had not deprived them of their senses of self-preservation.

'Sit down and recover,' she twittered. Major Rackstraw sighed. The woman had never understood supernatural life. Ghosts rarely sit down, even in a crisis, and there is a really good reason for that. Their ectoplasmic ability to glide through matter tends to deposit them in a heap on the floor.

'Whatever unmanned you?' demanded Sir Mawdesley, knowing the Major was a steady, thoughtful type. He had a mind of his own, as rebels usually do. He had besieged this castle valiantly in the Civil War and always said his capture was due to a Royalist trick.

'Did you *feel* something?' trilled the White Lady. 'A scent? A chill breath of wind?'

Ignoring her fancies, Sir Mawdesley asked gravely, 'Did you *see* something, sir?'

'It is...' began the Major slowly, 'a strange *device*.' He faltered, grasping for vocabulary.

The Black Dog gambolled out of the ether, reeking of bad breath and ready for play. 'Good boy,' said Sir Mawdesley absently as the Dog placed huge paws upon his shoulders and licked him. Mist wreathed about its head. Its red eyes blazed. Sir Mawdesley, once a fond owner of hounds, disentangled himself from the ghastly vision. The Black Dog rolled over on its back, seeking more attention. Major Rackstraw prodded its matted fur with one platform-soled

Roundhead riding boot, in a vague attempt to scratch its belly.

'Was it a Presence?' shrieked the White Lady, once more convincing the others that, tragic life aside, she was a damn silly girl. Even the Dog slavered uneasily.

'Where lies this Thing, sir?' rapped Sir Mawdesley.

'On the roof of Mad Jack's Tower.'

Sir Mawdesley sniffed down his long Elizabethan nose. His own improvements to this castle had been solid; he sneered at all subsequent flimflam. 'After my time!'

'Oh a pleasing bauble,' teased Rackstraw, who liked taking a poke at aristocrats. 'I should be obliged for your opinion, sir.'

'Let's to it then!'

On leaving the courtyard all the ghosts paused, needing to readjust to the current ground level, which had been raised when Capability Brown conducted a garden makeover. The Dog dashed ahead, scampering over a drawbridge. 'I hate,' confided the Major to the poet in a low voice, 'how that accursed creature snaps through a man's ankles.'

'And then disappears while you are shaking it off,' agreed Sir Mawdesley, glumly tidying his ruff. The Black Dog tunnelled straight through the Mound, which the Major remembered as an artillery base for cannon. Nowadays it was a children's play area, where some of the little hooligans seemed able to see them and hurled insults.

Noticing the Major reminiscing, the White Lady said, 'I mean to ask you one day, Major, why you came back?'

Major Rackstraw faintly smiled. He did not answer, for it was not yet a question. Mad Jack's daughter had been here with them less than two centuries, but even she hoarded interesting conversations, as precious as her long jet necklace, to be used in their eternal future, when desperate. Eventually, his answer would be that he never left. Captured during an attempted sally, he was thrown into the Dungeon, a desperate hole where his name was still shown to visitors, hopeless graffiti he had incised on the damp stonework alongside scratches counting off his days there. He died a prisoner.

One day, before neglect claimed him, a considerate jailer had thrown him a volume of Sir Mawdesley's poems. These were elegant comments on Time and Mortality – an irony, since their author had now defeated Time and immortally paced his own grounds as the most civilised of spirits. Alongside him, Rackstraw marched with sombre tread, eternally awaiting ransom which his friends never sent.

The White Lady had strayed into spectredom at the castle, like a house guest who was deaf to hints to leave; there was no question she had been and always would be socially inept. The Black Dog hung around as a wraith because he liked being a menace.

In the afternoon light the ancient walls and towers assumed a uniform mellow gold. This was no grey, bleak stronghold where discomfort ate into people's bones. The castle was sturdy, hospitable, business-like – and even in winter much visited by the public. At the massive oak door to Mad Jack's Tower, two anxious female tourists asked the ghosts the way to the public toilets. This question was regularly put to them by those who were spiritually aware yet who could not notice signs. Sir Mawdesley shuddered and gloomed, to no avail. Haunting could be hard work.

'Quiver your aura, Major!' giggled the White Lady. Rackstraw briskly waved an arm in the right direction. He honoured the rule that spirits could only hold conversations when warning sinful people they must change their lives or be damned. Needing a house-of-easement hardly came into that category. Warning people to repent and reform was equally hard work and the ghosts rarely bothered with it. This explains why so many serial killers, bankers and women who present decoupage kits on TV shopping channels are allowed to continue their terrible careers.

Even though the castle guide always told tourists the ghosts' stories when she reached the darkest passageway, they were rarely recognised as the apparitions who had been described. Now, they overheard the two women with the urgent mission decide these must be members of a historical re-enactment society, perhaps later to offer a presentation on ancient warfare or cookery. Annoyed, Major Rackstraw whizzed himself up the Tower at high speed.

'Shall we walk?' Sir Mawdesley asked the girl.

An unnecessary question. Of course they walked; that is what ghosts do. They progressed up the winding stair with graceful motions, barely needing to lay hands on the sturdy rope banisters.

They left the Black Dog outside, tearing about with its ears back in crazy joy at not being alive.

The door at the top of the stairs was never padlocked, even though the roof was too dangerous for public access. A simple notice that said 'No Entry' was sufficient because visitors to monuments know better than to start bells ringing by defying the rules. When they wanted to be mischievous, the ghosts had been experimenting in how to set off alarms, but so far a method had eluded them. Ghosts are never frightened by high rooftops that lack sensible parapets, so the poet and the girl eased themselves gently through the door and looked around without a qualm. They existed despite the worst Health and Safety can achieve.

'Oh what do you think it will be?' trilled the White Lady.

'An anxious soldier's lively imagination.' Sir Mawdesley nodded at Rackstraw as he wafted ahead on the leaded roof. 'He longs for the clash of arms and roar of cannon. Be calm. It may be a harmless bauble.'

'Some bad trifle he ate,' the White Lady agreed, missing the point as usual. Major Rackstraw could not remember the last time he had food. Even when he was alive, his cruel guards only threw him occasional mouldy crusts. Poor diet as a prisoner had killed him; at least it could not harm him now, or even cause him flatulence.

He pointed coldly to an object which lay against one of the fantastically ornamented drainpipes installed by Mad Jack. 'It is some piece of ordnance – yet none I ever saw in our armies.'

Sir Mawdesley bent and peered, with eyes that had ceased to be perfect after too many evenings penning quatrains by candlelight. He made out a solid box shape, with wires attached.

'A bomb!' declared the White Lady. This was nothing new. Foreign anarchists had brought bombs to London in her day. She was not troubled by this one; it could not hurt a woman who had already died heartbroken. Then as soon as she had spoken, second thoughts struck. 'Calamity! We cannot allow incendiarists to destroy my Papa's Tower!'

Sir Mawdesley felt almost pleasure at the thought of Mad Jack's aberration being blown to smithereens; he had always denounced it as a gimcrack Italianate pleasure pavilion and could not bear the thought that conservation officers, those tasteless hirelings of Machiavellian government, adored it.

The Lady's indignant tone brought the Black Dog bounding up to see what he was missing. Before they could stop him, he pawed the device then peed on it; fortunately paranormal widdle, though steamy, had no effect.

The Major considered logistics. 'On any other tower, where the walls are constructed thick, it would blast the top off with small damage, but this flimflam is liable to collapse entirely, crush-

64

ing everything below. We must take action. The bombarillo could be slung over and dropped below, to explode safely in the moat.'

'Good sir, not by us.' Sir Mawdesley was right. Ghosts could not lift objects physically. Nor was it likely they could attract attention and bring human help; the castle guide always declined to notice them, for she was a retired bookkeeper with a certificate in heritage studies, despite which she called herself a sensible woman. Although the security man felt funny in their presence, he knew he ate too much junk food so put his collywobbles down to that.

Major Rackstraw assigned himself the role of reconnaissance. He wafted to the belvedere, whence he looked down into the car park at the rear of the stables. The others flittered up to join him as he checked for enemy incursions or unwelcome earthworks. The area was virtually empty, with just a few vehicles, most of which were parked as close to the castle entrance as possible. One car stood alone, oddly situated under trees at the far end. Rackstraw sent the Black Dog to have a look and the creature reported two figures were sitting inside, apparently not doing much.

'Who visits our castle yet does not enter?' demanded Sir Mawdesley.

'Our terrorisers, by Noll's nose!' decided the Major.

'Awaiting the outcome of their iniquity!'

Major Rackstraw knew the car park was where he and his companions had once laid siege to Mordaunt Castle; they too had had to endure many hours of inactivity before the defendants emerged and captured him. He agreed that the two dallying individuals were quite likely those who had placed this device on Mad Jack's Tower, now waiting to observe the damage. He pointed out that visitors and staff were in danger of their lives if the tower fell on them. Whatever purpose the bombers had, such violence was a criminal act; it was contrary to the Ordinances of War to assault civilians or even attack property.

Sir Mawdesley, who enjoyed disputation, commented that those who took up arms in what they considered to be a worthy cause, generally believed they had no choice; they were driven to defy an authority that would not respond to reasoned debate. For them, their actions were not crimes. The crime, for them, was committed by those they opposed. He felt no need to draw comparisons with the Parliamentary rebels of the Civil War – though the White Lady did. Major Rackstraw would have reddened with annoyance, but was constrained by his ghostly rank, which made him remain ghastly.

Mordaunt Castle must be a target because it represented the fabric of the nation. They discussed what kind of people might be making this gesture. Sir Mawdesley thought marauding Musselman corsairs wanting slaves for their galleys, with the Major inclined to believe they were heartless European mercenaries paid by malignant monarchists to oppress the common people. The White Lady had no opinion. She had been brought up to bear nineteen children and thus have no time for politics. It had been thought sufficient preparation for the expectation of dying in childbirth to teach her to press flowers in tissue paper.

The three human relics were united in loathing the threat against innocent people. Death had not dwindled the consciences they possessed in life. They decided it must be their task to prevent murder.

'"The World's a bubble and the life of man Less than a span",' quoted Sir Mawdesley, thinking, I wish I had written that. Even so, yearning in perpetuity for the existence he had lost, he was highly opposed to the taking of life prematurely.

The Black Dog was indifferent to issues of conscience, but he wanted to thwart any activists who might be claiming to assert his animal rights. In life, the Dog had belonged to an extremely stupid peasant who had taught him deep suspicion of anything new – even if it might improve his own existence. Eventually, he bayed crazily and then produced a surprisingly good suggestion for dealing with the dangerous object: he had a friend in town, as all dogs of character do. His friend was not bound by normal spiritual rules about physical motion.

The others saw the sense of it. They would fetch the poltergeist.

Few people were aware of them as they made a stately procession from the Main Gate, floating out by the In lane, straight through a delivery van. Projecting themselves onto Mordaunt Street where, apart from the Dog, they rarely ventured, they gazed around curiously. Sir Mawdesley's eye was caught by a wine bar, decorated for Christmas with cotton-wool snow; in his previous life he had enjoyed a glass of sweet Canary. The White Lady exclaimed over the prettiness of the tinsel and lights, while the Dog tried in vain to knock over a Christmas tree. Major Rackstraw, who belonged to a strict puritan sect and abhorred Christmas, shuddered with dread that he was about to be lured into merriment or debauchery.

'No time for it, man!' quipped Sir Mawdesley cheerfully. He decided to come back later, without the others. Poets get better reviews if they have a reputation as debauched.

Much of Mordaunt Street was less vibrant. Shops stood boarded and empty. Times were hard. Commerce was in decline and the once thriving high street faltered; businesses had closed as clothes and craft shops ceased to make a profit. A bookshop which had barely survived on goodwill finally failed too. Sometimes sad incomers took short leases, then disappeared in turn. Abandoned premises that were no longer used even as charity shops stood as symbols of recession. The phantoms drew into themselves, as they understood with a sense of extra melancholy that where they now walked was in its death-throes, the very place now ghostly. Decay was something they knew intimately.

But people must eat (unless they are captives in dungeons). At the far end of the failing street stood a large modern supermarket. The Dog hitched a ride in a shopping trolley while the others slipped in unobtrusively.

The store was a revelation to them. Alarmed by its single-minded crowds and astounded by the aisles of unfamiliar produce in colourful packets, they made all speed to track down the polter-geist. He was invisible. Even the ghosts only saw him as a stressed bubble of spiky air, tearing about like a teenager. They gave thanks that in their times adolescents and children were minia-ture adults, subdued in the presence of their elders. Those were the days. Supposedly.

They corralled the poltergeist against a BOGOF rack. Introducing themselves, they ex-plained the problem at the castle. They told him how he could assist, since his role in life, or in the afterlife, specifically allowed him to lift things and move them about.

'Can't help. Gotta wreak havoc here!' The poltergeist was tempted, nevertheless. He led a miserable life-after-death. He wanted to retrain as a computer virus. Nobody noticed his in-store efforts. When he moved packet soups to the olive oil shelf or skimmed frozen fish packets down the hardware aisle, the staff just supposed this carnage had been caused by their customers, while customers blamed devious marketing decisions. He got no credit.

'Hmm,' mused Sir Mawdesley cannily. 'When our grenade goes off, methinks there will be a fine show of noise and fire!'

If the poltergeist had possessed eyebrows, they would have shot up. The poet had rightly guess-ed that the mad force of supernature loved ex-plosions. 'Can I play with the matches?'

'The device may roar enough, without benefit

of a match cord,' the Major assured him.

'Oh, you've twisted my arm!' Without more ado, the poltergeist wrapped himself up in a carrier bag, and bowled out of the store ahead of them, having fun looking like litter. Halfway up Mordaunt Street, a council refuse collector tried to spike him.

Back at the Castle, Major Rackstraw groaned. A coach had arrived, disgorging a large party who were now ensconced in the Buttery with hot tea and scones while they listened to a lecture on medieval fortifications. The guide trundled through her Motte and Bailey notes while people gave most of their attention to scoffing. The Buttery was manned by broad-bodied Middleswick women who made all the cakes themselves; crockery clearance was womanned by a youth in the throes of a sex change. Despite the generous portion control exercised by the counter-queens, his role was to ensure a fast through-put in order to boost scone sales.

The Major gasped, 'We must hurry! These innocents will swarm out into peril any moment.' He blew on the carrier bag, still containing the poltergeist, whisking it up in a puff of gesticulating plastic to the roof of Mad Jack's Tower.

'Ow!' complained their assistant, screwing himself out into the fresh air.

'Less fuss, varlet!' ordered Sir Mawdesley. 'Now, good Major, tell us your plan.'

Major Rackstraw smoked his long clay pipe as he honed final details and gave everyone their orders of the day; Sir Mawdesley, whose life predated Walter Raleigh, looked on enviously at the Virginian tobacco smoke.

'What about the two men lurking in their carriage?' asked the White Lady. The man-mad girl never forgot the presence of anything in britches. She took it upon herself to go and inspect them, bringing back news that two figures were still visible, keeping suspiciously low in their seats. 'As soon as they see they have been thwarted, they will make off at speed. We cannot let them escape!' Because of her pitiful history, she knew everything about men wanting to escape.

Sir Mawdesley and the Major admitted the justice of her plea; they tackled the poltergeist. 'Sprite, we must make these anarchists safe.'

'Do it yourself. I don't play with central locking.' Their helper was up to date, but bloody-minded.

'Oh, but none of us is as capable as you!' cooed the White Lady, in the tones of honeyed sincerity that had driven her suitor away. Unused to flattery, the malevolent imp felt confused. He was unhelpful, because his job was to cause human anxiety. But at heart, insofar as he had one, he was thrilled by the idea of locking the bombers in their own car, which was exactly the kind of prank for which he existed. He dashed down to do it. To jam central locking was easy; he even let down all the tyres, for extra devilment. The activists were trapped.

The rest of the plan went into action at once. The milling visitors in the Buttery were too close to potential danger. Sir Mawdesley manifested himself there, beckoning slowly with an eerie stare, as if summoning the group to a costumed reconstruction of historic laundering. Bemused, they were drawn after him into the safe inner courtyard, expecting dollies, coppers and starch to be demonstrated by a costumed wench.

Meanwhile, the White Lady preoccupied the guide by pretending to faint. Most guides live for a chance to use their First Aid training, which is so much more rewarding than apprehending misfits who try to walk off with Fabergé eggs from the study. Attempts at giving the kiss of life proved strangely difficult, though the White Lady became hysterical at the sensation upon her previously untouched lips.

Meanwhile Major Rackstraw made a dramatic appearance at the ticket office, raised his flint-lock, stood to and shot the Black Dog. The phantom bullet passed harmlessly through the unkempt beast – but the medieval monster loved to play; he let out a spine-chilling howl, then lay down with his paws in the air and his red eyes closed, for once apparently at rest.

It worked. 'That madman shot a dog! Someone call the police!'

Galvanised by this horror, the custodian rushed into the Gatehouse to telephone. A security guard bravely tried to fell the Roundhead with a rugby tackle, but the radical rebel was impervious to elitist sports.

Meanwhile high above them, the poltergeist was going to work. He gathered the bomb and all its wires together, teasing the bundle into his carrier bag. Whirling himself into a ball of air, he

lifted the handles. He spun upwards, then man-
oeuvred the bag high above Mad Jack's Tower.
With a delighted shriek, he jerked his burden
over the belvedere. The dangerous package
dropped down outside and into the neat moat at
the base of the Wardroom, where the castle walls
were over ten feet thick.

The bomb went off.

Its blast propelled the poltergeist all the way
back down Mordaunt Street and into the store
again, where he hurtled into more manic spite,
spilling strawberry yoghurt on the floor just
where the busiest shopping aisles met. As sirens
began wailing in the distance, the visitors in the
castle courtyard had covered their ears at the roar
from the explosion. Once they realised they had
so narrowly escaped injury or worse, even stout
women in tweed skirts and brogues found
themselves trembling.

By a miracle nobody, alive or dead, had been
hurt. Mad Jack's Tower survived intact. The
Dungeon where Major Rackstraw had been a
prisoner was the only part of the fabric to sustain
damage. The wall where he had carved his name
crumbled; all trace of his long misery vanished.

The White Lady threw herself upon him, full
of praise; he managed to free himself. The Black
Dog scampered around some bemused policemen who had discovered the bombers locked
helplessly in their vehicle and were thinking
about arresting them, when they could be ex-
tracted.

Sir Mawdesley Mordaunt, one-time owner of

the castle, gazed through the smoke and choking dust as it settled. Only those with the gift to hear him knew that, amazed at the destruction, the ghostly poet murmured, *'Zounds!'*

MR HALKETT'S HOBBY

Martin Edwards

Martin Edwards' latest Lake District Mystery is
The Frozen Shroud. The series includes *The
Coffin Trail* (shortlisted for the Theakston's prize
for best British crime novel), *The Arsenic Laby-
rinth* and *The Serpent Pool.* He has written eight
novels about Liverpool lawyer Harry Devlin,
and two stand-alone novels, including *Dancing
for the Hangman.* He has won the CWA Short
Story Dagger and edited twenty-one anthologies.

'Would you care to meet a murderer's daughter?'
   Stirring in my armchair, I forced my eyes open.
The smoking room in The Curiosity Club
possesses an agreeably soporific atmosphere.
Even on a winter's day, the fire is warm, and the
sultry perfume of Robertshaw's cheroots has an
effect akin to opium. I had been leafing through
a monograph recording the lamentable dissolu-
tion of the Phrenological Society of Cambridge,
before succumbing to a thankfully dreamless
slumber.
   Trentham's heavy jowls wobbled with amused
self-satisfaction. He takes pleasure in startling

people with unexpected remarks, in the childish belief that this marks him out as interesting and unpredictable. Meet a murderer's daughter? For her to have accompanied him here was impossible. Our club does not permit the presence within its precincts of any member of the opposite sex. A tremor of excitement rippled through my body, but it would never do to seem eager. Men like Trentham should not be encouraged.

I yawned. 'As you know, my studies into the psychological attributes of—'

'Yes, yes.' Trentham fiddled with his watch chain. Loquacious as he is, when others speak, his hasty manner suggests that he is itching to depart for the coast in a Tilbury, the moment the conversation can be concluded. 'Thought I'd look in, on the off chance you were here, and not closeted away at home in that damned laboratory of yours.'

I could not help but sigh. Trentham is not, for all his pretensions as a Linnean, a serious student of matters scientific. He is a dabbler, the summit of whose ambition is to be thought of as a scholar, rather than to do anything so challenging as to indulge in scholarship. His prized collection of botanical specimens amounts to little more, in my opinion, than a variegated collection of weeds.

'The offspring of a hanged man, seeking charity to avoid destitution...?'

Trentham shook his bald pate with his habitual testy vigour. 'No, no, Halkett, nothing of the kind. This young lady may be indigent, but her financial circumstances might soon change. You

76

need have no fear of my introducing you to an importuner.'

'Then...'

'Nor was her father hanged.'

I caught my breath. 'Yet you say he is a murderer?'

'I make no judgement, please do not misinterpret my remark. I merely repeat a commonly held view. Christabel believes the jury was right to acquit him. Yet to a man, the lawyers I know say he was as guilty as sin. And now the fellow has disappeared.'

I levered myself out of the chair as the Rimbaud long-case clock chimed the quarter hour. A few minutes earlier, I had intended to summon a waiter and order tea. What Trentham was saying, however, caused thoughts of refreshment to flee from my mind.

'Disappeared, you say?'

Trentham allowed himself a crooked smile. 'Ah, I see I have caught your interest, you old rascal! I am sure you will be able to put a name to Christabel's father.'

I inhaled the smell of calfskin from the bindings of the books on the shelf beside the curtained window. 'Not ... not Leicester?'

'You are acquainted with him, I gather?' Trentham coughed, in a vain attempt to conceal his enjoyment of my discomfiture. 'Calderbank tells me that he happened to observe the pair of you taking tea in a secluded corner at Mivan's Hotel, no more than six weeks ago.'

That wretched old gossip, Calderbank! I suspected at the time that he had noticed us. It would have caused him such mischievous delight, to see a fellow club member deep in conversation with a man who, despite acquittal in court by twelve good men and true, was regarded in polite society as a man whose reputation was tarnished beyond repair.

'I do not entertain the prejudices of the common herd,' I said coldly. 'Leicester's behaviour makes him an eminently suitable subject for dispassionate assessment.'

Trentham made an elaborate performance of taking a pinch of snuff. 'Well, I should say that one man's dispassionate assessment is another's inspired guesswork. But never mind that. Simeon, my cousin's boy, has taken a shine to Christabel Leicester, but his parents insist that he must not see her again. They fear there is bad blood in the family; it is entirely understandable.'

'Christabel's desire, then,' I said slowly, as the meaning of our conversation became clear, 'is to track down any evidence that might offer more comfort than a verdict of not guilty?'

'Precisely, Halkett! But nothing has been seen of Leicester for several weeks. He and the girl were estranged, and she cannot tell whither he may have fled. She suspects that the obloquy he suffered prompted him to leave for the Continent, or possibly the colonies. For all that anybody knows, he may already be living under an assumed identity, seeking to rebuild his life far from England.'

I nodded. 'With the consequence that it is difficult for anyone to clear his name.'

'In such circumstances, my thoughts turned to you. Knowing how it pleases you to indulge your hobby of playing the detective.'

'I am a scholar,' I said coldly, 'not a policeman, far less a player of games.'

'Of course, I say nothing about the reliability of your methods. But the boy is timid, and the girl headstrong. Pretty young filly, too, little as that may count with an ascetic such as yourself. Nevertheless, there is enough romance in my veins for me to clutch at straws. The girl's mother succumbed to a crippling lung disease a few months ago, so she is alone in the world. Simeon is a decent lad, and I should be glad to play a part in easing the course of young love.'

Clearing my throat, I said, 'I must confess that I am intrigued by what you say.'

'Then you will see the girl?'

Contriving to suppress my excitement, I inclined my head. 'It is always a pleasure to assist a fellow member of the Curiosity Club.'

'Mr Trentham has told me a great deal about you,' Christabel Leicester said.

When she smiled, it was as if the lobby of Mivan's Hotel was thrown into dazzling illumination. I had chosen precisely the same spot where – it seemed like yesterday – the girl's father and I had conversed. Facially, she resembled him. The snub nose, the wide mouth, the scattering of freckles across both cheeks, all those features spoke of his parentage. Yet her hair was long and thick, lustrous and golden, flowing down below her shoulders in such abun-

79

dance that it was impossible even to hazard a guess at the shape of her head. In contrast, Leicester's hair was dark and thinning and clung to his skull. He was small and wiry, whereas Christabel's figure was strikingly mature. Her mother, I surmised, must have possessed equally arresting looks. My interest, however, lay not in the poor creature that Leicester had seduced so long ago.

'My advice would be to discount every word. Trentham is an incurable romantic, whereas I consider myself a man of science.'

Her eyes sparkled. 'He told me to read those extraordinary stories of Mr Poe, concerning the Chevalier Dupin.'

I could not help but wince at the absurdity of the comparison. 'Put such nonsense out of your mind. Dupin's supposed analytic genius is a world away from the disciplines of academe. If I am to help you...'

'Yes?' She leaned towards me, unwittingly making a conspicuous display of her ample bosom. Lesser men would have found her eagerness as intoxicating as the ripe and youthful flesh. I concentrated my gaze instead on those cascading golden locks. 'Mr Trentham thought it possible that you might be able to establish that my father did not kill that wretched man.'

I sighed. Trentham scorned my science, and yet, unable to resist the temptation to make a favourable impression upon a comely young woman, he had encouraged her to believe what he did not.

'Are you not content to accept the verdict of

the court? Leicester was found not guilty of murdering Hubert Dalrymple.'

'Ha!' Her cheeks suffused with a pink glow. 'Very few people in this city doubt that he was the luckiest man in London, Mr Halkett, and that is why I am beseeching you for help. Simeon's family are set against our union. His father is a diplomat with an eye upon an appointment as ambassador. A scandal would ruin his prospects of promotion, and he has threatened to disinherit Simeon unless he desists from seeing me.'

'But Simeon's love for you...' I began, a little hesitantly, for I know little of love, except that it makes fools of men and women alike.

Her anguish was unmistakeable. 'Dear Simeon is the light of my life, but he cannot contemplate the prospect of estrangement from his family. For my father to have to be exonerated on a technicality is not enough. Unless and until his innocence can be proven, I shall never see Simeon again.'

'Your father did not treat you well,' I said.

She bowed her lovely head. 'No. Even my small allowance has ceased since my mother died. I am about to start work in a laundry-house in an attempt to make ends meet.'

Leicester had abandoned his wife and child when Christabel was young to pursue the avocations of a libidinous cad, preying on rich widows and indulging his coarser tastes with women of ill repute. His final conquest had, however, proved to be his undoing.

'Many would say that your father is best forgotten,' I ventured. 'The same, I fear, is true of

81

your young man Simeon.'

She looked up at me. Tears had formed in her blue eyes. Had I possessed a heart, it would have melted.

'I have no one else to turn to,' she said. 'You are my only hope.'

I closed my eyes, and leaned back in the armchair with a low sigh. The meeting had proceeded as if preordained. Her faith in me was as much as I could have dreamed of.

The death of Hubert Dalrymple did not, by common consent, rob the world of a soul worthy of redemption. Dalrymple had inherited a substantial fortune, and spent some fifty-five years squandering the better part of it on gambling and the sensual pleasures. His first wife had died in childbirth, and his second of a seizure. Some three years prior to his own demise he had married for a third time, after a young woman caught his eye at a racecourse. Emily had been affianced to a stable lad, but Dalrymple's practised charm soon turned her head, and his lavish way with money no doubt added to his allure. If his intention was to sire an heir, he was disappointed, and in due course he resumed his habit of dalliance with harlots. Yet Emily was too young and spirited to rest content with the lot of the dutiful wife.

William Leicester was twelve years Dalrymple's junior, and no less dissolute. The two men had long been thick as thieves, and Leicester often called upon the Dalrymples at their house in Bryanston Street, near to the Marble

Arch. In the fullness of time, a scandalous intimacy developed between Emily Dalrymple and her husband's friend. Dalrymple became aware of the liaison, and whether he was complaisant in the matter, or even offered Leicester encouragement, became a question of fierce dispute during the subsequent trial.

One week before his death, Dalrymple threw Emily out of his house. She scurried not to Leicester's arms, but to the home in Guildford of her married sister Mary. There she remained until news came that Dalrymple had died at the house of an elderly neighbour to whom he had complained of severe abdominal pains, accompanied by vomiting and sundry other symptoms of serious illness. The doctor who attended him ensured that his stomach and its contents were removed and examined. The investigation revealed the traces of eighty-five grains of arsenic.

The police were called in and quickly established that Dalrymple had told the neighbour of a visit by Leicester the evening before his death. In the final hours before his unpleasant life came to a fittingly dreadful end, and with his very last words before he lost consciousness, he accused Leicester of poisoning him. When challenged, Leicester did not deny having called at Bryanston Street, but maintained that he had come to apologise to Dalrymple for his conduct with regard to Emily. On his account, the men had eaten a hearty meal together and drunk heavily, parting with their friendship renewed, as firm as ever.

Enquiries revealed that, under the terms of the

recent Arsenic Act, an apothecary in Soho had recorded half a dozen occasions when he had sold white arsenic to Leicester. Again, the fellow made a ready admission of the facts. His counsel was to argue that his frankness was a sign of innocence, although, in truth, the evidence was unequivocal, and only a complete fool would have contested it. Whatever his failings, Leicester was not a complete fool.

According to the neighbour, Dalrymple had complained a week earlier of a serious digestive ailment, and enquiries rapidly established that the incidents had roughly coincided with a visit made by Leicester to the Bryanston Street house, whose arrival had been apprehended by the observant neighbour. Leicester maintained that he had come to visit Emily, only to find that she had left for Guildford. A terse conversation had taken place between Dalrymple and himself, but he refuted the suggestion that they had had anything to eat or drink together. He claimed that, after lengthy reflection, he had concluded his entanglement with Emily, and resolved to restore cordial relations with Dalrymple. Hence the supposed evening of reconciliation immediately prior to the older man's demise.

Leicester's trial proved to be a nine-day wonder. The prosecution alleged that Leicester meant to kill Dalrymple, in order to secure Emily for himself. The defence rested in part on the claim that the intrigue between Leicester and the young woman had reached a natural end. Emily insisted throughout that she had received no word from her lover from the moment she set foot in her sister's home in Guildford, and Mary and her husband corroborated her testimony. Leicester admitted to being a habitual arsenic eater, hence his purchases from the apothecary. He alleged that arsenic improved both one's complexion and virility. Dalrymple was, according to Leicester, also a notorious arsenic eater, and Emily confirmed that her husband indulged in various drugs, notably opium. However, she was unable to say where he made his purchases, and the only evidence uncovered indicated a frequent acquisition of modest quantities of laudanum.

Wisely, Leicester had secured the services of Sir Eustace Pilling, and that doubtless heavy investment reaped its dividend with a closing speech in which Sir Eustace lambasted the prosecution for its temerity in bringing the affair to court. The paucity of evidence to show that Leicester had administered poison to his mistress's husband was so marked that one would not, he assured the jury, hang a dog on it, far less a man. He said nothing about his client's morals, but Leicester was not on trial for licentiousness. If ever such ungentlemanly behaviour, however deplorable in itself, became a capital offence, many more notable men than his client, he thundered, would have to swing because of it.

The jury retired for no more than twelve minutes. Sir Eustace had earned his fee.

Unusually, however, there was a marked reluctance on the part of members of the public to cheer news of the acquittal to the courtroom's rafters. In common with almost every person of my acquaintance, when the verdict was delivered, I doubted that justice had been served.

Yet it was not quite beyond the realms of possibility. And even if Dalrymple had been murdered, it was not entirely certain that Leicester was responsible for the crime.

'What led to your encounter with my father?' Christabel enquired.

'I must make a confession to you,' I said, putting down my wine glass. 'I am possessed of a restless academic curiosity, and I found myself unable to overcome the desire to scrape acquaintance with him.'

She savoured the claret. 'But why, Mr Halkett? Following the revelations of his conduct at the trial, most decent folk would be sure to keep their distance from him.'

'Murder fascinates me,' I said. 'It has long been my belief that science can answer questions that perplex the most astute legal minds.'

'Mr Trentham told me that you are an adherent of the school of Herr Franz Joseph Gall.'

I bowed, and moved to refill our glasses. We were sitting in the drawing room of my house in Highgate. Thick velvet hangings at the long windows kept a cold and thick November fog at bay. The fire crackled greedily, and half a dozen candles burned in their silver holders. I care little for ornaments or decoration, save for a curtained alcove above the carved hearth, and two walls lined from floor to ceiling with bookshelves. My visitor, on inspecting the closely packed volumes, had remarked on the abundance of scientific texts. I have no use for Gothic romance or fantastic tales of mystery and imagination. Facts fascinate me; facts – and theories.

'Most criminals belong to the common herd. Your father, at least, is a man from a higher social echelon than many. I wanted to seek his aid in testing an idea of mine.'

Christabel frowned. 'You thought him guilty? Had I known that before coming here this evening—'

I held up my hand to still her outrage. 'I will not pretend otherwise. Would you have me lie? But it did occur to me that Hubert Dalrymple's wife might have had at least a part to play in his death.'

'Emily?'

'Indeed. Her absence from Bryanston Street at the critical times was uncannily convenient, and it suggested the possibility of a plot. I have heard it mooted that there was a conspiracy. Leicester arranged for her to be out of the way when Dalrymple was poisoned, in order to ensure that she could not be accused of the crime. The plan, on this view of events, was for the couple to feign an acrimonious estrangement, and then reunite, perhaps overseas, once the hubbub had died down, enjoying additional wealth from those remaining assets which Dalrymple had not had time to squander before his death.'

Christabel put a small white hand to her mouth. 'So you do believe my father is a murderer?'

'Hear me out, I pray. There is a flaw in the analysis I have outlined. As I understand it, Emily continues to this day to lodge with Mary and her husband. It is said that she is distraught, although whether that is due to her husband's death, her abandonment by her lover, or some other cause remains uncertain.'

'But do you suspect...?'

I leaned back in my armchair and drained my glass. After studying my expression, she did the same. I was glad to observe her growing realisation that all would soon be made plain.

'I speculated that your father might indeed be innocent. Suppose Emily had slipped away from Guildford? She was not, after all, under guard, and was free to come and go as she pleased. Conceivably, she assisted your father in the act of poisoning her husband. Yet she might have been solely responsible. Indeed, your father, as well as her husband, might have been a target of her wrath. What if she meant to kill them both, and your father was saved merely by his own tolerance to arsenic, resulting from its absorption into his system over many years? The peasants of Styria—'

'The court heard no evidence that he suffered illness after the food and drink he shared with Dalrymple.'

I shrugged. 'Perhaps he was too proud to admit it.'

She shook her head. The youthful exuberance of our first meeting was a fading memory. Her cheeks looked sallow, and her eyes were heavy-lidded. Yet that thick golden hair continued to dazzle in the candlelight. I found it hard to tear my eyes away from it.

'I ... don't know any more.'

I leaned forward. 'Suppose for a moment that your father was guilty of the crime. He would never admit the truth, even if I were stupid enough to put the question outright. I could, however, offer him the chance to prove to the world that he had been unjustly maligned.'

'But ... by what means?' She sounded frail and short of hope.

'Bumps,' I said. 'To put it with Trentham's crudity. Or, as I prefer to express it, by practising the science of phrenology.'

Christabel frowned. 'Mr Trentham said—'

'Nothing of merit, I would hazard. He lacks all understanding of the finer points of reading character from the contours of the skull. From a single examination, a skilled phrenologist can identify the signs of a criminal personality. We have broken with the metaphysical and theological nonsense of the past, and found an empirical science which explains even the most depraved behaviour. Your father, I fear, was sceptical, but consented to my request to examine him here, subject to an agreement that we observe conditions of strict secrecy. I suppose he thought he had little to lose.'

'He was right,' she said hoarsely.

I smiled. 'He regarded me as a charlatan, but presumably reasoned that if I proclaimed his innocence, it would be to his benefit. For every doubting Trentham, there may be another, more open mind, receptive to scientific proof.'

'You found my father is innocent?' This was little more than a whisper.

'Alas, I did not. I conducted the most thorough

and exhaustive assessment possible, and it left no room for contradiction. Your father, I regret to say, displayed phrenological characteristics more depraved than I might ever have imagined. Like others in my field, I have on occasion been granted the opportunity to study the severed heads of executed murderers. I found it quite enthralling, to come so close to some of the most godless creatures to have walked this earth. Never have I encountered signs of such inbred wickedness as in the skull of William Leicester. I have no doubt that he murdered Dalrymple, and did not need Emily's help to do so.'

Christabel gave a little moan. 'Then ... I am ruined. I shall ... I shall never be rid of the taint ... of my inheritance.'

'Inheritance, yes.' I breathed in deeply. 'You have lighted upon precisely the question that has me spellbound. To what extent are such characteristics passed from one generation to another?'

She gazed at me in horror. Her rosy lips parted, but no words came.

'You have a contribution to make of the utmost value,' I insisted. 'My researches will, in the fullness of time, make the most profound contribution to the betterment of society. Your sacrifice will be repaid a thousandfold.'

I strode to the fireplace, and took hold of the cord to the alcove curtain. It concealed a shelf that yet had space for a final trophy. 'You have nothing to fear, I give you my word. The narcotic in that splendid claret has already done its work. You will not feel the faintest nick from the saw when it touches your throat. And there is one last gift that I gladly bestow.'

She stared at me, unable to speak, but I only had eyes for her golden hair. I have no experience of physical lust, but perhaps the giddy excitement of scientific discovery mirrors its intensity. Once those long locks were shorn, what extraordinary findings would the skull beneath it yield? My mouth was dry, my temples pounding, my flesh aflame with anticipation.

'You may see your father again, one last time.'

And I pulled the cord.

KILLING THE SWANS

Ruth Dudley Edwards

Ruth Dudley Edwards is an historian and journalist. Her twelve witty crime novels tilt against the establishment: targets so far include the civil service, gentlemen's clubs, academia, the literati and conceptual art. She won the CWA Gold Dagger for Non-Fiction for *Aftermath: The Omagh Bombing and the Families' Pursuit of Justice* and has twice won the CrimeFest Last Laugh Award.

Pounding, pounding, pounding, pounding; back straight, arms pumping symmetrically, weight distributed evenly, Henrietta George jogged steadily down the towpath. She covered the ground at her customary six miles per hour, which her trainer had assured her was – at her age and weight – her perfect pace. After precisely thirty minutes and five miles, she would turn around and jog home.

She did not look about her for interesting flora or fauna. Instead she focussed on the path ahead, scanning it for anything she might trip over; an accident of any kind was not something she was prepared to risk in a busy life. She much preferred jogging on the treadmill, which was risk free, but the gym didn't open until six, which on crowded days was too late for Henrietta.

Too early even for the *Today* programme, rather than putting on her headphones and listening to news programmes she regarded as essentially frivolous, she reflected on yesterday's triumph. Her performance in the immigration debate had, she thought, been one of her best, if the cheers from her own side and the furious response from her opposite number were anything to go by. And with the elections for the National Executive Committee looming, crowd-pleasing was important. If she was to go up significantly in the party pecking-order, she needed to do better than just scrape in like last time.

Henrietta was under no illusions that her party would ever love her, but she was prepared to settle for respect. Despite her best efforts to dress less expensively and develop a more common accent and touch, she looked and sounded too posh for the rank-and-file's plebeian tastes. She had emulated Tony Blair by replacing her received pronunciation with 'peopw' instead of 'people' and 'govmund' instead of 'government', but 'creckly' for 'correctly' had been a bridge too far and Dave had told her she sounded ridiculous and that since she didn't have Blair's acting ability she'd better stick to being herself.

It was all right for Dave, who was probably still slumbering happily, she thought resentfully. His working-class Newcastle accent had survived grammar school and Leeds University, so he didn't suffer her handicaps in Labour circles. And what was more, he had chosen merchant banking over politics, where it didn't really matter what you sounded like. He might have done as well if not better than her in politics, if he'd been able to conceal his distaste for it. They could have been a power couple to contend with. But it was not to be.

As was her custom, rather than dwell too much on her husband's inadequacies, Henrietta tried to be positive by reminding herself how difficult life would have been without his money. This particular morning she luxuriated in thinking about the Commons debate and her clarion call to cherish diversity over Little Englandism. She smiled happily as she once more recited that excellent line she'd produced to demolish those who were whingeing about all the unexpected immigrants from Eastern Europe. 'We are proud as a party to have made our country better by opening our hearts and minds and national borders to our friends from the east,' she had cried, to great applause from the benches behind her.

'Any trouble with the Lithuanians?' asked Dave, as his showered, smartly-dressed and carefully made-up wife joined him at the breakfast table.

'Oh, for heaven's sake, stop harping on about the Lithuanians,' she said, adding yoghurt to her muesli and blueberries. 'You sound like some Tory bigot moaning about an influx of Eastern Europeans. Where would we be without Agnes?'

Henrietta picked up *The Times* and found the politics pages.

'And Pavel. And Irenka. And Lucacz. And Krystiana...'

'Oh, do shut up.'

'Sometimes I think we're well on our way to employing the entire population of Gdansk.'

'It's not as if they're expensive,' she said. 'And someone has to do all the domestic crap.' She squealed suddenly. 'What a bitch that woman is. I don't hector. And I'm not holier-than-thou.' Throwing down *The Times*, she fished in the pile for the *Guardian*. 'Where is Agnes anyway?'

'Cooking my breakfast, I hope. Why, are you missing something?'

'I'm off in a couple of minutes. There's a shadow cabinet meeting at nine and I've a ton of briefing to get through first and I need to give her some more instructions about tonight.'

He groaned. 'Do I really have to come? Can't you do without me? You know how I hate that crew.'

'This is important, Dave. You know there are a few political commentators coming too and we have to charm them.' She hurled her paper to the floor. 'Even the sodding *Guardian* sketch-writer has made snide head-girl remarks. It's so unfair. I hate this class warfare.'

'I thought class warfare was a governing principle of your party's present electoral strategy.'

'Not,' said Henrietta through gritted teeth, 'when it's directed at me.'

'Did you have to raise the bloody Lithuanians in

95

that company?' she hissed, as they closed the front door on the last guest.

'It was only a pleasantry. Joe had asked me something about the wildlife on the canal and I just happened to mention the decline in the swan population.'

'And blamed the Lithuanians.'

'He did ask the reason.'

'You could have sidestepped it. You could have found a different reason. But no, you had to make a racist allegation. In front of half the front bench and a sprinkling of hacks.'

A tall, blonde young woman emerged from the drawing room carrying a tray of dirty glasses.

'Good night, Irenka,' said Henrietta.

'Lidka,' she said. 'Irenka cousin.'

She vanished downstairs.

'Where's Irenka then?' Henrietta asked her husband.

'Downstairs washing up, I guess. Agnes said she needed reinforcements since she needed to go to bed early.'

'What do we pay her for?' asked Henrietta crossly, as she switched off the drawing-room lights and headed for the stairs.

'Not for a seventeen-hour day,' he said mildly, as he followed behind.

'Great do last night,' said Judith, Henrietta's closest political friend and ally, as they snatched a quick lunch in the Members' Tea Room. 'I thought the whole tone was very positive.'

'Except for that Lithuanian business,' said Henrietta, stabbing viciously at 'a harmless mound of shredded carrot. 'I could have slapped Dave. I can tell you I gave it to him with both barrels afterwards. We had a real row on the way to bed. He slammed off to the dressing room for the second time this week.'

'You're getting worked up about nothing, Hen. It was quite funny really. I'd no idea Lithuanians ate swans.'

'If that's their cultural preference, that's their business.'

'Swans are a protected species, though. I don't think foreigners have the right to come here and barbecue our wildlife even if they are in the EU.'

'We don't know that happened, Jude. Sounds like tabloid racism to me.'

'But Dave said he found the encampment near you and that he saw what looked like swan carcasses. He seemed particularly incensed about the black feathers.'

'Forget about the bloody swans.'

'Dave said there have been a lot of complaints about muggings too. And drunken carry-ons. That's why he thinks you shouldn't run there early in the morning. And wonders why you won't complain to the council. You are the MP after all.'

Henrietta put down her fork and looked at her friend with an expression Judith knew well and did not much like. 'These people are homeless because we have made them insufficiently welcome. I will not be party to their persecution.' She took one last sip of fizzy water and pushed her chair back. 'Anyway, I've never noticed any of them around at that time of the morning.'

'Probably still out of their skulls on vodka from the night before.'

'Judith, this kind of cultural stereotyping does you no credit.'

'We're not back in Benenden now, Hen,' said Judith as she stood up. 'Stop talking down to me. I think Dave's right. There are Lithuanians and Lithuanians, and these sound like scumbag Lithuanians. I just hope you don't carry any valuables when you jog.'

It was two weeks later when Dave checked his watch again and decided there was no obvious explanation for Henrietta's unprecedented lateness so he'd better go and look for her. Had she changed her plans, she would have called him. He tried her number again, but once more it went straight to answer. It wasn't hysterical to be worried that she could have had an accident or been mugged and injured.

Hood up and scarf across his face, he marched into the cold drizzle, turned the corner into the towpath and walked swiftly along scanning the undergrowth and the canal surface. The solitary early-morning runner he encountered denied having seen a tall, middle-aged woman jogging in a grey tracksuit. It took only twenty minutes for him to spot a floating grey-clad body, tear off his overcoat, pull off his shoes and plunge in. By the time he had dragged her up onto the path, he knew there could be no doubt that she was dead, but nonetheless he opened her mouth, rolled her on to her stomach and rang 999.

By the time two paramedics came running

towards him, he was sitting on the path hugging her body close and rocking to and fro. 'I couldn't do anything for her,' he said. 'My poor, poor Henrietta. Look at her head. She's been murdered. Oh, Hen, Hen, why couldn't you take my advice?'

The police got nowhere with the Lithuanians, all of whom claimed to have to have been asleep in their shacks at the time she was attacked. Then a close search of the undergrowth near their squalid camp revealed her money belt, in which – for Henrietta liked to be prepared for all eventualities – was her phone, a fifty-pound note, a few pound coins, a tissue, her keys and a debit card. Since even in death Henrietta was a VIP, this discovery led to the arrest of the couple of dozen occupants of the encampment, but even with the help of a team of interpreters over two days, none of them had anything helpful to say. What was more, enquiries suggested that while they were disposed to a bit of thieving, they had no record of violence except with each other after too much drink.

'What the fuck are we supposed to do?' asked the chief inspector of his superintendent. 'There isn't a shred of forensic evidence to implicate them. She was hit with a big stone on the side of her head and then thrown into the water. But even the dumbest of those scumbags would have known to chuck the weapon into the water, so even if we found it, it would be clean.'

'And anyway why would they kill her?' said the superintendent. 'They could have just snatched the money belt.'

'Dunno. She seemed the type to put up a fight. Maybe someone thick and drunk was trying to cover his tracks.'

'Definitely no dabs on the money belt except hers?'

'Nope. And we confiscated all their effing gloves, but forensic's found nothing. And the woolly gloves we found when we sent a couple of divers down weren't yielding up any guilty secrets neither.'

'Husband? Enemies?'

'Everyone says the marriage was happy and apparently the husband had been warning her against jogging alone. He said miserably that he should have kept her company but that he didn't have her energy. Apparently they slept separately when she was going to get up especially early, so he hadn't even heard her go out.'

He scratched his head. 'As for enemies? Well there seems to have been thousands of people who didn't like her, but then she was a politician.'

Henrietta's family, friends and colleagues were outraged that the police had to admit defeat, though not at all as outraged as the tabloids which she had so despised who did everything short of making direct murder accusations. When they went back to their miserable accommodation, the Lithuanians were terrified by the massed ranks of cameras and shouting media types, and in consultation with interpreters and the social services, packed up and headed off to stay with friends living rough near Peterborough.

The party leader appointed Judith to Henrietta's job and life in the Commons went on as usual. Dave went back to work, but his colleagues noted sympathetically that his heart seemed no longer in it. After a couple of months he went to his boss and gave in his resignation. 'It's no good, Gavs, I just can't do it any more. I don't know what I'll do next, but I've got to carve out some kind of life without my Hen.' And with the blessing of his superiors, he took an enormous golden handshake, held a subdued drinks party for his closest colleagues and walked away from the City.

The following morning, Dave lay in bed late with Agnes and counted his blessings. He no longer had to share his life with a woman whom he could barely stand, and he could enjoy playing the field. What was more, he was rich as well as free, having ensured he wouldn't be taken to the cleaners, as he well knew he would have been had he had the temerity to leave Henrietta. And as a bonus he'd got rid of those blasted Lithuanians who were disfiguring a neighbourhood he so loved and who had made his evening strolls unpleasant. He smiled when he remembered how often Henrietta had sneered at him because of his inability to multitask. 'You have got to hand it to me now, old girl,' he thought. 'It takes some operator to kill three birds with one stone.'

BRYANT AND MAY IN THE FIELD

Christopher Fowler

Christopher Fowler is the author of a series featuring Arthur Bryant and John May, who are members of the fictional Peculiar Crimes Unit. The Bryant and May series is set primarily in London, with stories taking place in various years between the Second World War and the present. Whilst there is a progressive narrative, many of the books focus on flashbacks to a major criminal incident from the detectives' shared past. His other publications include a study of unjustly forgotten authors, *Invisible Ink*.

'Remember that parachutist who was alive when he jumped out of his plane but was found to have been strangled when he landed in the field? Well, you're going to love this one, trust me.' John May took the car keys away from his partner and threw him an overcoat. 'Come on, I'll drive. You'll need that, and your filthy old scarf. It's cold where we're going.'

'I'm not stepping outside of Zone One,' Arthur Bryant warned tetchily. 'I remember the last time we left London. There were trees everywhere. It was awful.'

'It'll do you good to get some fresh air. You shouldn't spend all your time cooped up in here.'

The offices of the Peculiar Crime Unit occupied a particularly unappealing corner of North London's Caledonian Road. Most of the building's doors stuck and hardly any of its windows opened. Renovations had been halted pending a budget review, which had left several of the unheated rooms with asbestos tiles, fizzing electrics and missing floorboards. Bryant felt thoroughly at home in this musty death-trap, and had to be prised out with offers of murder investigations. 'Alright,' he said grudgingly, 'if I have to. But this had better be good.'

As the elderly detectives made their way down to the car park, May handed his partner a photograph. 'She looks like butter wouldn't melt in her mouth, but don't be deceived. The Met has had its collective eye on her for a couple of years now. Marsha Kastopolis. Her husband owns a lot of the flats and shops along the Caledonian Road. He's been putting her name on property documents as some kind of tax dodge. The council reckons it's been trying to pin health and safety violations on them, but no action has ever succeeded against her or her husband. I think it's likely they bought someone on the committee.'

'I take it she's dead,' said Bryant impatiently.

'Very.'

'That doesn't explain why we have to drive somewhere godforsaken.'

'It's not godforsaken, just a bit windswept. The

103

body's been left *in situ*.'

'Why?'

'There's something very unusual about the circumstances. Yes, look at the smile on your podgy little face now, you're suddenly interested, aren't you?'

'We'll see, won't we?' Bryant knotted his scarf more tightly than ever and climbed into the passenger seat of Victor, his rusting yellow Mini.

'Have you got around to insuring this thing yet?' asked May, crunching the gears.

'It's on my bucket list, along with climbing Machu Picchu and learning the ocarina. Where *are* we going?'

'We need to climb Primrose Hill.'

Bryant perked up. 'Greenberry Hill.'

'Greenberry?'

'That's what it was once called. After the executions of Messrs Green, Berry and Hill, who were wanted for the murder of one Edmund Godfrey in 1678. Although nobody really knows for sure if the legend is true.'

'Incredible,' May muttered, swinging out into Euston Road. 'All this from a man who can't remember how to open his email.'

The night before it had snowed heavily again. Now the afternoon air was crisp and frosty, and the rimes of snow that crusted King's Cross station had already turned black with traffic pollution. The Mini slushed its way past the grim bookies and pound stores of lower Camden Town, up and over the bridge still garlanded with Christmas lights, and into the wealthier environs of those who paid highly for living a few more

104

feet above sea level. It finally came to a stop at the foot of the fenced-off park, a great white mound surrounded by the expansive, expensive Edwardian town houses of Primrose Hill.

'The local officers have sealed the area,' said May, 'but the council wants the body removed before nightfall. The hill is a focal point for well-heeled families, and as the shops in Queen's Crescent are all staying open late over Christmas they're worried about the negative impact on local spending.'

Bryant wiped his glasses with the end of his scarf and peered across the bleached expanse, its edges blurred by a lowering silver sky. Halfway up, a green nylon box had been erected. 'You can tell them they'll get it cleared when we're good and ready to do so,' he said, setting off toward the body.

'Wait, you can't do that, Mr Bryant.' Dan Banbury, the PCU's Crime Scene Manager was sliding through the pavement slush towards them.

'Can't do what?'

'Just go off like that. I've established an approach path.' He pointed to a corridor of orange plastic sticks leading up the hill. 'You have to head in that way.'

'I'm a copper, not a plane,' said Bryant, waving him aside.

'There are already enough tracks out there. I don't want to have to eliminate any more.'

Making a sound like a displeased tapir, Bryant diverted to the narrow trodden channel, and the detectives made their way up the snow-covered slope to the tent, with Banbury anxiously darting ahead. 'She was found just after 6:20 a.m. by a man out walking his dog,' he told them.

'Why did it take so long to get to us?' asked May. 'It's after two.'

'There was a bit of a dispute about jurisdiction. They were going to handle it locally but all fatal incidents in Central North get flagged, and we picked it up.'

They reached the tent and Banbury went in ahead of them. The victim lay on her back on the frozen ground, her beige overcoat dusted with snow. From the alabaster sheen of her skin she might have been a marble church statue reclining on a bier. A single battery lamp illuminated the wound on her upper throat. Blood had coagulated around the parted flesh and had formed a hard black puddle beneath her left shoulder. Her eyes were still open but had lost their lustre as they froze.

'You've moved her,' said Bryant, noting the snow on the front of her clothes.

'That was the dog walker,' said Banbury. 'All he could see as he got closer was a woman's body lying in the middle of the common. There was a bit of a mist earlier. He thought maybe she had collapsed until he turned her over and saw she'd been stabbed.'

'Looks like a very sharp kitchen knife or a cut-throat razor,' said May. 'The wound's very clean, straight across the carotid artery. A real vicious sweep.' He checked her palms and fingers and found them crimson. 'Not defence marks. Maybe she raised her hands to the wound and tried to

106

stem the bleeding. Any other cuts to the body?'

'Not that I can see, but bodies aren't my field of expertise,' Banbury admitted. 'I'm more interested in whcre she fell.'

'Why?' May asked.

'She's in the exact centre of the common, for one thing, about 150 metres in every direction. The dog walker was met by a DS from Hampstead who called in his team. We've just taken a full statement from him. I picked up the initial report and established the corridor to the site.'

'Why did you do that before anything else?'

'Because there are no footprints,' Bryant cut in, waving his gloved hand across the virgin expanse of the hill.

'That's right, Mr Bryant. We've got hers, out to the middle but not back, the dog and his owner's, also there and back, and the DS's. Nothing else at all. Six is a bit early for the Primrose Hill crowd. Victim was last seen around 11:00 p.m. last night by one of her tenants. She was coming out of a restaurant. No more snow fell after about 5:00 a.m. According to the dog walker, there were just her footprints leading out to the middle of the hill slope and nothing else. Not a mark in any direction that he could see.'

'He must have been mistaken.'

'Nope – he's adamant, reckons he's got 20/20 vision and there were no other footprints.'

'Then it's simple – she must have taken her own life.'

'What with? There's no weapon.'

'You haven't had her clothes off yet, you can't be sure of that,' Bryant said. 'Can we take the body or do we have to use the local resource?'

'They're happy for her to go to St Pancras if you sign it off.'

Bryant didn't answer. He was peering at the victim, trying to conjure her last moments.

'Could someone have swept away their footprints?' asked May.

Bryant pulled a sour face. 'Look at this snow, it's crusted solid. Besides, why would anybody try to do such a thing? This is an urban neighbourhood, not Miss Marple country. There has to be a more obvious explanation. Got her mobile, have you?'

'Yes, she received a call from a nearby phone box just after six this morning. You might want to check last night's— No!' Banbury snatched the plastic bag back from Bryant, who had begun to open it. 'Can you not take it out until I've finished with it?'

'Just send us the call list, then,' said May, always keen to keep the peace. His partner was like a baby, reaching out to grab the things he wanted without thinking. Except that he was always thinking. 'Come on, Arthur,' he said, 'we've enough to be getting on with.'

'Where did she live?' Bryant asked as he was being led away. Below him the skyline of London formed an elaborate ice sculpture that shone pink and silver in the gelid afternoon air.

'Canonbury, I believe,' Banbury said.

'What was she doing over here so early on a Tuesday morning? Get those lads on it.' He indicated the members of the Hampstead constabulary who were standing around in the car park.

108

'See if they can find out if she stayed somewhere nearby, will you? And have them check taxis running from Islington to Chalk Farm early this morning.'

'Why Chalk Farm?' asked May.

'To get here from Islington you either have to drop off your fare by the footbridge near Chalk Farm Station or go all the way around,' Bryant explained. 'This place is a peninsular that's a pain in the arse to reach. That's why the rich love it. They don't have to rub shoulders with us plebs. And get someone to walk all the way around the perimeter, check for any kind of break in the snow. There must be something.'

After a brief stop at the PCU, the pair headed across to the gaudy offices of North One Developments Ltd, the property company Marsha Kastopolis had owned with her husband. Bypassing the confused staffers at their computer terminals, they found Phantasos Kastopolis in the building's basement, sweating on an exercycle. The red-faced property tycoon was leaking from the top of his dyed comb-over to the bulging waistband of his electric blue nylon tracksuit. He grabbed a towel and mopped at his chain-festooned chest, clearly annoyed at being interrupted.

'If this is about burst pipes, there's nothing I can do,' he said. 'It's bloody freezing, innit, and them students haven't paid their rent this month so they got no bloody complaining to do.'

'It's about your wife,' said May, and he proceeded to explain the circumstances of Mrs Kastopolis's death while Bryant wandered

109

around examining the gym equipment with ill-disguised distaste.

'What was she doing out at that time?' Kastopolis asked after he had demonstrably absorbed the news, a process that involved a fair amount of ranting but not much grief. 'She never goes for a bloody walk.'

'We were hoping you could tell us. Does she know anyone in Primrose Hill?'

'I don't know where her friends live.'

'Do you know if she had any enemies?'

'She had enemies because I have enemies!' Kastopolis exploded, throwing his towel on the floor. 'They all got it in for us, 'cause they don't like Cypriots owning their streets.'

'Your wife was English.'

'Yeah but she was married to me. I came here with nothing but the clothes I stood up in and bought the shops one by one. My father was a farmer, and look at me now. Thirty years of bloody hard work.' He raised his spatulate fingers before them in an attempt to prove the point. 'Of course I have enemies. They're jealous of me. They try to ruin me. But I tell you what, my friend, I do a lot of good in this community.'

'You infringe a lot of building regulations, too,' said Bryant, unimpressed. He pulled a plastic folder from his overcoat. 'Fire hazards, illegally blocked-off hallways, substandard materials, contractor lawsuits, environmental health injunctions, it's all here.'

'Listen, if I waited for council approval before starting to build, I'd never get anything done.'

'Let's get back to your wife,' said May. 'You

110

think someone was trying to get at you through her?' He thought, *If that was the plan, they didn't succeed. He's not upset or even surprised.*

'Why else would anyone bother with her?' Kastopolis pushed past them and began slicking down his hair before an elaborate gilt mirror. 'She didn't know nobody important.'

'But she worked for you.'

'Secretary stuff, posting the mail, making coffee, that sort of thing. I made her come to work just to keep her out of the shops, spending my bloody money. And to stop her eating. She was getting as fat as a pig.'

'When was the last time you saw her?'

'When she left the office yesterday evening. She was going out with her mates to some cocktail bar maybe, I don't know what she does no more.'

'She didn't come home?'

'We got a lot of places, and she's got keys to them all. She stays in different ones when she's had a few.'

'Alone?'

'Of course alone! What are you bloody saying?'

'And you, do you stay in these flats?'

'That's got nothing to bloody do with it.'

'It has if you can't vouch for your whereabouts between last night and today.'

Kastopolis nearly ruptured a vein. 'Ask my boys upstairs where I was. They was with me all evening. We left here at eight and went to the Rajasthan Palace until midnight. They was all with me again from six o'clock this morning. We work long hours here. Why you think we make so much money? Are you sure she's dead?'

'Very sure. She was stabbed.'

'Primrose Hill, eh? No blacks around there, don't know how she got stabbed. I can't bloody believe this. I gave her everything. She didn't have nothing when she met me, came down from Liverpool without a penny to her name. She owed me big time, and this is how I get paid back.'

'What do you mean?'

'Stands to reason, innit? She was seeing some-one behind my back.' Kastopolis checked his hair in the mirror and turned to them. 'Where do I pick up her body?'

'What a revolting man,' said Bryant as they headed back along the Caledonian Road. 'All that grey chest-hair poking out, it made me feel quite ill. Surely no one would speak about his wife like that if he'd killed her.'

'Obviously it's a long time since he cared any-thing for her. It sounds to me like the arrange-ment of staying in empty apartments was more for his benefit, not hers.'

'I think we should talk to someone she counted as a friend,' said Bryant, 'rather than a husband.'

They found Kaylie Neville seated alone in the Lion and Unicorn pub nursing an extremely large gin and tonic. Judging by her swollen red eyes and the number of lemon wedges in her drink, she had already been informed of her friend's death. The pub was so still and quiet that

112

the detectives stirred the dust-motes in the late afternoon sunlight as they sat down beside her at the copper-topped table.

'Phantasos called me and just started having a go, yelling and carrying on like I'm to blame,' she said, anxiously searching their faces. 'You mustn't believe anything he says about her. Nothing true or kind has ever come out of his mouth. He cheats, he steals, he has affairs. There's not a decent bone in him. The things he gets up to in those flats, you don't want to know.'

'Forgive me,' said Bryant, 'but if Mr Kastopolis is such a terrible man, why did Marsha marry him?'

'She'd had a rough time of it. She came to London to escape a bloke in Liverpool who said he would kill her.'

'Why did he say that?'

Kaylie tapped nervously at her glass with bitten painted nails. 'He was staunch Irish Catholic, and she had an abortion. He threatened to come down and cut her up. She was a lousy judge of men. But a kind heart, a good heart. I did what I could for her. You do what you can, don't you? She met Phantasos and he offered to look after her. Then she found out what that involved.'

'What did it involve?'

'Keeping the clients sweet. Doing anything they wanted. I mean, anything.'

'You're saying he prostituted her out to them?' said Bryant, always one to accurately title a gardening implement.

'She said no, of course. But he found plenty of

113

other ways to hurt her.' Kaylie took a sudden alarming gulp from her gin, nearly finishing it. 'She told me he started using her identity to hide cash in different accounts, all kinds of dodgy goings-on. I keep away from him. If he knew half the things I know, I wouldn't fancy my chances.'

'Do you think he had something to do with his wife's death?' asked May.

'He must have done,' Kaylie replied. 'See, she was smart. She kept everything written down in a little notebook, just in case there was ever any trouble.'

'What sort of things did she write down?'

'Account numbers, deposit dates, details of all the rental contracts he faked, the councillors he bribed, everything.'

'I don't suppose you know where she kept this book?'

'She never told me. Not at home, maybe in one of the rented properties, but there's fifty or sixty of those. He's got people everywhere. They're always on the lookout for trouble, that lot.'

'And you think that's why she died? Because she was keeping track of him?'

'You have to understand, he goes on about arriving in London without a penny, how he built up an empire, how no one can stop him. Then she started standing up to him. She told me she'd had enough. She was going to take the notebook to the police.'

'When was this?'

'She said it last night. She'd said it loads of times before, but this time I think she was really going to do it.'

'We're going to find out who killed her,' said May.

'If we can find out how he did it,' said Bryant.

The temperature was dropping again, and the brown pavement ice had become treacherous. May kept a tight hold of his partner's arm as the pair made their way around the corner to their unit. Central London in the snow was never picturesque for more than the first hour.

'It doesn't make any sense,' said Bryant. 'You can see the kind of a man Kastopolis is, a feral throwback, like something out of the 1970s, crafty but not too bright. His wife was lured out into the middle of that park and killed – that's why somebody called her from a phone box just before her death, to make sure that she was keeping her appointment. You heard what Miss Neville said; Kastopolis has men everywhere. Central North is his turf. Everybody knows the local villain, and that's the way he likes it. He needed this to happen off his patch. What I don't understand is how he did it, and he knows that we don't know.'

'Maybe he's smarter than you think he is,' said May. 'Perhaps he wants to divert our attention into trying to work out how it happened.'

'Let's talk to Giles,' said Bryant. 'He might have had a chance to examine her properly by now.'

They found Giles Kershaw in the darkened Forensic Pathology office at Camley Street, where he had recently taken up the position of coroner for St Pancras. 'You've caught us at a bad time,' warned Giles, ushering them in. 'The power's out. Ice pulled down the lines. The fridges are on a separate grid but we're working by torchlight until tomorrow morning. I don't know how Canada manages. A few millimetres of snow and the whole of London grinds to a halt.'

'What did you get from Mrs Kastopolis?' asked Bryant. 'Is there any tea going? I'm perished.'

'I didn't get much, and it's probably not what you're after. I don't think she stayed overnight in Primrose Hill. Went there first thing this morning, I imagine, but you'll know that once you've checked her Oyster card.'

'How do you know?'

'What, that she went by tube or that she'd been in Islington?'

'Both.'

'She had no purse, just the travel card. No make-up, and she'd dressed in a hurry. She was wearing boots that had some fragments of French gravel in the grooves. They hadn't been there long because there was ice underneath them. Islington uses different tarmac surfacing to Camden, so she crossed boroughs this morning. I've got a home address for her in Canonbury, Islington.'

'Her husband says she didn't come home last night, but she had several empty flats she could have gone to in the Canonbury area. Anything else?'

'We have a time of death because of the phone

call. She fell face down and died quickly. There was no weapon of any kind on her, or anything that could conceivably be used as one. It looks like therc were two wounds, one opening the carotid artery and the other grazing the trachea.'

'Grazing – you mean cutting it?'

'Yes, just lightly.'

'So the air escaped from her lungs and she couldn't breathe in,' said May.

'Exactly. Slashes rather than stabs – they're not very deep. She's five six, which would make her killer six feet at least, because the cuts are downward.'

'Except that he couldn't have been standing in front of her because he left no footprints,' added Bryant. 'How do you account for that?'

Kershaw flicked back his blond fringe. 'Well, I can't. Most seemingly impossible situations are the fault of poor information gathering. Are you sure Dan's got his facts straight? The obvious answer is that the dog walker killed her and threw the weapon away.'

'That won't fly,' said May. 'He walks his dog at the same time every day, along the same route. He was searched at the site and came up clean, and he has no connection with the deceased. The officer said he was pretty shaken up. There's no reason to suspect him.'

'Oh come on,' said Dan, 'you're a policeman, you suspect everyone. What about her enemies?'

'An ex-boyfriend in Liverpool. Turns out he died of a barbiturate overdose nearly a year ago. We've good reason to suspect the husband, but he has alibis in the form of half a dozen

117

employees, so he must have got someone else to do it. Dan's searching every inch of the field but so far he hasn't found any marks in the snow other than the ones we've accounted for.'

'A throwing dagger,' said Bryant suddenly.

'They'd have found it,' said May shaking his head.

'Not if it cleared the field.'

'Thrown 300 metres?'

'With rockets attached. Or a boomerang. Circus performers. A crossbow with razorblades on the front.'

'I'm going to take him back to the unit now,' May told Kershaw, patting his partner's arm. 'It's time for his meds.'

'Not yet,' Bryant insisted. 'Let's check Kastopolis's alibi. His employees are going to say anything he tells them, aren't they? The Rajasthan Palace, Cally Road, didn't he say he spent most of last night there?'

'Marsha Kastopolis died this morning.'

'But if he hired someone else to kill his wife, it was because of what she'd told Kaylie Neville, and maybe he planned it in the restaurant. Besides, it's been ages since I had a decent Ruby Murray.'

'Don't you ever stop thinking of your stomach?' asked May.

'I need to keep the boiler functioning in this weather,' said Bryant. 'If my pilot light goes out, I'll never get it started again.'

From the outside it was not the most appealing of restaurants. The splits in the yellow plastic fascia

118

had been repaired with brown parcel tape, and computer printouts of takeaway menus were plastered over the windows, but the staff were smartly uniformed and the interior was clean enough. May selected a salad while Bryant followed the time-honoured British tradition of ordering twice as much Indian food as he could possibly eat, topped off with a peshwari nan and a pint of Kingfisher. As the waiters got busy he attempted to question them, but they proved reluctant to be drawn on the subject of their customers and anxiously fetched the manager, Mr Bhatnagar, who tentatively tiptoed out toward them.

'Mr Eddie is our very great friend,' the manager explained, beaming eagerly. 'Everyone calls him Mr Eddie. He's coming here regularly for dinner and staying a very long time.'

'When was the last time you saw him?' asked May.

'Last night, same as always. He arrived soon after eight and stayed until we closed.'

'What time was that?'

Mr Bhatnagar silently calculated the validity of his drinks licence. 'Midnight,' he assured them.

'You remember who he was with?'

'His colleagues from the office, all very nice but very fond of a tipple, I think. Very ... energetic.'

'I assume you mean loud. Does he bring anyone else here apart from his colleagues?' Bryant asked.

'Sometimes he comes here with his lovely wife.'

'Does she eat here with her own friends?'

'No, just with Mr Eddie.'

'And who else does Mr Eddie bring to dinner?'

'Many people. Mr Eddie has many, many friends. He is very well known in this neighbourhood.'

'And your staff' – Bryant waved his hands at the young waiters illuminated by the pale light of their mobiles behind the counter – 'they were all working here last night?'

'All except these two, Raj and Said.'

'You manage several restaurants along this road, I suppose.'

'Yes, half a dozen or so.'

'And Mr Eddie owns them. Do your staff take shifts in the others?'

'What do you mean?'

'Do the waiters move around?'

'Indeed so.'

'I don't suppose you overheard any conversation last night?' asked Bryant, already sure of the answer.

'Oh no, sir,' came the hasty reply. 'We would never eavesdrop on our esteemed customers, certainly not.' Mr Bhatnagar gave them both a reassuring smile.

'What was all that about?' asked May as they stepped back into the street.

'I like to get a thorough picture,' replied Bryant evasively.

'Yes, and I also know when there's something funny going on in your head. One more stop and we'll go back to the PCU. The Islington Better

120

Business Bureau. It's the council's outsource in charge of the licences for properties along Upper Street and the Caledonian Road. Let's see what they make of Mr Kastopolis.'

'Do we have any friends there?' asked Bryant.

'We're not their favourite people. You gave them grief over a corpse found in one of their properties, remember? A headless murder victim stuffed into a chip shop freezer? Ring any bells?'

'Oh, *that*. Not someone called Anderson, by any chance?'

'The very one. He's Kastopolis's liaison officer. I'm sure he remembers you. You made him go to the old Bayham Street mortuary to identify the victim.'

'Why did I do that?'

'You didn't like him.'

'Ah. I wonder if he remembers.'

'I imagine it might have stayed in his memory, yes,' said May. 'Better let me do the talking.'

May held a twanging glass door open for his partner. They entered a lobby that resembled a spaceship's flight-deck from a low-budget film in the late 1980s. David Anderson came down to meet them, waving them anxiously toward a miniscule glass meeting room beside the reception area, a holding pen for those not worthy of being granted full access to the executive suites upstairs. He was slightly plump, slightly balding, slightly ginger, slightly invisible, the kind of man who makes you feel old when you realise with a shock that he's probably only in his early thirties.

121

'Our relationship with Mr Kastopolis has been somewhat fractious in the past,' he explained, placing himself between the detectives and the waiting area outside, for he was none too pleased about having the law visit council offices. 'He's quite a larger-than-life character, as I'm sure you've discovered.'

'We're more concerned that he may—' *Be a murderer*, Bryant was about to say, but May kicked him under the table. As this was also made of glass, everyone saw him do it.

'—have done more than just bent a few planning bylaws this time,' concluded May more diplomatically. 'Perhaps it would be better to discuss this in your office.'

Anderson was clearly upset by the idea, but was hardly in a position to argue. The trio rose to the third floor and settled themselves in plusher, more traditional surroundings. Bryant had to be surreptitiously cautioned against rummaging about on Anderson's desk. The meeting did not go well. The planning officer was prepared to admit that the bureau suspected Kastopolis of flouting property regulations, but was unwilling to divulge any personal doubts.

'What about outside of work?' Bryant asked. 'Do you see each other socially?'

'Good Lord, no.' Anderson seemed genuinely horrified by the idea. 'We're expressly forbidden from seeing clients outside of the building. There is a sensitivity about undue influence, you understand. And after the MPs' expenses scandal, it's more than our lives are worth. Can you give me more of an idea why he's of particular interest to you at the moment?'

'No,' said Bryant offhandedly, trying to read the liaison officer's paperwork upside down.

'The seriousness of the matter at hand means we must limit information until there's a case to be made,' said May, 'if indeed there is one to be made. But we appreciate the help you've been able to give us.'

'You're such a pussy,' said Bryant as they left the building. '"We must limit information until there's a case to be made." You don't get anything out of people if you don't frighten the life out of them. Typical council man, wet as a whale's willy, reeking with the stench of appeasement, utterly incapable of confrontation. Kastopolis runs roughshod over the lot of them and they do nothing.'

'You don't know that,' said May. 'He's spent the last thirty years finding ways to balance along the edges of the law. Men like that eventually make mistakes.'

'I can't wait for him to make a mistake. I'm old.'

'What do you want to do, then?'

'Head back to the PCU,' Bryant said. 'There's something I need to check.' May was glad they had brought the car. The iced-over pavements had become bobsled runs, and his partner was unstable at the best of times.

As the hours passed, May worked on with the rest of the PCU team while Bryant remained holed up in his office with the door firmly closed to visitors. Finally, when he could no longer bear the suspense of not knowing what his partner was doing, May went to check on him.

'You should put a brighter light on in here,' he said. 'You'll strain your eyes.'

'She's here,' Bryant said, looking up sadly. He had printed out everything he could find on Marsha Kastopolis, and had stacked it all in the centre of his desk. His hands were placed over the file, as if trying to conjure her presence. 'I can sense her.'

'What do you mean?' asked May.

'She was a bright girl. Then she was abused by her new stepfather. Her mother did nothing. The social services failed to protect her. She became withdrawn and lost. Her school grades dropped away. She was made pregnant by a junkie, came to London and started again. By this time she had grown a tough hide, and was determined to make something of herself. She must have been able to see through her husband, so why did she put up with him? What did she get from the relationship? Stability? Money? No, something else. That's the key to this.'

'Funny,' said May.

'What?'

'Nothing. I thought you'd be in here trying to work out how he did it. You know, the mechanics. The nuts and bolts. More up your street than people.'

'Don't be so rude. I hate to see promising lives ruined. As it happens, I know how it was done.'

'You do?'

'Most certainly. And I think I want to handle the last part by myself.'

'I don't understand you, Arthur.'

'I want to do the right thing for her. You can see that, can't you? I don't anticipate a problem, but it might be better if you stayed within reach of your mobile. I'm not going very far.' With that he rose stiffly, jammed on his squashed trilby and burrowed into his overcoat. May watched him go, flummoxed.

'What's up with the old man?' asked Banbury as he passed.

'You know how possessive some people are with their books?' said May. 'Arthur's like that with crimes. Sometimes I think I hardly know him at all.'

Bryant pushed open the wire-glass door of the Rajasthan Palace and seated himself by the window. An impossibly thin, hollow-eyed waiter who looked like he'd not slept since 1931 approached and placed a red plastic menu before him.

'I'll just have a hot, very sweet *chai*,' said Bryant. 'But you can send Mr Bhatnagar out to me. I know he's there, I just saw him peep through the curtain.'

Moments later the portly little manager appeared from behind the counter and made his way over to the table, bouncing on the balls of his feet. 'Mr Bryant,' he said, 'what a pleasure to see you again, so soon.'

'You may not think so in a minute.' Bryant gestured at the seat opposite. Mr Bhatnagar's smile showed sudden strain, and he remained standing. 'Mrs Kastopolis,' said Bryant. 'She ate at the Bhaji Fort last night. Your boy Raj saw her, didn't he? More to the point, he overheard her. Who did he tell you she was with?'

'Raj is a good boy,' said Mr Bhatnagar anxiously. 'Mrs Kastopolis was with another lady, a friend, that's all, not somebody my boy knew.'

'Then why did he bother to call you?' asked Bryant. 'I'll tell you why.' And he proceeded to do so. By the time he had finished, Mr Bhatnagar had visibly diminished. His mouth opened and closed, but no sound came out. Finally, he sat and dropped his head in his hands, not caring about his staff, who were nervously peering out at him from their counter. Mr Bhatnagar realised that his eagerness to please had finally been the undoing of him, and wept.

'I thought you didn't like the fresh air,' said May, slapping his leather-clad hands together in an effort to keep warm. His breath condensed in dragon clouds as he looked down from the pinnacle of Primrose Hill over the frost-sheened rooftops of London.

'I don't,' said Bryant, dislodging the snow from his trilby by violently beating it. 'I just wanted you to see this. How it was done.'

He pointed to the far edge of the hill, where several young Indian men were standing. May followed his partner's extended index finger up to the burnished winter sky. 'Can you see them now?' he asked.

Overhead, half a dozen diamonds of indigo and maroon silk soared and swooped around each other like exotic fish fighting for food. 'Kite

126

flying is a very popular pastime in Rajasthan. But it's far from a gentle sport. It's a matter of kill or be killed, and sometimes huge bets ride on the outcome. The idea is to destroy your enemies by bringing them down. The only way to do that is by severing their strings. So the kite-warriors coat their cords with a paste of boiled rice mixed with glass dust. It makes them as sharp as any cut-throat razor. And they can control the lines to go exactly where they want. Our assassin only had to bring it down from the sky and touch it across her throat.'

May was incredulous. 'You're saying Mrs Kastopolis was killed by a *kite*?'

'By the cord of a kite flown by an expert, yes,' said Bryant. 'Mr Bhatnagar looked out for his friend and protector, the landlord of all his properties. He made sure his waiters kept their eyes and ears open. When one of them overheard Marsha Kastopolis telling her friend that she was going to talk to the police about her husband, he stepped in to help. He called the man who had repeatedly asked him to stay vigilant.

'Obviously, if anything bad happened to Marsha on her husband's home turf suspicions would have been aroused. So one of the waiters was paid to draw her away. Mr Bhatnagar called her pretending to be an ally, and said he had important information for her. He lured her to the meeting on Primrose Hill. He thought he could get rid of her in a quiet place, and made his waiter, Raj, do the dirty work, using the one special skill he possessed. I don't suppose the lack of footprints in the snow even crossed anyone's mind. But it made the case unique enough to attract our attention.'

'Why would this Raj agree to do such a thing?'

'He had no choice. He was in debt to Mr Bhatnagar.'

'Have you sent someone around to arrest Kastopolis?'

'No, you've misunderstood,' said Bryant. 'Kastopolis didn't ask Mr Bhatnagar to keep an eye out for problems. It was the liaison officer, Anderson. Your first instinct was right; Kastopolis had bought someone on the committee. That was how he got away with breaking the law for so many years. Anderson got kickbacks and watched out for his client in return. Ultimately, it was Anderson who forced the waiter, Raj, to commit murder.'

May was mystified. 'But how did you know it was him?'

'Anderson vehemently denied ever consorting with his client, remember? But when I rummaged about on his desk I saw a receipt for the Rajasthan Palace. He'd eaten there the night before. He was slipping the dinner through on his expenses.'

'All these people, working to protect one corrupt man,' said May, 'and they're the ones who'll go down for him while Kastopolis walks away again. It's not fair.'

'You're forgetting one thing,' said Bryant. 'The notebook is still out there somewhere. We just have to find it before he does.'

The elderly detective turned back to watch a shimmering turquoise kite as it looped down and slashed the string of its nearest rival. The other kite, a fluttering box of emerald satin, was caught in a violent spin and plunged into a dive, shattering on the frozen earth.

'Alluring and dangerous,' said Bryant. 'The winners are raised up on the sacrifices of the fallen. That's how it has always been in this city.' He smiled ruefully at his partner and turned to watch the turquoise diamond weaving back and forth across the clouds, savouring its brief moment of glory.

FEDORA

John Harvey

Ever since he was awarded the CWA Cartier Diamond Dagger for Sustained Excellence in Crime Writing in 2007, **John Harvey** has been trying, unsuccessfully, to shrug off the implication that everything, henceforth, is downhill. No matter how hard he struggles, the label 'veteran crime writer' clings to him like a shroud. His latest effort to disprove the onset of senility is the novel, *Darkness, Darkness*, to be published by William Heinemann in 2014.

When they had first met, amused by his occupation, Kate had sent him copies of Hammett and Chandler, two neat piles of paperbacks, bubble wrapped, courier delivered. A note: *If you're going to do, do it right. Fedora follows.* He hadn't been certain exactly what a fedora was.

Jack Kiley, private investigator. Security work of all kinds undertaken. Ex-Metropolitan Police.

Most of his assignments came from bigger security firms, PR agencies with clients in need of babysitting, steering clear of trouble; solicitors after witness confirmation, a little dirt. If it didn't make him rich, most months it paid the rent: a second-floor flat above a charity shop in north London, Tufnell Park. He still didn't have a hat.

Till now.

One of the volunteers in the shop had taken it in. 'An admirer, Jack, is that what it is?'

There was a card attached to the outside of the box: *Chris Ruocco of London, Bespoke Tailoring*. It hadn't come far. A quarter mile, at most. Kiley had paused often enough outside the shop, coveting suits in the window he could ill afford.

But this was a broad-brimmed felt hat, not quite black. Midnight blue? He tried it on for size. More or less a perfect fit.

There was a note sticking up from the band: on one side, a quote from Chandler; on the other a message: *Ozone, tomorrow. 11am?* Both in Kate Keenan's hand.

He took the hat back off and placed it on the table alongside his mobile phone. Had half a mind to call her and decline. Thanks, but no thanks. Make some excuse. Drop the fedora back at Ruocco's next time he caught the overground from Kentish Town.

It had been six months now since he and Kate had last met, the premiere of a new Turkish-Albanian film to which she'd been invited, Kiley leaving halfway through and consoling himself with several large whiskies in the cinema bar. When Kate had finally emerged, preoccupied by the piece she was going to write for her column in the *Independent,* something praising the film's mysterious grandeur, it's uncompromising pessi-

131

mism – the phrases already forming inside her head – Kiley's sarcastic 'Got better, did it?' pre-cipitated a row which ended on the street outside with her calling him a hopeless philistine and Kiley suggesting she take whatever pretentious arty crap she was going to write for her bloody newspaper and shove it.

Since then, silence.

Now what was this? A peace offering? Some-thing more?

Kiley shook his head. Was he really going to put himself through all that again? Kate's com-panion. Cramped evenings in some tiny theatre upstairs, less room for his knees than the North End at Leyton Orient; standing for what seemed like hours, watching others genuflect before the banality of some Turner Prize winner; another mind-numbing lecture at the British Library; brilliant meals at Moro or the River Café on Kate's expense account; great sex.

Well, thought Kiley, nothing was perfect.

Ozone, or to give it its proper title, Ozone Coffee Roasters, was on a side street close by Old Street station. In full view in the basement, industrial-size roasting machines had their way with care-fully harvested beans from the best single-estate coffee farms in the world – Kiley had Googled the place before leaving – while upstairs smart young people sat either side of a long counter or at heavy wooden tables, most of them busy at their laptops as their flat whites or espressos grew cold around them. Not that Kiley had any-thing against a good flat white – twenty-first-century man, or so he sometimes liked to think, he could navigate his way round the coffee houses in London with the best of them.

Chalked on a slate at the front of one of the tables was Kate Keenan's name and a time, 11.00, but no Kate to be seen.

Just time to reassess, change his mind.

Kiley slid along the bench seat and gave his order to a waitress who seemed to be wearing mostly tattoos. Five minutes later, Kate arrived.

She was wearing a long, loose crepe coat that swayed around her as she walked; black trousers, a white shirt, soft leather bag slung over one shoulder. Her dark hair was cut short, shorter than he remembered, taking an extra shine from the lighting overhead. As she approached the table her face broke into a smile. She looked, Kiley thought, allowing himself the odd ageist indiscretion, lovelier that any forty-four-year-old woman had the right.

'Jack, you could at least have worn the hat.'

'Saving it for a special occasion.'

'You mean this isn't one?'

'We'll see.'

She kissed him on the mouth.

'I'm famished,' she said. 'You going to eat?'

'I don't know.'

'The food's good. Very good.'

There was an omelette on the menu, the cost, Kiley reckoned, of a meal at McDonald's or Subway for a family of five. When it came it was fat and delicious, stuffed with spinach, shallots and red pepper and bright with the taste of fresh chillis. Kate had poached eggs on sourdough

133

toast with portobello mushrooms. She'd scarcely punctured the first egg when she got down to it.

'Jack, a favour.'

He paused with his fork halfway to his mouth.

'Graeme Fisher, mean anything to you?'

'Vaguely.' He didn't know how or in what connection.

'Photographer, big in the sixties. Bailey, Duffy, Fisher. The big three, according to some. Fashion, that was his thing. Everyone's thing. Biba. *Vogue*. You couldn't open a magazine, look at a hoarding without one of his pictures staring back at you.' She took a sip from her espresso. 'He disappeared for a while in the eighties – early seventies, eighties. Australia, maybe, I'm not sure. Resurfaced with a show at Victoria Miro, new work, quite a bit different. Cooler, more detached: buildings, interiors, mostly empty. Very few people.'

Skip the art history, Kiley thought, this is leading where?

'I did a profile of him for the *Independent on Sunday*,' Kate said. 'Liked him. Self-deprecating, almost humble. Genuine.'

'What's he done?' Kiley asked.

'Nothing.'

'But he is in some kind of trouble?'

'Maybe.'

'Shenanigans.'

'Sorry?'

'Someone else's wife; someone else's son, daughter. What used to be called indiscretions. Now it's something more serious.'

Following the high-profile arrests of several

134

prominent media personalities, accused of a variety of sexual offences dating back up to forty years, reports to the police of historic rape and serious sexual abuse had increased fourfold. Men – it was mostly men – who had enjoyed both the spotlight and the supposed sexual liberation of the Sixties and later were contacting their lawyers, setting up damage limitation exercises, quaking in their shoes.

'You've still got contacts in the Met, haven't you, Jack?'

'A few.'

'I thought if there was anyone you knew – Operation Yewtree, is that what it's called? – I thought you might be able to have a word on the quiet, find out if Fisher was one of the people they were taking an interest in.'

'Should they be?'

'No. No.'

'Because if they're not, the minute I mention his name, they're going to be all over him like flies.'

Kate cut away a small piece of toast, added mushroom, a smidgeon of egg. 'Maybe there's another way.'

Kiley said nothing.

As if forgetting she'd changed the style, Kate smoothed a hand across her forehead to brush away a strand of hair. 'When he was what? Twenty-nine? Thirty? He had this relationship with a girl, a model.'

Kiley nodded, sensing where this was going.

'She was young,' Kate said. 'Fifteen. Fifteen when it started.'

'Fifteen,' Kiley said quietly.

'It wasn't aggressive, wasn't in any sense against her will, it was ... like I say, it was a relationship, a proper relationship. It wasn't even secret. People knew.'

'People?'

'In the business. Friends. They were an item.'

'And that made it OK? An item?'

'Jack...'

'What?'

'Don't prejudge. And stop repeating everything I say.'

Kiley chased a last mouthful of spinach around his plate. The waitress with the tattoos stopped by their table to ask if there was anything else they wanted and Kate sent her on her way.

'He's afraid of her,' Kate said. 'Afraid she'll go to the police herself.'

'Why now?'

'It's in the air, Jack. You read the papers, watch the news. Cleaning out the Augean stables does not come into it.'

Kiley was tempted to look at his watch: ten minutes without Kate making a reference he failed to understand. Maybe fifteen. 'A proper relationship, isn't that what you said?'

'It ended badly. She didn't want to accept things had run their course. Made it difficult. When it became clear he wasn't going to change his mind, she attempted suicide.'

'Pills?'

Kate nodded. 'It was all hushed up at the time. Back then, that was still possible.'

'And now he's terrified it'll all come out...'

136

'Go and talk to him, Jack. Do that at least. I think you'll like him.'

Liking him, Kiley knew, would be neither here nor there, a hindrance at best.

There was a bookshop specialising in fashion and photography on Charing Cross Road. Claire de Rouen. Kiley had walked past there a hundred times without ever going in. Two narrow flights of stairs and then an interior slightly larger than the average bathroom. Books floor to ceiling, wall to wall. There was a catalogue from Fisher's show at Victoria Miro, alongside a fat retrospective, several inches thick. Most of the photographs, the early ones, were in glossy black and white. Beautiful young women slumming in fashionable clothes: standing, arms aloft, in a bomb site, dripping with costume jewellery and furs; laughing outside Tubby Isaac's Jellied Eel Stall at Spitalfields; stretched out along a coster's barrow, legs kicking high in the air. One picture that Kiley kept flicking back to, a thin-hipped, almost waif-like girl standing, marooned, in an empty swimming pool, naked save for a pair of skimpy pants and gold bangles snaking up both arms, a gold necklace hanging down between her breasts. Lisa Arnold. Kate had told him her name. Lisa. He wondered if this were her.

The house was between Ladbroke Grove and Notting Hill, not so far from the Portobello Road. Flat fronted, once grand, paint beginning to flake away round the windows on the upper floors. Slabs of York stone leading, uneven, to the front door. Three bells. Graeme Fisher lived on the ground floor.

He took his time responding.

White hair fell in wisps around his ears; several days since he'd shaved. Corduroy trousers, collarless shirt, cardigan wrongly buttoned, slippers on his feet.

'You'll be Kate's friend.'

Kiley nodded and held out his hand.

The grip was firm enough, though when he walked it was slow, more of a shuffle, with a pronounced tilt to one side.

'Better come through here.'

Here was a large room towards the back of the house, now dining room and kitchen combined. A short line of servants' bells, polished brass, was still attached to the wall close by the door.

Fisher sat at the scrubbed oak table and waited for Kiley to do the same.

'Bought this place for a song in '64. All divided up since then, rented out. Investment banker and his lady friend on the top floor – when they're not down at his place in Dorset. Bloke above us, something in the social media.' He said it as if it were a particularly nasty disease. 'Keeps the bailiffs from the sodding door.'

There were photographs, framed, on the far wall. A street scene, deserted, muted colours, late afternoon light. An open-top truck, its sides bright red, driving away up a dusty road, fields to either side. Café tables in bright sunshine, crowded, lively, in the corner of a square; then the same tables, towards evening, empty save for an old man, head down, sleeping. Set a little to one side, two near-abstracts, sharp angles, flat planes.

'Costa Rica,' Fisher said, ''72. On assignment. Never bloody used. Too fucking arty by half.'

He made tea, brought it to the table in plain white mugs, added two sugars to his own and then, after a moment's thought, a third.

'Tell me about Lisa,' Kiley said.

Fisher laughed, no shred of humour. 'You don't have the time.'

'It ended badly, Kate said.'

'It always ends fucking badly.' He coughed, a rasp low in the throat, turning his head aside.

'And you think she might be harbouring a grudge?'

'Harbouring? Who knows? Life of her own. Kids. Grandkids by now, most like. Doubt she gives me a second thought, one year's end to the next.'

'Then why...?'

'This woman a couple of days back, right? Lisa's age. There she is on TV, evening news. Some bloke, some third-rate comedian, French-kissed her in the back of a taxi when she was fifteen, copped a feel. Now she's reckoning sexual assault. Poor bastard's picture all over the papers. Paedophile. That's not a fucking paedophile.' He shook his head. 'I'd sooner bloody die.'

Kiley cushioned his mug in both hands. 'Why don't you talk to her? Make sure?'

Fisher smiled. 'A while back, round the time I met Kate, I was going to have this show, Victoria Miro, first one in ages, and I thought, Lisa, I'll give her a bell. See if she might, you know, come along. Last minute, I couldn't, couldn't do it. I sent her a note instead, invitation to the private view. Never replied, never came.'

He wiped a hand across his mouth, finished his tea.

'You'll go see her? Kate said you would. Just help me rest easy.' He laughed. 'Too much tension, not good for the heart.'

Google Map said the London Borough of Haringey, estate agents called it Muswell Hill. A street of Arts and Crafts houses, nestled together, white louvred shutters at the windows, prettily painted doors. She was tall, taller than Kiley had expected, hair pulled back off her face, little make-up; tunic top, skinny jeans. He could still see the girl who'd stood in the empty pool through the lines that ran from the corners of her mouth and eyes.

'Lisa Arnold?'

'Not for thirty years.'

'Jack Kiley.' He held out a hand. 'An old friend of yours asked me to stop by.'

'An old friend?'

'Yes.'

'Then he should have told you it's Collins. Lisa Collins.' She still didn't take his hand and Kiley let it fall back by his side.

'This old friend, he have a name?' But, of course, she knew. 'You better come in,' she said. 'Just mind the mess in the hall.'

Kiley stepped around a miniature pram, various dolls, a wooden puzzle, skittles, soft toys.

'Grandkids,' she explained, 'two of them, Tuesdays and Thursday mornings, Wednesday afternoons. Run me ragged.'

Two small rooms had been knocked through to give a view of the garden: flowering shrubs, a small fruit tree, more toys on the lawn.

Lisa Collins sat in a wing-backed chair, motioning Kiley to the settee. There were paintings on the wall, watercolours; no photographs other than a cluster of family pictures above the fireplace. Two narrow bookcases; rugs on polished boards; dried flowers. It was difficult to believe she was over sixty years old.

'How is Graeme?'

Kiley shrugged. 'He seemed OK. Not brilliant, maybe, but OK.'

'You're not really a friend, are you?'

'No?'

'Graeme doesn't do friends.'

'Maybe he's changed.'

She looked beyond Kiley towards the window, distracted by the shadow of someone passing along the street outside.

'You don't smoke, I suppose?'

'Afraid not.'

'No. Well, in that case, you'll have to join me in a glass of wine. And don't say no.'

'I wasn't about to.'

'White OK?'

'White's fine.'

She left the room and he heard the fridge door open and close; the glasses were tissue-thin, tinged with green; the wine grassy, cold.

'All this hoo-ha going on,' she said. 'People

digging up the past, I'd been half-expecting someone doorstepping me on the way to Budgens.' She gave a little laugh. 'Me and my shopping trolley. Some reporter or other. Expecting me to dig up the dirt, spill the beans.'

Kiley said nothing.

'That's what he's worried about, isn't it? After all this time, the big exposé, shit hitting the fan.'

'Yes.'

'That invitation he sent me, the private view. I should have gone.'

'Why didn't you?'

'I was afraid.'

'What of?'

'Seeing him again. After all this time. Afraid what it would do to all this.' She gestured round the room, the two rooms. 'Afraid it could blow it all apart.'

'It could do that?'

'Oh, yes.' She drank some wine and set the glass carefully back down. 'People said it was just a phase. Too young, you know, like in the song? Too young to know. You'll snap out of it, they said, the other girls. Get away, move on, get a life of your own. Cradle-snatcher, they'd say to Graeme, and laugh.'

Shaking her head, she smiled.

'Four years we were together. Four years. Say it like that, it doesn't seem so long.' She shook her head again. 'A lifetime, that's what it was. When it started I was just a kid and then...'

She was seeing something Kiley couldn't see; as if, for a moment, he were no longer there.

'I knew – I wasn't stupid – I knew it wasn't

going to last forever, I even forced it a bit myself, looking back, but then, when it happened, I don't know, I suppose I sort of fell apart.'

She reached for her glass.

'What's that they say? Whatever doesn't kill you, makes you strong. Having your stomach pumped out, that helps, too. Didn't want to do that again in a hurry, I can tell you. And thanks to Graeme, I had contacts, a portfolio, I could work. David Bailey round knocking at the door. Brian bloody Duffy. *Harper's Bazaar.* I had a life. A good one. Still have.'

Still holding the wine glass, she got to her feet.

'You can tell Graeme, I don't regret a thing. Tell him I love him, the old bastard. But now...' A glance at her watch. 'Mr Collins – that's that I call him – Mr Collins will be home soon. Golf widow, that's me. Stops him getting under my feet, I suppose.'

She walked Kiley to the door.

'There was someone sniffing round. Oh, a good month ago now. More. Some journalist or other. That piece by Kate Moss had just been in the news. How when she was getting started she used to feel awkward, posing, you know, half-naked. Nude. Not feeling able to say no. Wanted to know, the reporter, had I ever felt exploited? Back then. Fifteen, she said, it's very young after all. I told her I'd felt fine. Asked her to leave, hello and goodbye. Might have been the *Telegraph*, I'm not sure.'

She shook Kiley's hand.

When he was crossing the street she called after him. 'Don't forget, give Graeme my love.'

The article appeared a week later, eight pages stripped across the Sunday magazine, accompanied by a hefty news item in the main paper. 'Art or Exploitation?' Ballet dancers and fashion models, a few gymnasts and tennis players thrown in for good measure. Unhealthy relationships between fathers and daughters, young girls and their coaches or mentors. The swimming pool shot of Lisa was there, along with several others. Snatched from somewhere, a recent picture of Graeme Fisher, looking old, startled.

'The bastards,' Kate said, vehemently. 'The bastards.'

Your profession, Kiley thought, biting back the words.

They were on their way to Amsterdam, Kate there to cover the reopening of the Stedelijk Museum after nine years of renovations, Kiley invited along as his reward for services rendered. 'Three days in Amsterdam, Jack. What's not to like?'

At her insistence, he'd worn the hat.

They were staying at a small but smart hotel on the Prinsengracht Canal, their's one of the quiet rooms at the back, looking out onto a small square. For old times sake, she insisted on taking him for breakfast, the first morning, to the art deco Café Americain in the Amsterdam American Hotel.

'First time I ever came here, Jack, to Amsterdam, this is where we stayed.'

He didn't ask.

The news from England, a bright 12 point on

144

her iPad, erased the smile from her face. As a result of recent revelations in the media, officers from Operation Yewtree yesterday made two arrests; others were expected.

'Fisher?' Kiley asked.

She shook her head. 'Not yet.' When she tried to reach him on her mobile, there was no reply.

'Maybe he'll be OK,' Kiley said.

'Let's hope,' Kate said, and pushed back her chair, signalling it was time to go. Whatever was happening back in England, there was nothing they could do.

From the outside, Kiley thought, the new extension to the Stedelijk looked like a giant bathtub on stilts; inside didn't get much better. Kate seemed to be enthralled.

Kiley found the café, pulled out the copy of *The Glass Key* he'd taken the precaution of stuffing into his pocket, and read. Instead of getting better, as the story progressed things went from bad to worse, the hero chasing round in ever-widening circles, only pausing, every now and then, to get punched in the face.

'Fantastic!' Kate said, a good couple of hours later. 'Just amazing.'

There was a restaurant some friends had suggested they try for dinner, Le Hollandais; Kate wanted to go back to the hotel first, write up her notes, rest a little, change.

In the room, she switched on the TV to catch the news. Over her shoulder, Kiley thought he recognised the street in Ladbroke Grove. Officers from the Metropolitan Police arriving at the residence of former photographer, Graeme

145

Fisher, wishing to question him with regard to allegations of historic sexual abuse, found Fisher hanging from a light flex at the rear of the house. Despite efforts by paramedics and ambulance staff to revive him, he was pronounced dead at the scene.

A sound, somewhere between a gasp and a sob, broke from Kate's throat and when Kiley went across to comfort her, she shrugged him off.

There would be no dinner, Le Hollandais or elsewhere.

When she came out of the bathroom, Kate used her laptop to book the next available flight, ordered a taxi, rang down to reception to explain.

Kiley walked to the window and stood there, looking out across the square. Already the light was starting to change. Two runners loped by in breathless conversation, then an elderly woman walking her dog, then no one. The tables outside the café at right angles to the hotel were empty, save for an old man, head down, sleeping. Behind him, Kate moved, businesslike, around the room, readying their departure, her reflection picked out, ghostlike, in the glass. When Kiley looked back towards the tables, the old man had gone.

LAST EXIT TO FUENGIROLA

David Hewson

David Hewson is a former journalist with *The Sunday Times* whose series featuring Italian detective Nic Costa opened with *A Season for the Dead* in 2003. In addition, he has written a number of stand-alones, as well as novels based on the acclaimed Danish TV series, *The Killing*.

When he finally got out of the Scrubs, Eileen had taken matters into her own hands. The terraced house in Plaistow, the place he'd grown up, was gone, she told him as they stood on the prison steps, Alf with his duffel bag in hand, blinking at the bright July sun. Then she mumbled something that sounded like 'Sleazyjet' and pushed him into a minicab to Gatwick where they flew down to Spain in what appeared to be an orange bus with wings.

Her mum had died not long before his twelve years were up. She'd owned a decrepit pile near the waterfront in Whitstable. While Alf was in jail, trying to teach his cellmate Norm the Chisel there were better ways to spell 'ink-arse-

147

erashun', it seemed the place had turned from Hoxton-by-Sea to Islington-sur-Mer. Eileen had sold the dump to a TV producer with funny glasses and a stupid haircut. Best part of a quarter of a million for dry rot, fungal damp and four squawky cats.

Now *that* was robbery, Alf observed mid-flight only to get a whack round the chops in return.

Their new home, a place that 'would keep him out of any more of that trouble he liked so much', was a tiny villa not far from the last motorway turnoff for Fuengirola. Two and a half bedrooms, a patio with a weedy palm tree, a table for drinkies with their new-found friends. Who weren't really friends, not to his way of thinking, and tended to show that after a couple of glasses of industrial strength Larios and tonic. Especially after he put a sign outside the front door that read 'Dunblagging'.

Irony, he said when she started kicking up a fuss. There'd been a lot of it about ever since the men from the Yard came a-knocking in the night.

He was sixty-three now, a big bloke, still muscular, all his own teeth, good for something better than hanging round the Costa del Sol and listening to Radio 2 off this weird iPad thing she'd bought. Bald as a coot, he'd turned walnut after two weeks of Spanish sun. That was the first time he'd looked at himself and thought: you're getting old. Time's running out. And there's still a nasty black mark on your life you never deserved.

Eileen reckoned retirement was nature's way of telling you it was time to 'adjust your lifestyle'. Not that she'd much idea what counted as lifestyle in B Wing of Wormwood Scrubs. Or that he was minded to tell her.

The truth was, she said, they could retire with a little peace for a change, away from his old scallywag mates and the reporters she now referred to as 'the meejah'. He could play golf whenever he liked and once a week she'd drive him into Fuengi town so's he could go boozing with the blokes she called 'your fellow East End villains'.

The most popular watering hole was called the Wonky Donkey. Every other Tuesday from 6.45 p.m. on Alf could be found there nursing one of the two bottles of San Miguel that would see him through the evening, listening to tales of what the old East End was like before the immigrants and the Olympics came along. Never once saying that he was, like most of them, an immigrant himself, his old dad coming over from Poland after falling out with Hitler. Or that, from what he saw on the Scrubs telly, the Olympics looked pretty good really.

They were a decent enough bunch in the Donkey even if the chatter had a distinctly circular nature to it. By week three he'd lost count of how many times he'd heard it said things were better when the Krays were around. Weren't no hoodlums robbing you in the street then. You could leave your door unlocked without some toerag kid sneaking in to nick your valuables. And when people did get hurt ... well, they asked for it usually. What harm was done was done inside as it were, kept within the criminal fraternity. For the average honest East End citizen, life was safe and calm and happy when the brothers walked the streets.

Alf listened. Sipped his San Mig. Kept quiet. Was almost glad Eileen had taken a fifty per cent share in a struggling cake shop in Benalmadena to keep her busy. Because if all he had was this lot and her trying to redecorate Dunblagging in traditional Andalucian style, all bright tiles and plates on the walls along with strings of plastic peppers and tomatoes, he'd be wishing himself back in B Wing before long.

The drinking club was called the Gentleman's Estuarial English Zoological Association. GEEZA for short. Strangers to a man, with not the least interest in animals except the eponymous donkey. Everyone appeared to have congregated there on the basis of accent alone. As Eileen put it, 'All you've got to do is open yer trap, Alfred Hawkins, and everyone knows where you's coming from.'

Plaistow. A long time ago. And his real name wasn't Hawkins either. That was his dad's invention when things got a bit sticky after the war.

The drinkers in GEEZA ranged from Barking to Bow with one northerner from Hornsey tolerated on the principle he was a nice bloke who couldn't help it. Certainly no one from the west, a part of London that always made Alf Hawkins shiver, even before they banged him up in White City's finest slammer. Or that endless sprawl below the Thames that everyone called, simply, 'sarf'.

These men weren't bad people. Being the kind

150

they were they never asked questions. Never once wondered what you'd done back home. Or who with.

It was best that way as everyone understood. Until one Tuesday night round nine o'clock, close to the point when he was wondering how soon Eileen would turn up to ferry him home. The conversation had turned once more to a learned discussion about how the social decline of modern Britain could be directly traced to the moment Walthamstow Greyhound stadium shut up shop sending everyone who wanted to go to the dogs out to Romford which wasn't really London at all. At least three in the present company declared this to be the point at which they knew Britannia was doomed to Third World penury and upped sticks for the Costa accordingly.

Alf was minded to question this assumption when the door opened and Norm the Chisel walked in, all white-faced and pop-eyed.

'Lordy,' he said, coming over, throwing his big arms round the baffled, speechless figure at the bar. 'Lordy me, Alf Hawkins. Ain't I just been looking for you everywhere? And here you are.'

The rest of them stared at him.

'Where else would he be?' Bob, the mouthy one from Canning Town, asked. 'Here's where you always are, innit? You ain't Cockney, friend. Are ya? See, this gatherin's a bit exclusive like—'

'Peckham,' Norm broke in. 'Proud of it. Any argiments needed there?'

Silence.

No one ever wanted any argiments with Norm

151

the Chisel.

He grabbed Alf Hawkins by the arm and dragged him into the corner with the stuffed donkey's head.

'How's the reading and writing going?' Alf asked. 'Fancy a drink? I never knew you were in these parts.'

'Sod the reading. I seen 'im, Alf. He's 'ere.'

'Who's here?'

'Only that toff who fitted you up for murder. Mr Poncy-Woncy Detective Chief Superintendent Owen 'Ardcastle. That's who.'

Alf walked to the door, called Eileen and told her to give him another hour. Said it in a way that meant she didn't argue.

Then got a pint of lager for Norm and a third San Mig for himself, came back and plonked them on the upturned barrel next to the donkey's head.

'No one knows where Hardcastle is, Norm. Scotland Yard've spent three years chasing him. Got nowhere. You must be dreaming.'

He didn't much like the Spanish beer. Or Fuengirola for that matter. Alf Hawkins didn't want a lot out of life. Just to live and die in the busy terraced streets where he'd grown up, watching them change with the years. He'd been robbed of that and it hurt just to think about it.

'I ain't dreaming.'

'Besides,' Alf added, thinking of what Eileen would say. 'That was in the past. I'm out now. A good boy. All I've got to do is...' He looked round the Wonky Donkey. The crowd at the bar were staring at the two of them, as if an unwritten rule of etiquette had been broken. 'All I got to do is...'

He didn't finish the sentence. Couldn't.

'You're sure?' Alf asked.

'On my mum's life.'

'Your mum's dead.'

'Figger of speech. I'm sure. So what we gonna do?'

All the other inmates called him Scarface which was odd since Norm had the soft, pink cheeks of a baby even if his head was a touch small for his body, that of a prop forward on steroids.

It took a while before Alf realised he was hearing this wrong. Men in jail talked easily about their families, where they came from, what they'd do when they walked free into the smoggy air of west London. Not so much about what got them in there. Only gradually did he discover that Norman Barker – the Chisel bit came from his day job as a carpenter – had nearly killed a debt collector who'd been collecting more than debts from his missus in Peckham. Against her will, Norm insisted, not that she was waiting for him when he finally came out.

No previous. Not much sign of a temper. Just a long day at work then he came home, found them, lost it bad. Beat the debt collector black and blue, threw him onto the landing of the flats and half-strangled the man with his silk Burberry cravat.

Alf wondered why anyone would be rash enough to go to Peckham wearing a silk Burberry cravat. It seemed to be asking for trouble, just as much as fooling around with the wife of a gigantic bloke like Norm. But he didn't pursue that point.

The Scrubs being a place where people had lots of time to play with words, the customers of Her Majesty's Prison Service had dragged this story out of Norm and come up with the nickname.

It wasn't scar-face as Alf had thought. It was scarf-ace on the grounds that Norm's skill with the aforesaid neck warmer had proved so devastating the debt collector had been left in a wheelchair for a while, a fact the judge, a well-known hanger, had made much of when sending him down for attempted murder.

'I know I'm fick. Just a big stupid ug,' Norm whispered when they retreated further into the Donkey's darkest corner. 'But I seen 'im with my own two eyes. Seen the proof too. I'm telling you, Alf. Owen 'Ardcastle is living high on the hog no more than ten minutes up the hill from 'ere. Calling hisself Matthew Warman. Retired City financier. Pad like you wouldn't believe. Ten bedrooms, mebbe more. Jag in the drive and some young tart sunning herself on the patio who ain't the cleaner either. Veranda an' a pool you could drown Millwall in, which wouldn't be a bad idea if you ask me. It's not right. So what we gonna...?'

'Nothing,' Alf insisted. 'Even if it is him. Nothing at all.'

Norm took a swig of beer and stared at him sulkily. He'd been released from the Scrubs six weeks before Alf. Had said something at the time about skedaddling out of the country and putting all the bad stuff behind him.

'You taught me to read and spell proper,' Norm said.

Poring over books and newspapers, showing his cellmate a few tips on joined-up writing, passed the time. And Norm was a good, decent man, one whose temper had briefly and tragically broken. Another judge – a lawyer who liked the appeal system – he might have got a couple of years at the most. But being the quiet, resigned bloke he was Norm had never pushed it, and wouldn't even though Alf had nagged him.

'It was a pleasure. You're no idiot. You got to stop thinking that.'

'Didn't need to teach me difference between right and wrong though, did ya? What that 'Ardcastle did...'

Twelve years. They should have been good ones. Then, a strange Thursday in October, the door comes down, men in masks, yelling, shoving him into a corner, arms behind his back. Eileen crying. Wanting to know what was happening. And he couldn't tell her. Because, as the nightmare fell around them, Alf Hawkins, while no stranger to such situations, hadn't a clue himself.

Innocent people were always the easiest ones to fit up. DCS Owen Hardcastle proved himself to be a master of that. The night before a consignment of gold worth the best part of three million quid had been busted out of a bullion van on the way to Heathrow. Two of the security guards got shot. One died on the spot, the other in hospital. Eileen was down in Whitstable. Alf Hawkins had been at home at the time watching telly on his own, too lazy to go down the pub. Owen Hardcastle must have known that somehow because when the evidence got laid out in court it seemed so strong, so incontrovertible, the briefs never even put the case into the review system when the evil bastard fled the Met and Britain leaving a nasty string of allegations in his wake.

He'd been one of the new breed of media-friendly officers, university-educated and prone to quoting literature at press conferences. Popular in the newspapers and on TV. Seemingly sent down more than a few real villains too, one of them being Alf Hawkins, a criminal master-mind masquerading as a decent, honest citizen. Dead boring and invisible when in truth he was an animal who shot dead a couple of security guards without a second thought, which Alf still found remarkable given that at the time he was actually watching *EastEnders*, bored to bits.

'That man's the crim,' Norm said, jabbing a big finger into Alf Hawkins' chest. 'Not you. We're as bad as 'im if we let 'im get away with it. You read what the newspapers said when he legged it from London? Reckoned he was wanted for all manner of stuff. Murder. Robbery. Corruption. Rottenest copper the Yard ever 'ad. An'...'

'Didn't help me, did it?' Alf said, putting his hand on the big man's arm. 'I know all this. It's done with. I'm here. I'm free. I can't get those years back. I got Eileen to think about.'

'He murdered people. Good as killed you. I

saw what you were like in the Scrubs.' He hesitated then said it anyway. 'You still don't look right to me. I gave 'em reason to make me do time. You didn't. We all knew what you was. Not what 'Ardcastle made out.'

The little GEEZA gathering at the bar had gone silent. You weren't supposed to have serious conversations Tuesday nights in the Donkey. It was a time to sink beer and talk man crap.

'I never asked you for nuffink before.' The big finger was jabbing again. 'Not till now. This sod's evil. A monster...'

'Tell the police...'

'You think they'd believe a big, stupid ug like me? Peckham villain fresh out of chokey?'

'Then—'

'No arguing. You preached a lot about justice when we was inside. About how it mattered. You're coming with me tomorrow. We're going to take a look at this palace of his. See it for yourself. Tell me there's justice there.'

Alf finished his San Mig, said nothing.

'I'll meet you in the Lidl car park next to Burger King,' Norm said. 'You know that?'

'Would I dine or seek provisions anywhere else?' Alf asked.

'Still a sarky old bugger, aren't you? Something I s'pose. Ten o'clock sharp. Be there.'

He didn't like lying to Eileen but there didn't seem much choice. So he told her GEEZA had fixed a fishing trip to the reservoirs, looking for carp. Took out the rod and gear, got her to drop him off where Norm said, ten minutes early.

The stuttering cake shop was 'developing a new business strategy', she said. It seemed to involve doughnuts. There was a suspicious cast in her eye all the same. The fishing tackle was a gift when they turned up in Spain, a way of trying to give him things to do. He'd never got an inch of it wet.

Norm turned up with a red van, lettering on the side: *English Carpenter, Excellent Work, Great Value, No Siestas*. He said he'd sunk every last penny of his meagre savings into coming to the Costa, renting a little flat on the edge of town and trying to build a new life, a new business out of nothing.

Everyone in the Scrubs reckoned he'd been a great chippie on the outside, though how they knew ... That life seemed oddly remote now. As if it happened to a different man. Jail wasn't a place he ever wanted to see again. Something had been taken from him there and he knew it was never coming back. Maybe that was why the idea that fugitive Detective Chief Superintendent Owen Hardcastle was living high on the hog just round the corner got to him. Norm was a smart man, whatever he thought of himself. He understood that too.

The story was simple. Just into his new career as a bespoke carpenter for the expats of southern Spain, Norm had been given a job up in the hills behind Mijas. A remote place, surrounded by pines and exotic vegetation. Cash in hand, no questions asked. Refurb requiring some fancy woodwork and maximum discretion.

The man who answered the door was middle-aged, tall, a bit aristocratic. Posh London voice, smart clothes, dolly bird by the huge infinity pool overlooking the hills down to the sea. Lived there a year, he said. Needed some work done out back in the private quarters.

Tap of nose with that. *Private.*

Norm usually worked the tower blocks of south London. But he could handle mahogany and walnut veneers when required which was right up the street of Mr Matthew Warman, retired financier from the City of London (ha, ha). Gun cases, polished wood and glass, a proper little private armoury. And not just shot-guns either. Revolvers. Assault weapons. Knives. Stuff Norm couldn't guess at.

Alf listened then said the obvious.

'Doesn't mean it's him.'

They were sitting in the front of the van. The chippie reached behind, searched inside his tool-boxes, came back with a set of photos, placed them on Alf's lap and said, 'I 'appened upon these when I was clearing out his old cabinets. Purloined a few as it were.'

Men in uniform. Upper-ranking police officers at receptions, getting medals, meeting politicians and a few celebs. One face in every picture. The lean, smiling, supercilious features of DCS Owen Hardcastle.

'Our man's 'ad the surgeons in,' Norm said. 'Don't look quite like that today. Weeny little moustache not far off 'Itler's and the kind of tan you don't get from Tetleys. But you know 'im, Alf. You must have seen 'im often enough what with the court case an' everything. We get close

159

enough today. You'll cop that smug-faced bastard. Then tell me I'm an idiot.'

Norm's hand went to the keys. Alf stopped
him.

'If it is Hardcastle he's filthy rich, settled here
and armed to the teeth. The man's not going to
take warmly to us marching in there, is he?'

'Thought of that,' Norm said and they set off
for the hills.

It took twenty-five minutes. A different part of
the Costa. Vast mansions hidden in trees behind
high gates. Midway between two such palaces
Norm stopped the van next to a smart new Fiat
parked wheels-up on the slope to a stone wall. A
man got out, Spanish-looking, white shirt and
blue jeans, about forty, short, didn't smile, face
mostly hidden behind a pair of large sunglasses.
Norm introduced him as his friend Bruno. He
said he was from Madrid and spoke good
English but with an accent. After a handshake
Bruno passed over a serious pair of binoculars.
Then said they ought to talk after Alf had eye-
balled the man in the big house and made up his
mind.

There didn't seem a lot of point in asking
questions.

Half a mile up the road Norm told him to stay
by the gates, got himself in through the intercom
and walked up the drive.

Alf Hawkins stayed behind the pillar out of
sight. If he knew Owen Hardcastle then Owen
Hardcastle surely knew him.

After a few minutes Norm came out with a tall

160

man in tight swimming trunks, a tanned beer gut flopping over them. A slim blonde in a bikini emerged briefly, gave Mr Speedo a drink then disappeared inside.

From a comfortable position close to the gate Alf turned the binoculars on Norm's new acquaintance and kept them there.

The moustache was new, more British military officer than Hitler.

They talked for all of two minutes. When he came back through the big security gates Norm said, 'That bugger's so high up on his horse it's a miracle he can see us little people down here. I offered to build him a gazebo. Seemed a gazebo sort of bloke to me. Could use the work. But nah—'

'Norm...'

The man from Peckham shushed him.

'Let's not talk now.'

Bruno took them to a roadside bar for beer. There he gave a little talk about how different Andalucian food was from that in Madrid, then ordered a few plates of tapas: mushrooms, prawns, *patatas bravas*, some live clams called *conchas finas*.

'Is it him?' he asked squeezing lemon on a blob of orange and white shellfish, watching it wriggle with shock, then popping a cocktail stick into the shiny flesh and wolfing it down.

Alf stuck with the mushrooms and the potatoes.

'Had some work done on his mush. That tash looks dead stupid. It's him.'

Bruno squeezed lemon juice on another shell

161

and sighed.

'This Warman's a big man around here. A supporter of many charities. An attendee at all the great functions.' A smile, the first Alf had seen. 'A friend of the mayor and the chief of police. Very close, I believe.'

'He's a hood,' Norm said. 'Got enough guns in there to start a small war. I seen them. I made his damned cabinets, didn't I?'

'I told you, Norm. He's a person of importance around here. What's that English expression?' the Spaniard asked with a brief smile. 'Ah, I remember. Thick as thieves.'

When he shrugged his shoulders the corners of his mouth went right down, further than seemed possible. Like that football manager who used to be with Chelsea, except he was Portuguese.

'You're the man he sent to prison,' Bruno added looking straight at him. 'Whose life he ruined. This is your job if it's anyone's. There would be...' He took a sip of beer. 'Compensation, I believe. Considerable, I imagine. Life-changing.'

He looked round. They were outside, overlooking a small garden. No one to see them but a half-slumbering dog and a few chickens.

'You'll want this,' the man said and passed over a handgun and a pack of shells.

Alf Hawkins was no stranger to this particular weapon. Common or garden Glock 17.

Then Bruno looked at his watch and said, 'I must go now. Tomorrow, Señor Hawkins. It cannot wait.'

Nine o'clock the next morning, thirty minutes

162

before Norm was meant to pick him up, Eileen walked into the front room, deposited the gun on the table and said in a voice stiff with fury, 'What the hell's this? Care to tell me?'

'It's a gun, dear,' he replied. 'What's it look like?'

Arms folded, standing over him as he sat in the living room, she muttered, 'I can see that.'

They never rowed much, not in forty years of marriage.

'You shouldn't go looking through my things,' he said as mildly as he could manage.

'I wanted to know if you'd used that fishing rod I bought you. That was a lie too, wasn't it?'

'Yes,' Alf agreed straight out.

Her eyes turned glassy at that. He remembered the first time they met after Hardcastle's snatch team took him into custody. How she didn't even ask the obvious question: was it true? Did he really do those terrible things?

She was the only one who'd believed him from the start. Even the brief they found fell for Hardcastle's clever fit-up in his own head, or so Alf reckoned.

'I don't want to lose you again. All them years wasted. I can't go through it twice.'

He didn't know what to say. So he pulled up a stool, got her to sit on it, took her hands, leaned over, kissed his wife on the cheek, held her.

'Truth is,' he said, 'sometimes things come along you can't walk away from. 'Cos if you do they'll just follow you anyway.'

'What's that supposed to mean?'

'It means you need to trust me. One last time.

And then...'

Then what? Compensation, said Norm's friend Bruno, a curious stranger who came offering a gun. Life-changing. But rewards came in different guises. And the Spaniard, if that's what he was, didn't get specific.

'Drop me off on the way to the shop,' he said. 'Tonight...'

She was crying full on now and he hated to see that. So he took out his freshly-ironed hankie and wiped away the tears.

'You stop that now, love. It's not needed. Tonight we'll go out for dinner. Somewhere nice. My treat. You deserve it.'

Two hours later he was with Norm and Bruno watching Hardcastle's bit of stuff manoeuvre her Mercedes soft-top out of his palace then disappear down the road to Malaga, the word 'shopping' etched across her pretty, vacant face.

'Lithuanian,' the man from Madrid said. 'The man has no class.'

'All that money,' Norm grumbled. 'Who needs class?'

He looked at Alf.

'You want me to get him to open up again? I can say I'm back to do a bit more work.'

'Nah,' Alf said. He had his best jacket on, the Glock tucked inside it. 'He'll let me in.'

Then he walked up the road, went to the gate, pressed the bell and smiled at the camera lens above it.

A voice. Calm, English, familiar.

'DCS Hardcastle,' Alf said quickly. 'Long time

no see. We got matters to discuss, Owen. Don't you think?'

A long pause. Then the gate buzzed. He pushed it open and went inside.

The man himself was standing by the front door, phone in hand, pink Bermuda shorts and a green polo neck with the name of a golf club above the pocket. The tash was so bad it looked stitched on. He was smiling, which was never a pretty sight, and seemed leaner, richer, nastier.

'You'll want a stiff one after all this time,' Hardcastle said.

On the way up the drive Alf had shifted the handgun from his jacket pocket to the back of his trousers, stuffing it under the belt. Wouldn't be easy sitting down like that. But Owen Hardcastle was no fool. He'd have seen it otherwise.

Alf gazed at the pink shorts and shook his head.

'Just a chat'll do.'

He looked just as much at ease now as he did giving his lying evidence in court. Phone still in hand as they sat down.

Alf said, 'I'm not interrupting anything...?'

'Good Lord, no. I'm retired. Enjoying myself.'

Hardcastle's voice sounded posher than ever. It wasn't hard to imagine him mixing with the mayor and chief of police, regaling them with stories about his former life as a financial wizard back in London. And the rest.

They were in a long room, lavishly decorated, Alf on the leather sofa in front of a low coffee table, the Yard's most wanted renegade officer on a winged chair opposite, fidgeting from side to side.

'What's it you're after?' he asked. 'Money, I imagine.'

'Everyone likes money. But most of all I'd like an explanation. Why me?'

A glance at the watch. A brief sigh.

'Because you were there. Because it was easy. I don't want to talk about this.'

'Shame,' Alf said, then leaned forward, took out the Glock, placed the handgun on the coffee table. It was uncomfortable where it was anyway. 'I do.'

Hardcastle shook his head.

'I thought you were the wronged innocent, Alf. Above all this. Smart.'

'If I was smart I wouldn't have spent twelve years inside for something I didn't even know about. Let alone do.'

'I told you. It was easy. You were there ... Nothing else to say.'

Alf picked up the Glock, aimed it, watched Owen Hardcastle stiffen with alarm then pulled a shot into the floor-length mirror behind him.

Long time since he'd fired a gun. It was louder than he remembered.

The man opposite jumped in the air, came down in his seat. Glanced across the room, scared. Looked at his watch again.

'You need to find something to say,' Alf told him. 'Fill in the gaps. Now please.'

Twenty laboured minutes it took, as if Hardcastle was spinning it out as much as he could. Alf had suspected most of the tale anyway but it was nice to get the sequence of events, the pre-planning, the job itself, the laying of evidence, all down and clear.

'That wasn't hard, was it?' he asked when the man was done.

'None of it was aimed at you. Could have been anyone.'

'I'll try to remember that the next time I'm thinking about those twelve years I spent in the Scrubs.'

'What do you want, Alf?'

'Five million. Real money. Pounds. Not euros. Cash on the nail. Nothing wired. Nothing on tick. All in my sweaty palm by tomorrow lunch-time. Think you can do that?'

'No,' Hardcastle replied. 'Give me three days.'

'You got two.'

'Two then.' He looked at the door. 'And then you're gone? I don't hear from you any more?'

'You have my word. Which is worth some-thing, by the way, but I imagine you know that.'

A short, mirthless laugh.

'Oh yes. Mr Honest. Why do you think it was so easy? I have to emphasise this. It wasn't—'

Alf waved the gun at him again.

'Don't say it wasn't personal, Owen. Please.' He stood up. 'Do we have an agreement?'

Hardcastle got to his feet, nodded, held out his right hand.

'I'm sorry. If that helps.'

'Not really,' Alf replied but he put the Glock on the coffee table and reached out anyway.

It was quick. He had to give Owen Hardcastle that. One brisk step and he'd dodged Alf's outstretched hand, was down snatching the gun, grabbing it greedily.

The mask dropped then. Alf listened. Tut-tutted. When the barrage of profanities and threats ended he said, 'I'll never know how you got through university, let alone made DCS, with a trap on you like that. Really...'

More curses. The Glock waved in his face.

'There's people on the way here who are gonna take care of you,' Hardcastle spat at him, a touch of estuarial leaking into his voice. 'They can pick up the bloody pieces now. They can clean up the mess.'

Alf shook his head.

'You don't mean that, Owen. Not really.'

Another flurry of foul words. Alf was tut-tutting when Hardcastle pointed the Glock in his face and pulled the trigger.

Nothing.

Two more clicks.

Two more nothings.

Alf smiled, retrieved the rest of the shells from his jacket pocket, scattered them round the marble floor where they bounced and tinkled like ice cubes just let loose. Then he retrieved the wired mike from inside his shirt and, just for good measure, said into it, 'All yours now, gents.'

A thought.

'Hang on...'

Memories. It was all coming back.

'Let me do this,' he said, prising the gun from Hardcastle's shaking hands and lobbing it behind the sofa. 'If I can remember.'

Of course he could. It had been a part of his life
– the best outside Eileen – for more than twenty
years.

'Detective Sergeant Alfred Hawkins. West
Ham serious crime squad, sir. I would caution
you but for the life of me I don't know what
passes as a caution in this warm and foreign
land. So let me just say...'

Voices, the sound of a door coming down,
windows smashing, men coming in behind him.

Alf reached forward and grabbed Owen Hardcastle by the front of his golf club polo shirt,
pulled his smooth, scared face close enough to
smell the sickly aftershave.

'Your nickedness knows no bounds, sunshine.'

The funny Spaniard stood there grinning,
Norm the Chisel too.

'Book him, Bruno,' Alf said. 'We're done
'ere.'

By three o'clock the team from Madrid had
Hardcastle in custody in a special incident room
they'd set up down the coast in Marbella. In the
neighbouring cell they had the four Ukrainian
hoods they'd nabbed on the way to the villa,
summoned by the fugitive copper to deal with
his unexpected visitor.

An hour later the mayor was in another custody suite, with the local chief of police in the
adjoining one. Bruno was well prepared. Once
he had Owen Hardcastle on tape admitting to
fixing the bullion job there was enough to pull
him in as a local crim, along with his chums.

'Take you back to when you was working?'

Norm asked as they were getting ready to leave.

'Not really.'

The lines weren't quite so blurred then. There were bent cops, true. But the idea someone would fit up one of their colleagues...

They walked out of the temporary HQ Bruno had set up and went to a café round the corner. The story was on the news. Reporters and TV teams were flying in from London to cover the biggest crime bust to hit the Costa del Sol in years. Norm was going to make himself scarce with a quick holiday to Gibraltar. Bruno had fixed for Alf and Eileen to spend a couple of days at a posh hotel in the mountains at his expense.

Scotland Yard said they were sending out an assistant chief constable who wanted to talk to Alf about compensation and the reinstatement of his lost pension. The Spaniard had leaned forward when he heard that news and said, very firmly, 'Don't sign anything, Alf. Those people screwed you over. Get a lawyer and take them to the cleaners.'

Norm had winked at that and said, 'You're minted, mate.'

Alf kept quiet at that but in the café he raised his glass of San Mig, proposed a brief toast then asked, 'Bruno's what then? Spanish Special Branch or something?'

'Kind of. And a bit of Interpol or whatever they call it now.'

The man from Peckham answered so easily.

'Was he waiting for you when you got out of the Scrubs?'

Norm put down his glass and looked bashful.

170

'I'm not mad about this,' Alf added. 'I'd just like to know.'

'Saw me three times while we was in there together. Thought you might have noticed. I didn't get many visitors.'

'Oh,' Alf said.

'They were on to you as soon as Eileen bought that place. Bruno reckoned you and 'Ardcastle was in it together. I told 'im not to be so stupid. That bastard sent you down. But he reckoned sometimes it worked like that. Someone did the time and got their reward afterwards. I wasn't 'aving that.'

Alf lifted his glass again and said thanks.

'I told 'im you was a good 'un,' Norm went on. 'They'd been hunting all these locals for years apparently. Couldn't quite get enough evidence. Not surprising if the local boss copper was in on it, eh?'

'True.'

'I couldn't level with you, Alf. It wasn't part of the arrangement. He fixed the job for me. The flights. Told me to find you in the Donkey and...'

He was a gentle, kind man and starting to get upset. So Alf put a hand on his, said a few quiet, comforting words then asked, 'What now?'

'I'll try and get some work,' Norm said. 'Not much back for me in London, is there?'

They didn't have much to say after that. Close to five Alf wished him luck and left. Bruno had laid on an unmarked squad car to take him home then pick up Eileen and head off for their unexpected treat.

* * *

171

The place the men from Madrid took them was somewhere Alf would never have found, or paid for, on his own. A hunting lodge high in the forests of the Sierra Blanca. Almost empty for some reason. Quiet, well-dressed staff, an elegant suite as big as the ground floor of their little villa. A restaurant looking back to the busy lights of the coastline. No sound except birds in the trees and the low chatter of the staff. They ordered some food and sat alone on the terrace at sunset, lost for words for a while. At the view. And events.

'A man from the *Daily Mirror* offered an awful lot of money if you wanted to talk to him,' Eileen said as the waiter came with the first course: lobster.

'He can sod off.'

'A gentleman from the *Guardian* wants to talk too but he wasn't offering nothing at all.'

'He can sod off too.'

Alf had taken down the Dunblagging sign before they left. She'd liked that but they hadn't spoken much along the way, not with Bruno up front talking about the countryside and its history.

'I suppose you want to go back now,' she said quietly. 'To Plaistow. Wasn't such a good idea coming down here anyway. I don't think the cake shop's going to make it.'

He prodded his lobster and thought for a moment.

'Alf? Did you hear what I said?'

'If you hadn't bought that place in Fuengi none of this would have happened, would it? How can

172

that be a bad idea?'

'Well no, but ... London. I mean ... it's where you grew up. It's home.'

'Nah,' Alf said, then took the decision to dive in and try the thing in front of him. Lobster. First time ever. A good call. It was new and it was nice.

'You're just saying that...'

'Home's where you are, sweetheart,' he said and squeezed her hand across the table. 'If we've got money we can put some of that into the cake shop. Do an extension on the house too. Maybe build a little pool. I know a good chippie. Wouldn't mind learning a bit of the lingo either. Quite fancy knowing what I'm eating for one thing. And...'

And lots of things when he came to think about it. It wasn't just Bruno's sly and engaging talk about how the Arabs lived here once and left behind some beautiful buildings if only you knew where to look for them. There was a travel book with pictures in the hotel bedroom full of stuff he ached to see: cities and castles and cathedrals, all manner of spectacular places. He could hardly stop talking about it once he started. Especially when he saw how Eileen's face lit up along the way.

Then she was crying again. Women all over. Blub when you're happy. Blub when you're sad.

'Oh please, love...'

'You got your glint back, Alf. That's all. You got it back and I thought I'd never see that again.'

He grinned, felt happy, truly happy, for the first

173

time since he'd stepped out of the Scrubs.

'Only 'cos you kept it for me all them years.'

There was a Spanish word Bruno'd taught him that afternoon after they nabbed Owen Hard-castle, the first of many to come.

'Salud,' Alf said and chinked his glass against hers.

CLICK

Alison Joseph

Alison Joseph's first book about Sister Agnes was *Sacred Hearts*, published in 1994, and the most recent title in the series is *A Violent Act*. She has worked in local radio, and is the author of a number of radio plays; she has also adapted books written by other writers for radio. She is the current Chair of the CWA.

'You'd know if he was dead, though, wouldn't you? Your own husband...'

She stared into the black water. Around her the trees dripped with recent rain.

Would I? she wondered.

It was all very well for Rosemary to say that, pouring her yet another cup of coffee in her warm kitchen. Trying to help, of course. 'I mean, put it this way, Sheila, no news is good news, in my view David has just wandered off, memory loss, you know the kind of thing, I saw a programme on the telly about it, people just forget who they are sometimes, they'll find him safe and sound, trust me...'

Safe and sound.

She left the lake and headed through the trees,

her Wellingtons squelching in mud. Six days he'd been missing. Five and a half days since her phone call to the police, reporting that her husband hadn't come back. Yes, she'd said, uncharacteristic. Very out of character, she'd agreed. A solicitor, she said. Semi-retired. Concentrating on the garden these days, and his antique collecting, a bit of tennis too, although his knee had been playing up ... Our marriage? We'd been married thirty-two years last August. 'Any problems in your marriage, madam?' No, she'd said. No problems. 'Ours was a happy marriage,' she'd told the police officer.

The damp branches shivered in the cold wind.

A happy marriage.

How do I know? I know nothing about my marriage. I know nothing about my husband. All I know is that he set off for Waitrose in the Volvo, as he did every Thursday, and he never came back. There it was, our car on the news, last night, abandoned, police crawling all over it.

A happy marriage.

For all I know, he might be anywhere. He might be dead. For all I know.

She reached the path that led out to the Otley Road. The sky was heavy with impending rain.

Click. Camera 722, Otley Road. '11.04,' the timecode said. Click. Camera 723. '11.21' Click.

He zoomed in. The black and white image on the screen grew fuzzier, but the number plate was visible. That's the car all right, he thought. Click. Camera 724 ... 725 ... Silver Volvo, there it is. And then it disappears. And reappears, six days later, abandoned in a side street, they'd had the call this morning.

He checked the map. So, he leaves his home, heads on to the Otley Road, Waitrose, the wife said, and then vanishes. CCTV of the Waitrose car park, no sign of him there—

There was a knock at his door. 'Matt...?' She stood in the doorway, black hair, black trouser suit, red lipstick.

'Samira. Hi.' He swivelled his chair.

'The SIO sent me.'

'He did, did he?'

'He said he wants you to photograph the car.'

'Me? I'm doing the CCTV.'

'There's no one else. A new shout, little gangster rude-boy found shot dead in Yeadon. They're all out there.'

Matt sighed. 'Sure, I'll do it.'

'He said...' she hesitated.

'DS Shah,' he said. 'I know what he said.'

She laughed.

'He said, "Shame we've only got Novak".'

She shook her head, still laughing.

'Novak living in the fucking nineteenth century. Didn't he say that?'

'No,' she said. 'Course not.'

'Usually that's what he says. When he's not complaining about having given the job to an "Art Gallery nancy boy".' Matt got to his feet. He picked up two camera cases. One was hard black plastic with silver edges. The other was a battered brown leather bag.

Samira glanced from one to the other.

'Told you,' Novak said.

177

'He did say...'

'What?'

She shrugged. 'What you said. About the nine-teenth century.'

'I like the old stuff,' Matt tapped the brown leather. 'Don't suppose you've ever seen such a thing.'

'I have, so. My grandpa has a funny old camera like that.'

'Your grandpa?' He stared, appalled. 'I'm not that old.'

'Course you're not.' She patted his arm. 'SIO wants the pictures back by lunchtime.'

The door shut behind her. He looked at both camera cases. He put down the brown leather one, slung the black one over his shoulder and left.

In the car he glanced at himself in the mirror. He saw a tired-looking white man, brown hair fading to grey.

Samira's grandfather must have twenty years on me.

He imagined him, sprightly and upright, still black-haired, pottering in his well-tended semi, devoted wife, Samira was always talking about her nan, children, grandchildren.

Family life.

Perhaps it keeps you young.

What do I know?

It was a quiet residential street, taped off with blue and white. The car was neatly parked. One of the Scenes of Crime team was sitting on the

wall, a community constable, Barbara something, they'd met before, strange taste in hip hop,
he remembered, even stranger taste in shoes.

'All right?' she said, as he approached.

'Aye,' he replied. Her boots were black with
chunky silver heels.

He got out his tripod and camera and set to
work. The neat clean car made neat square
images. Barbara said something about getting a
coffee.

He was aware of someone standing at his
shoulder. She reached out across the police tape,
as if to stroke the bonnet of the car.

'Madam!' His hand caught hers, a brief touch
before she snatched hers away.

'Sorry. Of course.' She blushed. 'Forensics and
all that. I've seen it on the television.'

'Everyone has.'

Her gaze was still fixed on the car. 'I suppose
everyone hopes, don't they?'

'Hopes what?'

She turned to him. 'That it won't be the car. Or
the ... whatever ... that it will be a mistake.'

'You must be Mrs...?'

She held out her hand, strangely polite, formal.
'Sheila,' she said.

He shook her hand, clumsily. 'And this is—'

'Oh yes.' She interrupted him. 'This is our car.
Well, his car, really. I tend to drive the Polo.'

She surveyed the car, leaning to one side as if
checking the tyres. She turned back to Matt. 'Do
people do this? Disappear like this?'

'Well...' He straightened up. He wondered
when the SOCO would be back.

'Suicide,' she said, suddenly. 'That's what one of the reporters asked me. No, I said, no, of course not. He wouldn't leave me like this, not knowing...'

Matt fingered his camera.

She hunched her shoulders. Her coat was too thin for the weather. 'Chilly, isn't it?'

'Yes,' he agreed.

'They keep asking me, what was he like?' She spoke suddenly, loudly. 'Well, I said to them, he's my husband. He liked his work. He likes his tennis. And antiques, he'd become quite a collector since he was working less, porcelain, clocks...' She looked up at him. 'What can I tell them? He's my husband. I love him...' Her voice cracked.

'Mrs Logan,' he began.

Her eyes welled with tears.

'I have to go,' he said.

She was still standing there, staring at her husband's car.

He fished in his pocket. 'Here,' he said, handing her a card.

She took it, read it. 'Matt Novak. Imaging Officer,' she said. 'Is that what you are?'

He nodded.

'Anything you can think of...' he said. He could see Barbara, hobbling along the street, paper cup in hand.

'I can ring you?' She gazed up at him.

He nodded. 'Sure.'

She watched as he knelt by the car, packing his camera case. She was still watching as he got into his car and drove away.

Who do I think I am? he thought, driving back into town, giving her my card like that? She's got the DI to talk to, she doesn't need me.

He watched the rain spatter on his windscreen, the to and fro of the windscreen wipers.

I know why, of course. Another wife, elsewhere. Another story of abandonment, of pain.

Not that she'll be crying.

The familiar clench of despair, dark as the rain clouds that hunched over town.

He slammed his car door, breezed through reception, strode along the corridor to the Operations Room.

'Novak, old son.' A thin, slouching man in a pale suit looked up at him. 'Didn't need a dark room, then?'

Samira glanced across, laughing. 'Leave him alone, Terry.'

Novak scanned the wide, light space. 'SIO in?'

Terry shook his head. 'He's off with the Yeadon shooting.'

Samira handed three photographs to Matt. 'These are the suspects so far. The current view is that the victim was dealing and trespassed on another gang's patch. He's a lad called Cavin Jackson. Found dead in scrubland by the industrial estate. Single gunshot wound. He was carrying a blade, but no sign he went armed apart from that. He lives alone, one of the flats on the Grange estate there. He's known to the local team. Drug dealing, and rumours of something nasty with the local girls, some kind of pimping scene. He's got one brother, a half brother, technically. He identified the body. Darren, he's called, lives in London. Said he didn't have much to do with him. We're doing house to house, no one's talking. Single bullet, retrieved, forensics are having a look.'

Matt stared at the images. Three scowling male faces stared back.

'We've talked to the mother,' Samira said. 'You can listen if you want.' She handed him a CD, patted his arm. 'I'd get the images to the SIO as soon as you can. He's been making comments about how they'll all turn up in pretty frames.'

Alone, at his desk, Matt stared at the CD. Mrs Evelyn Jackson, it said, scrawled in black marker pen. He loaded it and pressed Play. He could hear Samira's voice, quiet, sympathetic, prompting. Then the mother spoke.

'I told him myself, loads of times I'm telling him, don't you go running with them, them's bad, they are, but he want money, he want to be the big guy, you see the car he drive, how does he get the money for that, BMW, you see it?'

There was another question from Samira, and then the mother's voice again. 'They pulled back the sheet, and I saw my son's face ... And I lay me down and wept. And when I done weeping, I looked at him, at his face that weren't him no more, and I wanted to cry to the heavens, I wanted to shout out loud, Lord knows I did. I wanted to say to him, "What you go doing this for, Boy, going armed? Didn't I always say, you go out

182

there carrying blades, there's always someone carrying something bigger and better than what you got..." I told him so many times, so many times...' The voice cracked into tears. After a moment, she spoke again. 'I went to take him in my arms, but the officer there, she tries to stop me. So I says to her, I ain't never going to see my baby again. Even the mother of Our Lord got to hold her dead child in her arms...'

Matt pressed Stop.

The mother of Our Lord.

A memory. An image. He clicked on Menu, scrolled through his documents. I know it's here, he thought. I know they're both here.

Click. Two images. One, a Madonna and Child, china-white skin against rich folds of red, the light and shade of the painter's brush.

The second was a seaside snap, a woman and a little girl, holding hands. The woman is smiling down at the child. The child is laughing at the camera. He sees blue sky, blue sea, blurred white cliffs, windswept blonde hair.

Under the first image it said, 'The Amati Madonna. Restoration, Cremona Museum Service. Restoration team, Maziotti, Pedoni, Novak.'

It had been a time of colour and light and laughter. The painting was discovered in a little church, cobwebbed, sticky with neglect. An early Anquissola, they thought, as they worked on it, brushstroke by brushstroke, bringing it back to life.

He gazed at the images. I spent my working days with art and colour and joy, my evenings with my wife and child.

Click.

His finger on the mouse. The image had gone.

He stared at the blank page of his computer screen.

I will not...

Click. A black and white image of the Otley Road. Click. A car number plate. Click. Woodland. Click. Not art. Not paint. Not joy, hope, colour. Just shades of grey. Just evidence. Just facts.

Just the mother's voice, ringing in his ears. 'I ain't never going to see my baby again.'

His phone rang.

'Novak?'

'Yes, sir.'

'Busy, are you?'

'Well...'

'Another case. Body been found over by the reservoir. Young woman, looks like strangulation. Been there a week or so. Not nice. Although mostly in one piece, at least, foxes too busy eating burgers these days. They're doing the ID now. Can you do the SOC stuff?'

'Yes, sir. Of course.' He glanced at the brown leather camera case on the floor.

There was white canvas shielding the body. She was pale and young, a tangle of dirty blonde hair, skin grey as clay, tiny skirt, missing sandal.

He set up his Leica and began to work. Her eyes were open, the whites muddied with blood. Her swollen face lay at an odd angle.

Click.

If this was my daughter...

A wave of rage.

Click.

There is no beauty here, he thought. I should have used the other camera. I should be generating ones and noughts in black and white.

His phone rang.

'My husband,' the voice said.

'Mrs Logan...'

'One of his pistols is missing,' she said. 'I noticed doing the dusting, don't know why I'm bothering but you have to keep busy, don't you?'

'Pistols?'

'Antique pistols. He'd acquired a pair of duelling pistols. They're quite valuable, it turns out, he was very pleased...' Her voice cracked. 'I'm sure it's nothing to do with his disappearance...'

'Are they in working order?'

She went quiet. 'Yes. He fired one of them at the shooting club about six months ago. Just to see if it worked, he said. Some old colonel there described him as a good shot, David was delighted.'

'Mrs Logan,' Matt said. 'If there's any sense that he might have—'

'Taken his own life?' Her voice was sharp. 'There are two reasons why he wouldn't do that. We're Catholic, you see, it's against our beliefs.'

'And the second?'

'He was happy. Perfectly happy. There's no reason for him to ... to do such a thing.'

She'd gone. Matt began to pack up his camera kit.

We're Catholic, she'd said, as if that was some

185

kind of protection.

He left the taped area, walked to his car.

I was Catholic once, he thought.

It doesn't help.

'Are you Feds?'

He turned at the voice. The girl had big afro curls, a bright red sweater and very skinny jeans.

'Yes,' he said. 'Yes, I am.'

'What did he do to her?'

'I'm afraid I can't tell you anything about the case. I'm just an imaging officer—'

'That bastard. She should have stayed away from him, I told her enough times, God knows I did, that Cavin don't care about no one but himself. She wouldn't listen.'

'Cavin?' Matt leaned against his car.

'They had a row last week. Man, it was a big row.'

'What about?'

The girl stared at her feet in her cheap heels.

'The gear he give her, y'know, he said she had to pay for it. And she goes to him, how am I going to pay for it then, and he says to her, girl, you going to earn it, like everybody else.'

'Gear?'

She met his eyes. 'She was using, y'know?'

'Go on.'

The girl took a cigarette from her bag, lit it, breathed in a deep breath. 'So she goes to him, I ain't going to, Cav, and he's saying how he weren't charity, it was business, it was time she paid her way...' She stopped, exhausted by speech.

Matt studied her through the curls of smoke.

'When you say he wanted her to earn the money...?'

'How do you think a girl earns money round here?' She raised her brown eyes to his.

'And she refused?'

The girl nodded. 'She said, if he loved her he wouldn't ask her. And he just laughed. And then she were angry, really angry, and she said that was it, it was over, she didn't want to see him again, and they had this row, and then...'

'Then what?'

'She left. But he followed her. He were right angry, he were. I was scared. I wanted to go too but the rest of them said I shouldn't, said they should sort it out themselves ... I wish I'd gone now. I might have saved her...' Her eyes filled with tears.

Matt touched her arm. 'What's your name?'

She stared at him, childlike. 'Macy.'

'Could you go to the police, Macy? Could you tell them all this?'

She glanced nervously around her.

'You could come with me now, in my car, if you like.'

She nodded, shivering.

He put his jacket around her shoulders and led her to the car.

'Black, no sugar.' Samira put the mug down on his desk.

'No biscuits?'

'Don't push it, boy. I'm only doing this because you brought in a key witness in the Faiman case.'

'Faiman?'

'The strangled girl. Abbie Faiman.'

'Ah.'

'She was only seventeen.'

Seventeen, he thought.

'That's pretty.' Samira peered at the screen. 'That's the crime scene?'

The image showed the reservoir, shrouded in mist, black branches against haloed clouds, raindrops teetering on twigs.

He clicked it to close.

Samira was eyeing the old brown leather camera case.

'You got that all developed and scanned since you came back?'

'It doesn't take long if you know what you're doing,' he said.

'Not bad for a nancy boy,' she said.

'I'm not a nancy boy.'

'I know,' she said. 'Well, if one of your pictures shows us who strangled the poor cow, then you get two biscuits, I reckon. Chocolate ones, even.'

He smiled. 'Any more on the Logan case?'

'Yes,' she said. 'First the lab boys said it was an unusual bullet – 214 grain, the boys said. So they were looking for a different kind of weapon, at least a point 52. And look what they found.'

She handed him a photograph.

'It was in one of the factory bins,' she said. 'Carefully buried, but not carefully enough. It's a duelling pistol, apparently. The boss said these gangsters are sourcing their weaponry from funny places these days. He blames the Russian mafia.' She touched his shoulder and then was gone.

He looked at the photograph. He looked at the number on his mobile phone.

He pressed Call.

'Mrs Logan. It's Matt Novak.'

'Have you found him?' Her voice was hoarse with hope. With fear.

'No, not yet.' He hesitated. 'I just wanted to ask you. This missing gun of your husband's – can you describe it?'

'Yes, of course,' she said. 'It's like its twin. It's just here, wait a minute, I'll get the box, lovely box, mahogany, he was as pleased with the box as the guns, I think. Here we are, well, it's silvery colour, very ornate wooden handle thing...'

He looked at the image in front of him. A steel duelling pistol with an ornate wooden handle.

'On the metal bit, there are sort of flowers,' she was saying, 'a rose, maybe two, you can see the thorns...'

He looked at the photo in front of him. The barrel of the gun showed two roses, their stems entwined.

'Deane and Sons, London Bridge,' she was saying. 'That's the maker.'

Deane and Sons, London Bridge, he read.

'Any reason?' she said.

'Oh,' he said. 'No. Just to be sure. In case it turns up.'

'OK.' There was a silence. 'Thank you,' she said. 'For earlier. I'm rather on my own with this.'

'Yes,' he said, 'I can see that.'

'Well, I'd better go. Dinner to cook. Although just for one person...' her voice tailed away.

'We'll keep you posted, Mrs Logan,' he said.

'Thank you.' Another hesitation. 'Well, good-bye, then.'

He stared at the photograph on his screen. A silver duelling pistol, used for a drug-related shooting on an industrial estate in Yeadon. Its pair now in a mahogany box in the well-kept respectable home of a missing semi-retired solicitor.

He walked through the office to the Operations Room, to Samira's desk. He put the photograph down in front of her.

'What?' she looked up at him.

'The twin of this pistol. It's sitting in David Logan's house. His wife's just told me.'

She stared at him. She patted the seat next to her and he sat down.

'Look,' she said. There was a sheaf of papers on the table. 'Bank records,' she said. 'David Logan's bank account.'

Matt looked at the columns of figures.

'He had an account that was separate from the one he shared with his wife,' Samira said. She pulled a page towards her, pointed at the figures with a red-painted nail. 'She seemed to know nothing about it when we spoke to her. It has very few records – a regular standing order into it, and weekly cash payments out of it, at the Yeadon branch. Fifty pounds, a hundred pounds, not huge amounts. But it goes back at least three years, look.' She tapped one of the pages. 'I'm

190

getting the CCTV from that branch. Can you go through it?'

'Sure,' he said.

The quietness of the night settled around him, pierced from time to time by a siren and a slash of blue light from the car park below. Matt trawled through the images on his screen.

Dates. Times. Days, weeks. Thursdays.

The cashpoint camera feed was old and scratchy. People came and went. He saw hats, umbrellas, bald patches, numbers punched, cash counted, all in bad quality, jerky movements, like a silent movie without the laughs. Without the story either.

Unless ... He wound back, played forward. Here we are ... Cash withdrawal from the Logan account. 11.05 a.m. Thursday before last. Blonde-looking girl, denim jacket, short skirt. Thursday before, same girl. Denim jacket, jeans. Thursday before that. Same girl. Same jacket. She must be bloody freezing, he thought.

Zoom in. And again. The screen crunched into digital steps. He froze the girl's image. He pulled up the ID picture they'd given to the press. Abbie Faiman, it said. Blonde hair. Same denim jacket.

So, every Thursday morning, Abbie Faiman would draw money out of an account that David Logan paid into.

His hand went to the internal phone. I'll tell the SIO, he thought. He picked up the handset. He put it down again.

The photos he'd developed lay in a pile next to him. He looked at the tangle of her limbs in the

191

powdery light. He felt a sudden wave of rage.

She'd been a child once. A child like his own.

The night faded into dawn. And in his mind, the story played again. Angie, the mother of his child. Sunny, Italian Angie. And then the London job, and Angie, homesick and lonely, turned away. He had taken refuge in the arms of someone else. Only briefly, and mistakenly, but it was enough. After that, there'd been rage, and guilt, and he'd found himself ejected. She'd stayed in London, always threatening to return to Italy. He'd limped back to Yorkshire, his home, once. If anything could be called home.

As the sky began to lighten, he looked at the image of the dead young woman and thought, you are someone's child. And now, the windows bright with sunlight, he stands up, stumbling through the litter of coffee cups, goes down to the car park, gets into his car.

It was a busy Thursday morning. He parked the car. He sat, holding a photo in his hand. He watched.

People came and went. There was a queue outside the post office.

There. There he was. A distinguished, upright man, tailored wool coat. Thinning hair. The coat was missing a button. His shoes were thick with mud. Matt could see the stubble on his chin as he walked towards the cashpoint.

Alone, a queue of one, the man glanced around him, holding his collar up with both hands as if to hide behind it. Matt checked the image. He got out of his car and crossed the road.

The man saw him. For a second their eyes met. Matt went up close to him, very close. He spoke in his ear. 'She won't be needing your money any more. Not where she's gone.'

The man was tall, Matt realized. Well proportioned. Elegant, even, despite the several days' growth of his beard, the tear in his coat. He gazed at Matt, as some kind of comprehension filled his expression. He shook his head.

'Seventeen,' Matt said to him. 'I have a daughter too. I'd have done just the same as you, Mr Logan.'

'You would?' His voice was rough. His eyes watered, with cold, with feeling, it was difficult to tell. He held Matt's gaze.

Matt spoke. 'Yes,' he said. 'I would.' The two men stood, their eyes locked.

'I assume you're police,' David Logan said.

Matt nodded, waited.

'Are you going to arrest me?' The voice was low, authoritative.

Matt took his arm. 'You look like you could use some breakfast.'

They sat by steamed-up windows with mugs of tea. David drank, thirstily, ate a large piece of toast.

'How did you know?' he said, wiping his mouth.

'I couldn't think why else...'

'Oh, it was the usual story, to start with,' David said. 'She was called Linda. I met her at the tennis club. She was everything I thought I wanted.

193

Glamorous. Sexy. Full of life. An affair, that's what it was, cliché I know, it's all bloody clichés.' His voice was loud, and people glanced up from their plates. 'In the end,' he said, lowering his voice, 'I refused to leave my wife. The whole thing was over. I didn't know anything about Abigail until...' He stared at the table. 'Linda, her mother, died, you see. Three years ago. Linda's sister tracked me down, told me there'd been a child. My child. There she was, this orphaned girl. I didn't know what to do. How to tell Sheila ... it would have destroyed us. I was a coward...' He covered his eyes with his hand.

Matt waited.

He composed himself. 'You have a daughter?' he said, suddenly.

'Yes,' Matt said.

'Look after her,' David said.

'I don't see her. Her mother and I ... we're estranged.'

'How old is she?'

'Twelve,' Matt said. 'Thirteen in seven, no, six, weeks.'

'When did you last see her?'

'Two years ago. Two years, two months.'

David stared at him.

'The divorce, you see,' Matt went on. 'Acrimonious, it was. Never resolved. My fault, in many ways. They live in London. But her mother moved last year, wouldn't tell me where. For all I know they're back in Italy. All I've got is a mobile number which I'm scared to try.'

David was silent. Then he looked at Matt.

'Cowardice, you see. It can be fatal, it turns out. All these years, and I did nothing. And now I've paid the price.'

In the car David told Matt the rest of the story, sitting quietly beside him. About the money. 'It was all I felt I could do ... the coward's way out...' How Abigail fell in with the wrong crowd. 'She was a vulnerable girl. About a month ago, I tried to intervene, she was on my conscience, it was all I could think about. She would go to that cashpoint every Thursday. Sometimes I'd meet her there, try to talk to her. This time I asked her what I could do. "Nothing," she said. She was terrified of him, she could barely speak from terror. I didn't know what to do. I resolved to take action, I've no idea what, kidnap her, take her home, face the music ... I don't know what, I just knew I should do something. I began to follow her, from a distance. I saw her with him, around that estate where he lived. And I thought, I shall save her. I'll be there on Thursday and I shall rescue her, whatever the cost, she's my daughter.

'And so last week, I went to the cashpoint ... And she wasn't there. And I knew, deep down, I knew in my bones that something terrible had happened. I went home, Sheila was out, luckily, she knows I go to Waitrose every Thursday, so I knew she wouldn't miss me. I picked up my pistol, I loaded it, like the colonel had shown me. I went to the estate, and he was there. He saw me. I said, "Where is she?" And he was taunting me ... He ran, and I ran after him, shouting, what

195

have you done? And he was laughing and jeering. And somehow, I caught up with him, I don't know how, a young man like that, down on the industrial estate there. And he said, "You'll never see her again." And my hand was on the gun, and everything I felt, such loss, such grief, such ... rage...' His voice tailed away.

'And you fired your gun?' Matt said.

David fell silent. Then he said, 'I knew he was dead. The blood ... the pumping ... twitching ... then nothing. And all my anger left me. I stood there. I felt terribly terribly sorry for him. For them all ... And I realized, the only person I was angry with, was me.'

They drove in silence. After a while David said, 'I went looking for her after that. I knew I'd never find her. Not alive, in any case. When I couldn't find her, I didn't know what to do. I sat out in the woods there all night. After that, it was impossible to go home. Sleeping rough ... Until you found me.'

'Why did you go to the cashpoint again?'

'Wishful thinking. Madness. I don't know. Those were the times when I'd try to talk to her, try to get her to get help. All I know is that I failed my daughter. My only child.' He fell silent, and then began to cry, a rough, male sobbing.

They arrived at the police station. Matt helped him from the car, walked him into reception.

Much later that day, Matt went to see him. He was sitting in a police cell. He looked clean and calm, despite the flat fluorescent light.

'They've charged you, I hear.'

'Yes,' he said. 'I'll appear in court tomorrow.'

Matt sat down on the single chair. 'How are you pleading?'

David seemed surprised by the question. 'Guilty. Of course.'

'But—'

'Sheila came to see me,' David interrupted. 'I have ruined my wife's life. Of course I'm pleading guilty.'

'Did she know any of it...?'

'None. Entirely unsuspecting. She has an innocence ... one of the things I loved about her.' He breathed, then gathered himself. 'We could not have children ourselves, you see. It has broken her heart.'

Outside there was the slamming of a door, distant shouting.

'I asked Sheila if she'd ever forgive me,' David said. 'She thought for a bit. Then she said, it was too much to ask, but that she would pray that I might be forgiven. I'm not sure what she meant, but it was a strange comfort.' He leaned forward on the narrow bed. 'I have been a coward. That's what I'm pleading guilty to. Cowardice. Terrible, fatal cowardice.'

Novak stood on the steps outside the court, stamping his feet against the cold. The wind gusted through the pillars, blew across the banks of journalists who were waiting behind the barrier. A woman appeared from the side entrance. He saw her well-cut grey hair, a navy wool coat. She came up to him.

'Mrs Logan ... I'm sorry,' he said to her.

She gripped his hand. She looked up at him. 'What it is, you see...' She struggled to find the words. 'This is not the life I was leading. You think you're living one life. And then ... and then everything changes. Everything is lost...' Her eyes filled with tears. She patted his hand, then turned away to a waiting car, as the reporters shouted and called behind her.

Matt watched her go.

To pray that I might be forgiven.

He turned and headed for his car.

Samira, leaving the court, saw him waiting there. He was holding his mobile phone, staring at it. As she joined him, he clicked the phone off.

'Who'd have thought,' she says. 'A man like that. You just can't tell, can you?'

'No,' he agreed, putting his phone away. 'You just can't tell.'

ANGELA'S ALTERATIONS

Peter Lovesey

Peter Lovesey is the author of four crime series, starting with the Victorian mysteries about Sergeant Cribb, which were adapted for television. In recent years, he has focused mainly on books featuring either the Bath-based detective Peter Diamond, or Hen Mallin. His stand-alone novels include the award-winning *The False Inspector Dew*, and he is a former Chair of the CWA, as well as a recipient of the CWA Cartier Diamond Dagger.

Second time around for Marcus, first for Sophie. He was thirty-nine, she three years younger. The wedding was non-religious, held in a seventeenth-century barn with two hundred guests, a jazz band, delicious food and dancing until dawn.

But Sophie was realistic. She knew the wedding had been the fairy-tale beginning. The rest of their married life would be more humdrum and she was prepared for the dull routine enforced by the need to earn a living in these tough times. The one shining thing was that she loved Marcus and he adored her. His first wife had not been worthy of him. That was Sophie's opinion. He rarely spoke about her and resisted the chance to blame her for the break-up. But she must have been a rotten wife and a poor mother because the judge had given Marcus full custody of Rick, their son. Everyone knows the woman normally gets priority. It's not sexist. It's practical. She must have been wholly unsuitable as a parent.

Marcus had a steady job at a petrol station. He did a bit of everything there, keeping the pumps clean and functioning, seeing to the deliveries when the tankers arrived, working the till, stacking the shelves in the shop and sometimes mopping out the toilets. He said there was plenty of variety and he was reasonably secure in the knowledge that cars always needed filling up. The hours weren't so good because it was an all-night place and he had to take his turn at the shifts. One week in three was the night shift. But as Sophie said, she was used to being alone at night. She'd lived all her adult life up to now as a single woman. Being separated from Marcus one week in three meant she really appreciated his company for the other two.

Sophie's job had more sociable hours. She was a *barista* in the local branch of Costa, the coffee shop chain. When she'd first gone out with Marcus and he asked her what she did for a living he thought she said she was a barrister. He asked if she worked for the defence or the prosecution and it was some time before she guessed what he was on about. It had become a running joke between them with saucy remarks about silk and briefs and being called to the bar.

With two salaries they managed well enough, renting a small house in Derbyshire that they made into a cosy home. Good neighbours, a garden where they grew their own beans and tomatoes, and a corner shop that supplied almost everything else they needed.

The one problem was Rick, her new stepson. Maybe the divorce had upset him. More likely (in Sophie's opinion) he'd been deprived of the love and attention he should have had from his mother. Certainly Marcus couldn't have been a more caring father. Whatever it was, Rick was a difficult young man, and that was putting it mildly. Fifteen at the time of the wedding – which he refused to attend – he came with a history of antisocial behaviour. Sophie wasn't told for a long time about the childhood misdemeanours. She was certain Marcus kept quiet from the kindest of motives. But gradually things filtered through. The boy had been excluded from nursery school for persistently attacking the other children, head-butting, spitting and scratching. He threw an old lady's cat into a pond. He ran a kind of protection racket at secondary school, demanding regular money from certain children who feared having their bicycles smashed or their backpacks thrown over fences. As he got older and the hormones kicked in, he started pestering girls, touching them at every opportunity. When they objected he spread rumours about them though the social media. He was suspended from school for a time for rigging up a camera in the girls' changing room. He tried drugs, got drunk, carried a knife. He was a constant worry for Marcus. And as the incidents grew more serious, he became known to the police. They called at the house twice and spoke to Marcus.

Rick left school at the first opportunity and joined the unemployed. Somehow he managed to fund the lifestyle he wanted, out most of the night clubbing, sleeping through much of the day and arguing with his father whenever they were in the house together. Mostly he ignored Sophie – apart from a few muttered obscenities which she didn't mention to Marcus. But she had a suspicion he was taking money from her handbag and she took to keeping it within reach at all times.

Her neighbour Paula called one Sunday morning when Rick was still in bed and Marcus at work. They enjoyed coffee and a chat.

'What are you going to do about that stepson of yours?' Paula asked out of the blue.

'What do you mean?'

'Anyone can see he's getting you down. He's trouble. I saw him yesterday shoplifting in Tesco. With that long blond hair of his he doesn't seem to realise he stands out. He took a basket in and collected a magazine and slipped several packets of condoms into his pocket.'

'Oh, don't!'

'Well, at least he's taking precautions. I suppose you ought to be grateful for that. But I wouldn't want a daughter of mine going out with him. He'll end up in the courts if you're not careful. Does Marcus have any idea what his son gets up to?'

'I'm afraid it's the usual story. A broken home, a mother who was never there when she was needed.'

'Yes, but what about Marcus?'

'He's well aware of it. He tries, he really does.'

'My husband wouldn't stand for it. He'd beat some sense into the little perisher and kick him out if he didn't behave. How old is he now?'

'Going on seventeen.'

'A lot of kids his age fend for themselves. Some look after disabled parents as well.'

'We're hoping he'll come to his senses now he's virtually an adult. He's not without ambition. He wants to learn to drive.'

'God help us all when he does,' Paula said, and they both laughed.

Two evenings later, Sophie and Marcus had a visit from a clergyman. He was the vicar at St John's, the local church. They were surprised to see him because they weren't churchgoers, but Marcus invited him in.

'You're wondering what this is about,' the vicar said. 'I'm responsible for three churches altogether. Most of my time is spent at St John's, and I conduct the occasional service at the other two, St Matthew's at the end of North Street, and St Barnabas, the little one beside the green at Barn End. They're lovely old buildings, of much interest architecturally, and people visit them just to look round. We put out leaflets just inside the door and there's a box for contributions. Some people are most generous and pay more than the suggested token amount.'

Sophie's stomach clenched. She could already

see where this was going.

'Some time last week, the box at St Barnabas was broken into,' the vicar went on. 'It's made of wood with a padlock and regrettably someone had forced it open and taken the contents. We don't know how much money was in there, but we usually empty it once a month and the contributions can range from twenty to thirty pounds. I expect you're wondering why I'm telling you this.'

Neither Marcus nor Sophie answered

'There's a lady – you don't need to know her name – who lives in the row of terraces opposite St Barnabas. She does some cleaning in the church and arranges flowers. She was in there one afternoon sweeping between the pews and she was surprised to see a young man come in. He just stepped inside for a moment and took a lot of interest in the box, tapping it with his hand and rattling the padlock. Then he saw her and went away. But an hour later, she was at home and saw the same young man enter the church and come out a few minutes later, looking furtively to right and left before walking quickly away. Suspecting something was wrong, the lady went back and discovered the box broken and emptied of money. I suppose I should have gone to the police as soon as she phoned me, but I didn't. Sometimes the Lord has ways of rectifying transgressions. I spoke to the lady, of course, and promised to investigate. She said she was sure she would recognise the young man if she saw him again.'

'Is this why you're here?' Marcus asked.

'I'm afraid so. I believe you have a son by the name of Rick.'

'I do.'

'The lady identified him as the thief and I don't think there's any question she is mistaken. She's reliable and has no axe to grind. Let me say at once that I believe in second chances. If you can persuade Rick to return the money and give an undertaking that he'll never steal again, I'm prepared to forgive and forget. This, I think, is a watershed moment and he must understand why I'm being lenient. I don't wish any young lad to start on a life of crime. I fear that's what will happen if he goes through the penal system.'

'That's very understanding,' Marcus said.

'I thought perhaps you wouldn't believe me.'

Sophie said, 'If we can't believe a man of God, who can we believe?'

'Shall we see if we can help him between us?' the vicar said.

'You mean, convert him?' Marcus said.

'Not at all. That's far too much to aim for at this stage.'

'You'd just like the money back?'

'Not from you. That would be too easy. I'd like Rick to return it in person to me. He'll surely see the sense in doing that, rather than being up before the courts. Then I'll have a chat with him about his future. If you can do the same, we may set him on a better path. He'll need much support and encouragement from you both.'

'We appreciate this,' Marcus said, 'and I hope Rick will, as well.'

* * *

Rick returned from the nightclub too late for a fatherly chat and was still in bed at noon the next day, but as soon as he appeared, bleary-eyed and unshaven, in the T-shirt and shorts he'd obviously slept in, and told Sophie he was hungry, she offered to cook for him and left the room as if to collect something from the freezer in the garage and instead called Marcus at work. He took a lunch break and came home.

They had agreed that this would come best from both of them, so Sophie stayed in the room when Marcus told Rick about the visit from the vicar.

At first, Rick appeared to ignore his father, staring at a music magazine as he ate the last of his late breakfast. But when Marcus spoke about the collection box, Rick looked up and said, 'So what?'

'So you could go to prison,' Marcus said.

'Not for that,' Rick said. 'I might get community service.'

'What you're getting is a second chance.' Marcus went on to explain the vicar's offer. 'Considering that you stole the money – you did, didn't you?'

A nod.

'Considering it's a criminal offence, you're being treated with exceptional consideration.'

'He wants the money back?' Rick said. 'He can't have it. I spent it.'

'Then you'll have to find thirty pounds from somewhere else.'

'Only twenty-three fifty.'

'That's not the point. You'll find thirty and go

206

and see him with it. He's got to have the box repaired or buy a new one.'

'Haven't got it. I'm skint,' Rick said.

'Then you can spend a few evenings at home instead of paying to get into the nightclub.'

'I don't pay. One of the bouncers lets me in. I happen to know he's gay and he hasn't come out yet, so he does favours for me.'

'That sort of thing's got to stop,' Marcus said. 'If you stay at home and do a few jobs round the house, I'll pay you, and then you can go and see the vicar when you've got the money to return to him. It had better be this week. Shall we call him now and make an appointment on Friday?'

Rick shrugged.

Marcus passed his phone across. 'It's pre-dialled. All you have to do is press the key.'

Rick stared at the phone and did nothing.

'But if you'd rather not, I'll phone the police,' Marcus said.

Sophie was proud of him.

Rick pressed the key.

'But has he learned his lesson?' Paula asked when Sophie told her about the incident.

A sigh. 'If I'm completely truthful, I doubt it. The vicar talked to him about mending his ways. But since then I've noticed more money missing from my purse. Dishonesty seems to be ingrained in him.'

'That's awful.'

'It's an awful thing for me to say it, but I see no prospect of him changing his ways.'

'Does Marcus feel the same?'

'He's never said so. The boy's his flesh and blood. But deep inside, he knows, I'm sure.'

'This puts such strains on your marriage.'

'You don't have to tell me, Paula. I'm in despair.'

Silence took over for a time.

'I don't think I've ever mentioned this,' Paula said. 'It would be a long shot, but there is a local woman who is said to have had remarkable results in turning people's lives around. I'm not entirely sure how she does it. Some homespun psychology, I suppose, force of personality and a bit of witchery for good measure.'

'*Witchery*?'

'There are white witches, aren't there, who do good deeds? Wise women, they are sometimes called. They have some sort of power that can't be explained.'

'Is that what this woman claims?'

'No, it's more of what people say about her. She's a little eccentric. But she seems to know what she's doing.'

'Is she expensive?'

'I don't know about that. You'd have to ask.'

'I bet she's never had anyone like Rick to deal with.'

'Probably not, but I heard she's straightened out several young people going through crises in their lives.'

Sophie wondered what Marcus would think of this suggestion, let alone Rick himself. 'What's her name?'

'Angela. I don't know her surname.'

'Nice name.'

'Yes, I'm sure she's on the side of the angels with a name like that. She's only about twenty-six herself, but she has a successful business in the town. She took over that tiny little shop where the cobbler used to be, next to the optician.'

One of the difficulties with working in the High Street was that Sophie didn't get to see changes in the other shops. 'What sort of business?'

'Altering clothes. You want a hem turned up or a seam put in – let out, in my case – and she does it on her sewing machine, while you wait, sometimes. It's a useful service, especially when new clothes are so expensive.'

'Does the shop have a name?'

'Angela's Alterations.'

'Nice idea, but he'd never agree to anything like that,' Marcus said. 'You saw how difficult it was getting him to see the vicar. I had to twist his arm, really.'

'We'd go and see Angela ourselves, in the first place,' Sophie said, refusing to have the suggestion brushed aside. 'She'd need to know what the problem is.'

'What the problems are, you mean. Thieving, shoplifting, blackmail, pestering girls, drugs, drink and defying his parents. She wouldn't know where to start.'

'Sometimes a fresh approach can make a difference. Let's at least go and see her, Marcus. If she thinks he's a lost cause, I'm sure she'll tell us.'

He agreed to take an hour off work on Saturday morning and so did Sophie.

While waiting in the tiny shop, they watched Angela attach a new zip to somebody's skirt. She completed the job remarkably quickly, handling the garment with total confidence. She looked younger than either of them expected, with a streak of bright green in her dark hair and silver clippings in her nose and ears. She wasn't good-looking in the model girl sense, but she had an intelligent, open face with wide brown eyes that took in her visitors in a way that made them feel as if they were kids themselves. 'What can I alter for you?'

Marcus explained, with some prompting from Sophie. They didn't actually name Rick, but they covered his story comprehensively.

When they'd finished, Angela said, 'So it isn't a sewing machine job,' and they all laughed. The tension eased.

'I'll need to know his name,' she said. 'I can see why you haven't mentioned it so far, in case I don't take him on.'

Marcus exchanged a glance with Sophie. It sounded as if Angela hadn't been put off. 'He's called Rick. I'm sorry to be so direct, but what would it cost us?'

'The same rate as all my alterations,' she said, 'but you wouldn't have the cost of materials. Ten pounds an hour.'

'I doubt if you'd fix him as quickly as you did that zip.'

'No, but I don't charge unless the job is com-

210

pleted to my customers' satisfaction.'

Marcus did a double-take. 'No success, no fee?'

Angela nodded. 'But you must allow me to go about this in my own way, with no interference. Don't ask Rick to visit me. I'll make sure we meet. If he speaks about me – which is unlikely – treat it as if you hadn't heard about me. And of course don't let him know you're paying me.'

Marcus cleared his throat. 'I'm sorry to insist. We ought to put this on a businesslike footing. We're not terribly well off.'

'From all you told me, I would think five weeks might do the trick. I wouldn't charge you all those hours, of course. I have a business to run. To give you a general idea, two hours a day would be the maximum. I work a six-day week.'

'That's about six hundred pounds,' Marcus said.

'Maximum,' Angela said.

Marcus turned to Sophie, who nodded eagerly. She'd been impressed with what she'd heard. Witch or wise woman, Angela radiated confidence.

They left her reaching for another garment and giving it a shake. With the sewing machine on its table, the ironing board and the racks of clothes under alteration, there was scarcely room to shake anything.

Three days later, Rick said, 'I'm going to learn to drive. I've applied for a provisional licence. Before you freak out, I won't be paying for lessons. A friend is going to teach me in her van.'

'That's nice,' Sophie said before Marcus could speak, just in case he hadn't cottoned on. 'You've always wanted to get behind the wheel.'

'It's on the level, Dad, I promise you.'

Marcus said, so smoothly that Sophie knew he'd worked out what was happening, 'Go for it, son. When you're ready to take the test, we'll pay for it.'

After Rick had gone out, Sophie said, 'Angela's on the case, then. What a clever way of getting his confidence.'

'I hope he doesn't crash her van.'

'He won't. She'll see to that.'

At the end of the week, Marcus returned from work and said, 'I had a chat with Angela today. She stopped by at the garage to fill up. She has this little white van with Angel's Alterations on the side in large lettering. And she has L-plates fitted front and rear.'

'What did she say?'

'It's going well. He's a confident driver and he'll soon pick it up. She thinks the lessons are bringing something positive to his life, a sense of achievement.'

'Did she say how they met?'

'No, and I didn't ask. She seems to have her own way of doing things and prefers not to say much about it. I get more impressed with her each time we meet.'

Paula from next door said, 'Angela seems to have taken your stepson in hand. I watched him reversing round a corner in her little van this morning. He looked different to me, much more at peace with himself and the world.'

'Yes, we're so grateful for your recommendation. She's a miracle worker. He's better at home, gets up earlier in the morning and even helps a bit around the house.'

'Speaking of helping, has he stopped helping himself from your purse?'

'He has. What is more, he's on better terms with his dad. They actually talk about music and football.'

'I'm happy for you all. At what point can you say the alteration is complete?'

'I don't know. She'll tell us, I expect. She promised it wouldn't make paupers of us.'

'I've heard her terms are reasonable. And she takes on all kinds of work. It isn't just the troubled teenagers.'

'Such as?'

'I think she cures warts and chilblains and stuff like that. Folk medicine, she calls it. More alterations really.'

'Things witches are traditionally supposed to do?'

'Right, but I wouldn't mention witchcraft if I were you.'

Sophie laughed. 'I wouldn't dream of it. We want to keep on the right side of her while she's altering Rick.'

Marcus, too, was altering. He was becoming more relaxed as the days went by and his relationship with Rick improved.

'Don't ask me how she managed it,' he told

Sophie, 'but it seems to be permanent. He and I are going for a drink on Saturday. The first time!'

'I noticed he tidied his room and threw a lot of old junk away. It's remarkable. There must come a point soon when we settle up with her.'

'She said five weeks. We're not there yet.'

'How will you do it when the time comes? We don't want Rick to find out.'

'God, no! She knows where to find me. She'll come to the garage, I expect. I'm going to feel like hugging her.'

'Have we got six hundred in the account? That's the figure she mentioned.'

'I think so. I'll make sure. She may prefer cash.'

The transformation in Rick continued. Instead of being so secretive he announced over breakfast one Sunday morning, 'That woman I mentioned, who is teaching me to drive, is called Angela. We met by chance in the street. Actually I was having a bit of a run-in with a copper who said I'd been shoplifting. She came right up and said it was a misunderstanding and she'd sort it out.'

'Were you shoplifting?' Marcus asked.

'That was then,' Rick said. 'I don't do it any more. Any road, she took me for a coffee and we got on really well. She has a small business in the high street mending clothes and that. She's in her twenties, I think, and she has a van and she offered to let me drive it round the car park. I must have done all right because she offered to teach me. She says when I pass the test she'll let me do deliveries for her and she'll pay me.'

'That's terrific,' Sophie said. 'Isn't it wonderful, Marcus?'

'Brilliant,' Marcus said.

'I'd like you to meet her some time,' Rick said.

'Actually, if she's the Angela of Angela's Alterations, I have met her a few times,' Marcus said. 'She fills up sometimes at the garage. And I agree – she's a super person.'

The five weeks were up and Sophie reminded Marcus. 'As far as I'm concerned, she's turned him round. He's a reformed character. He doesn't swear any more. He's given up the nightclubbing. I feel safe with him for the first time since we married.'

'Do you think we should pay her the six hundred?' Marcus said.

'That was the understanding. We must keep our side of the bargain.'

'Shall we see her together?'

'It looks a bit heavy, both of us. Why don't you call in at the shop with the money and tell her how grateful we both are?'

'Good idea,' he said.

'Be careful, just in case Rick is somewhere in the shop. It would be dreadful if he ever found out the truth.'

'It's such a poky little place he couldn't possibly be hiding there. Just to be sure, I'll go at a time when I know he's somewhere else. He's much more open these days about how he passes his time.'

'It was all a bit strange,' Sophie told Paula when

she went in for a coffee three weeks later. 'Marcus withdrew six hundred from the bank and went to the shop and said what a difference there is in Rick and how grateful we both are, and what do you think Angela said?'

'The money wasn't enough?'

'No. She said rather than taking the cash, she'd like to be treated to a day's shopping.'

'I don't follow you.'

'It was "treated" that was the operative word. She could easily have spent the six hundred on herself, but she wanted someone – a man – to take her shopping and buy everything for her.'

'Weird.'

'I thought so at first, but then I saw it from Angela's point of view. She works really hard, stuck in that shop all week and doing things for other people. She's not used to having a man take her shopping. It was a one-off opportunity, so I don't begrudge it at all.'

'What did Marcus say?'

'The funny thing is, he hates shopping. But we were so much in Angela's debt that he agreed. You have to laugh, really.'

'And did it happen?'

'Yes, it's done. We're all square now.'

'Where did she choose to be taken?'

'Paris, by Eurostar.'

'Oh my God – and you allowed it?'

'It was just for a day. They went early and got the last train back. She had boxes of goodies, he said.'

'I hope that's all she had,' Paula said, and added quickly, 'Sorry, darling. I'm sure it was all very proper.'

'I trust my Marcus and we're both very grateful to Angela. She's more than ten years younger than we are. Poor little soul, why shouldn't she have her treat? She's worked a miracle with Rick. Did I tell you he passed his driving test and now she employs him part time?'

Later that summer, Rick asked his father how much it would cost to buy a van of his own. He was thinking of doing deliveries on a bigger scale, full time instead of the odd jobs he still did for Angela.

'I think we should buy it for him,' Sophie said at once. 'We could get a loan, if necessary. It shows such good intentions on his part.'

'I don't know,' Marcus said. 'It's still early days in his rehabilitation. A few months ago I wouldn't have dreamed of letting him anywhere near a van. I'll tell you what. I'll ask Angela's advice next time I see her.'

Secretly, Sophie was a little hurt that her opinion counted for less than Angela's, but she didn't say anything.

'I saw your Rick driving his new van yesterday,' Paula said. 'He gave me a wave, which he would never have done in the old days.'

'It isn't new. It's reconditioned,' Sophie said. 'Good idea.'

'Angela's idea, in fact. She'd heard about it going cheap. Rick spruced it up with Marcus's help and he's really proud of it. He's found one or two regular delivery jobs, thanks to Angela knowing people.'

'And he's still on the straight and narrow?'

'From all I can tell, he is. Instead of night-clubbing he does potholing.'

'Does *what*?'

'You know. Blokes in helmets with lamps going underground on ropes. There are some really deep holes and mineshafts out there. He puts his kit in the van and drives off and we don't see him for hours and hours.'

'Is it safe?'

'They're very professional about it.'

'Some of those holes are so deep you wouldn't stand a chance if you fell. And the mineshafts are notorious.'

'He's getting to know them all and he knows which ones to avoid. From our point of view it's a lot less dangerous than clubbing, what with the drugs and everything.'

'I'm impressed. I won't go on about it, then. What a relief for you both. Is Marcus at work?'

'Upstairs, catching up on his sleep. He's working nights at the garage this week.'

'All this week?'

Sophie nodded. 'One week in three, nine till seven. I thought you knew.'

'Well, I thought I did. I ran out of milk late yesterday and I always have a cocoa at bedtime or I can't sleep, so I nipped round to the garage. About ten, it was. Marcus wasn't on duty. That Asian guy was serving. I asked if Marcus was about and he said he was on a week's holiday.'

'He's not. That isn't true,' Sophie said, her heart thumping.

'You'd better keep an eye on him.'

'I can't understand it. He was gone all night, for sure.'

'Somebody got their wires crossed, I expect,' Paula said. 'Don't look so worried.'

She was deeply worried. She'd noticed Marcus behaving strangely in the last few days. Tight-lipped and twitchy, he almost seemed to shun her at times. She didn't like to dwell on it, but her beloved husband seemed to be undergoing an alteration.

Of all the people to confide in, she chose Rick. He'd become so much more mature now, running his own delivery business, paying his way and being upfront with people.

'I'm worried about your father. He's been behaving strangely. It's like a personality change.'

'I've noticed,' Rick said. 'I didn't want to interfere.'

'I'm so unhappy, Rick. I think he's having an affair.'

'My dad? Get away!'

'Really. I don't think I've lost him entirely, but it could happen if I don't do something about it. I couldn't bear to let him go.'

'Are you sure about this?'

'There are too many signs. People who know me, customers in the coffee shop, drop hints that they've seen something going on, something they can't discuss with me. And Paula from next door is more outspoken. She says she's seen them together several times.'

'Seen who?'

'Your dad with Angela.'

'*Angela*? That's crazy.'

'That's what I thought at first, but everything points to it.'

'It's not possible,' Rick said, flushing all over his fair skin. 'I see her all the time. I'm running my business through her shop. We're in partnership now. We share the profits and I'm part-owner. Of course I'd know if anything like that was going on with Dad.'

'I couldn't believe it myself for a long time,' Sophie said. 'He visits her when he's supposed to be working nights at the garage. He pays Sanjit to stand in for him.'

Now the blood drained from Rick's cheeks. 'She's my partner.'

'Business partner. Her love life is another thing altogether.'

Rick was silent, seeming to bite back what he had been about to say. Finally he managed to speak. 'But she was my discovery. I found her and she's turned my life around.'

Sophie, too, bit back the words that were ready to spring from her. She didn't care any more about Angela, but Rick would fall apart if he learned the truth about the arrangement.

Now the words poured from Rick. 'Why would he want to take up with her when he's got you? She's far too young for him. I'm closer to her age than he is and she really put herself out to help me through a difficult time. I was on the skids heading for some kind of hell and she reached out to me and pulled me up. I owe everything to her. She thinks I'm young and still in need of help, but our relationship is changing day by day. We're almost equals now. I'd move in with her if she asked me.'

Sophie was on the verge of tears. 'I had no idea. I wouldn't have mentioned it. Oh, this is terrible. I don't want to hurt you. I shouldn't have told you. I should have had the courage to take it up with Marcus.'

'How could she be so cruel – to you and to me? She knows how I feel about her. She must.'

'I'll speak to him.'

'Don't,' Rick said. 'Leave him out of it. If this is true, I know exactly how to deal with it.'

'How's it all going now?' Paula said towards the end of the year. 'Got your life back together, have you?'

'We're doing fine now,' Sophie said, and meant it.

'Marcus came to his senses, did he? I see he's pulling his weight at the garage these days.'

'It was just a silly little episode and we're over it.'

'Men. They all need pulling into line at some stage.'

Sophie smiled, trying to think of a way of changing the subject.

Paula changed it for her. 'She seems to have left the district, that Angela. Strange woman. Disappeared overnight. I don't think anyone knows where she went. Rick's the one who ought to know, but he doesn't say a word.'

'I don't suppose he knows anything.'

Paula gave a faint, disbelieving smile. 'It

hasn't done him any harm, seeing how he was in partnership with her. He can still use the shop for his own business. I see the sewing machine has gone. No use to a man running a transport company. I wonder where it went, with the ironing board and the clothes racks. Down one of those old mineshafts where he does his potholing at weekends, I shouldn't wonder. Has he stopped being a worry to you both?'

'Completely.'

'He's made a success of his life, hasn't he, after such a shaky start? Stunning, I call it. You and Marcus must be proud when you see the vans with his name on the side. And it sounds just right – Rick's Removals.'

THE LAST RESORT

Claire McGowan

Claire McGowan was born in Northern Ireland, but later moved to England and worked in the charity sector after taking a degree in English and French. Her first novel, *The Fall*, was published in 2012, and she has followed it up with *The Lost*.

'Do you think ... You think they forgot about us?'

Neither of them wanted to say anything at first. Lucy's voice was muddy and tentative in the silence of the hotel dining room.

Rob crossed the floor, his flip-flops slapping on the concrete. He was trying to walk purposefully, but he didn't feel it. It was weird, really weird. Where was everyone? They'd woken up in their luxury tent as dawn broke; pink, worn-out. Safari dawn. And now it was breakfast time, but no one was here.

'What about the safari drive? We were meant to go out today.'

'I don't know.' He raised his voice. 'Hello?' The whole of the safari lodge was silent, the only movement the fluttering of the plastic tablecloth clipped to the buffet table. When they'd arrived last night, after a long drive round the park to the isolated northern side and this lodge on the hilltop, they'd been sweating in equatorial darkness. There'd been lots of staff, dark uniforms blending politely into the night as Rob and Lucy were led, exhausted, to their tented room. But this morning, no one.

Rob could see Lucy's face slide. The whole time they'd been in Africa, it was as if she'd been holding herself together with both hands. He'd promised her that this, the last hotel, would be a nice one – not somewhere she'd have to shower under a thatched roof teeming with insect life, or pee in a darkened latrine that was full of the most alarming rustles. The last hotel was supposed to make up for the feeling he'd had the whole trip, as she lumbered behind him through virgin forest alive with chimpanzee hoots, or shrieked as a cockroach ran under the bed. The feeling he'd been trying not to name, until he woke up one morning to find it square on his tongue like an after-dinner mint: *embarrassment*. Even the clothes she wore, God. As if she'd coated herself in glue and run through a branch of Millets. The trousers that unzipped into shorts, the wilderness hat that tied under her chin. All trip he'd been watching her burnt face bob under it, anxious and scared. She always had one finger in the guidebook, as if putting it down would mean they'd be struck by civil war, or plague, or those worms that burrowed into your eyeballs which she'd once seen on a Channel 4 documentary. It didn't help that she'd ignored the actually sensible advice of not eating the

224

salad, and been stuck on the toilet for days, the smell of pumping sewage not adding to the atmosphere of their cramped room, where every corner scuttled with shadowy life.

Worst of all, it was the last hotel before they went home, and he knew somewhere in the shared mind space that all couples have she was expecting more. Why else after six years would you go to Africa, and see chimps and lions and walk in the bush, if you weren't going to get engaged at the top of a waterfall? He'd even looked at rings in H. Samuel in Brent Cross, on yet another Saturday searching for jeans that would fit her 'curves', trips that left her tearful and needing to be soothed with Krispy Kremes and rom-coms starring Katherine Heigl.

Lucy stood before him now, six years together, four living in the flat they owned together in Harrow. There was nowhere else to go except the altar. Then have babies, die. Her first, or him. Him probably, since he was a year older and a man.

'Are you listening? Where do you think they went?'

Rob dragged himself to the present, where he was 32 and Lucy was 31 and standing anxious in her safari shorts and sweat-stained T-shirt, size 14 (though she'd told him it was a 12). She perched on one trainer-sandal and with the other scratched at a bite on her calf.

'Maybe it's their day off.'

'All of them?' It was a small hotel, just the dining room/reception and the individual luxury tents, but there'd been lots of staff the night before. They'd just gone. A hose had even been left trickling into pink shrubs, and Rob had conscientiously turned it off on their way up.

'Do you remember what they said last night?'

He shook his head. 'I was too tired.' She always expected him to remember, follow instructions, know the way. 'I suppose it *might* be their day off.'

'What should we do?'

'Let's just enjoy it,' he soothed. 'We've got the whole place to ourselves. They'll be back later.'

On the first day, the power was still on, and they found the fridge full of food – ham, eggs, slices of pale European cheese. They sat in the dining room and ate rough sandwiches, the only sounds the cheep of the birds landing for crumbs, and the breeze ruffling the plastic tablecloths.

She giggled nervously. 'I feel we should be whispering. Do you think there's any way we can hear the news? A radio or anything?'

There was no TV in the hotel – it was meant to be a retreat into nature.

'There might be. Hang on.' He went into the kitchen, his voice echoing off the tiled walls. 'Hello?' No one. Some eggs lay in a cast iron pan, thick with congealed oil, as if someone had run off in the middle. 'Hello?' He searched the racks for a radio, something the staff might listen to while cooking, but there was nothing. The bar area had a CD player but nothing that received. Glancing outside, he could see all the Jeeps were gone, and there must be no other guests, because the parking space was entirely empty. He didn't

226

tell her this.

'And your phone's still not working?' Lucy was keeping her voice light, curious, but he could hear the effort in it.

'No. No reception.' It hadn't worked since the capital.

'What can we do then?'

He slipped his hand into her clammy one; it was as much of an effort as her speaking. 'Let's relax. I'm sure there's a reason.'

The first day they spent at the pool, helping themselves to beers from the bar. 'Should we write down what we had?' She was worried.

'They left us.'

'Good point.'

They went to sleep beer- and sun-drunk, like children without a babysitter. That first night, he was convinced all the way down to his ankles that the staff would be back come morning, with towels draped on their arms and glasses of fresh orange juice in which ice cubes clinked like jettisoned crates in a dirty river. But you weren't supposed to have ice cubes, were you? Bottled water. He had to remember. He drifted off to sleep listening to Lucy's snuffling breath, the rise and fall of her chest under her pyjamas, wondering as he often did at what point in a relationship you first undressed yourself, instead of tearing each other's clothes off. The first time you didn't have sex. The last.

The second day, nobody came. The resort was as silent and still as before. Tiny night-birds had pecked at the fruit platter from breakfast, so it was ruined, sticky and ant-eaten.

'What should we do?'

'They have to be here on Friday, surely? They are supposed to drive us back to town.'

'So we just wait till then?'

'I dunno. What else can we do?'

She didn't answer the question, but he felt she expected him to do something all the same. Anything. Just something.

The second day they were freer, going into the kitchen, taking beers from the bar. Two days without cleaning and the pool floated with leaves and insects, spinning delicate shadows on the tiled bottom. When she swam Lucy left in her wake an opalescent slick of DEET and sun-cream, like a wrecked tanker. The sun beat down, fierce, burning. Rob fell asleep at lunch-time and woke to find an ant crawling over his damp foot. He jumped up, itching and grouchy. 'I might walk to the village.'

She looked up from her paperback, flesh spilling over the sides of her bikini. 'What village?'

'Remember we passed through one on the way? It was only a few miles, I think.' He recall-ed the colourful wraps of the women, and a row of tinpot shops, and the stares and the mutters of '*Mzungu*'. Whites.

She turned a page. He was expecting her to talk him out of it. 'That might be a good idea. Be careful, though.'

Rob regretted it hugely after just ten minutes. He was so hot his skin had gathered a coating mixed of sweat and the red dust that rose up with every step of his hiking boots. He'd put them on in case of snakes, then slapped himself all over with corrosive DEET until his flesh stung. All through the banana-lined trail that led to the hotel, there was not a single person. He emerged onto the main road, such as it was. No vehicles. A sign for the resort swaying in the faintest breath of breeze. He was exhausted and sopping but he trudged on down the red road. How far had it been? Three miles?

It seemed to take hours. He'd never been so aware of time. Each second stretched and sloshing like a water balloon full of sweaty discomfort. His feet ached and chafed in the boots, and a band of black flies buzzed thickly round his ears. The cluster of shacks, which had seemed nearby, receded further and further with every bend in the cracked road. And the whole time he walked, not a single car passed, not a person was to be seen among the banana plantations. Eventually he came to the outskirts of the village, the ground littered with a strange collection of rubbish, from fish bones to bottle tops. 'Hello?' His voice sounded weak in the silence. On an empty shop, a metal Coke sign creaked to and fro.

Rob felt the sweat cool and prickle on the back of his neck. No one was there, not in any of the little shops or shacks. The only human figures were headless mannequins dressed in hideous nylon clothes. There was also no food in the shop, just a broken fridge full of Coke and Sprite, but he'd noticed this in other towns in the country. You could always get Coke. Some dusty shelves of biscuits, nothing that was fresh, no connection to the deep red earth outside. The till when he pinged it had money in. Why would anyone leave that behind? In one home a fire was still smoking, as if it had just been extinguished by running feet.

He filled his rucksack with warm drink cans, leaving too much money in the till, and tramped back the hours to the hotel. When he got back, Lucy was sitting in the dining room, uncomfortably, as if she hadn't wanted to breathe properly until she saw him. She sprang up. She'd showered and her hair was wet down the back of her flowered dress, face red with sunburn. As he walked up he was already thinking what words to say, how to frame it so she wouldn't get that look in her eyes again.

That night the power went off. Getting up in the dark to pee, Lucy fumbled for the dim bulb and nothing happened. 'The light's off,' she said, an edge of panic in her voice as it woke him. At first he wasn't worried.

'It happens. Use the torch.' But in the morning there was still nothing, and the food in the fridge smelled hot and spoiled. They ate bread, and cooked the last of the eggs on the stove, which was gas. Neither of them talked about how little food was left. The day followed a rhythm – pool, reading, lunch, pool, reading, dinner, bed. The pool wasn't being filtered, and had taken on a warm greenish tinge. Lucy went in that day but Rob didn't. He sought shade instead and thought how different heat became when you had to work round it, not enjoy it. Their plug-in mosquito coil no longer worked, so they spent all night slapping and cursing. It was dark as hell by the stroke of 6 p.m.

That night they heard the gunshots. Rob started awake and found a huge hot spider had him under its web. He was tangled in the mosquito net.

Lucy was out of bed, peering through the mesh windows of the canvas room.

'What's wrong?'

'I heard something. Shots maybe.'

'It's for the elephants, to scare them. Remember they told us.'

'No ... I don't know. I can see fires.'

He swung his legs out of bed, moving gingerly across the floor in case of insects. Far away on the edge of the immense plain, the horizon was tinged with orange. For the first time he was very aware that their room, for all its expense, was a glorified tent. A pricey tent, a £200 a night tent, but still just canvas. Canvas and one steep hillside stood between them and whatever had caused all the staff to vanish in the night, taking the Jeeps and leaving the eggs to cool on the stove.

They didn't sleep much more that night, fitful and sweaty. He had to keep a hand on a part of Lucy at all times, a bitten ankle or a sunburnt arm. His greatest fear was to wake up and find her gone too. He couldn't take this vast African emptiness, not alone. Both were up with first light, sensing some kind of movement on the site, and they ran up the stone steps in their sandals, reaching the dining room and pool. Ahead of him, Lucy froze. The hem of her khaki shorts

231

had ridden up, showing the red rash of her thighs.

'What is it?'

She reached round, fumbling into him. He craned his head. What he saw made a sudden and terrible sense – of course, they'd come to drink.

The animals were gathered at the pool. The lion was on its haunches, tongue lapping at the scummy green surface like the cat Rob had loved as a little boy in Taunton. The elephant and its calf were on the other side, frantically ignoring the lion, their skin grey and crusted. Rob saw behind that the fence had been trampled down. Several large birds had also come – marabous? There was a rustle in the bushes and he seized Lucy's arm. 'Go back. Slowly. Don't make eye contact.'

After that Lucy wouldn't leave the room at all. The water in the pipes had slowed to a trickle, so they conserved it in plastic bottles, brown and sluggish. They no longer bothered with showers and the room began to smell.

'We shouldn't flush the toilet,' he said to her on what was maybe the sixth day. He waited for her to protest; she hated to be dirty, hated the latrines they'd had to use on this trip, but she just nodded, not meeting his eyes. When the sun was at its highest point, Rob would tramp round the grounds, looking for what, he didn't know. He moved all the packet food down to their room, and they ate biscuits and bread rolls. Neither was hungry.

He wasn't sure when he realized Lucy had been drinking the water. She knew not to, of course. He'd lectured her before they got on the flight, no ice, no juice, no soup, no stew, bottled water for brushing teeth. But on one of the last days he found himself coming to on the bed. That happened a lot during those days. It wasn't like sleeping. It was more like the boundaries of the world were creeping and blurred, like he wasn't sure when he was actually awake or when he was asleep.

In whatever this was, Lucy was in the bathroom. She had taken off her pyjamas and was naked, crouching at the bath like an animal. Her breasts hung down over her stomach. She was craning her neck to lap water from the tap, the last dirty drops that clung in the pipes. There'd been nothing for days, though they left all the taps fully on, and they'd grown used to the continuous grinding noise as the system slowly failed. He remembered how they'd filled the rolltop bath to the brim that first night, after the bloody sun went down on the plain below. Poured it all away, all that water.

Lucy, he said, but no sound came out. 'Lucy.' She didn't move.

'Don't drink that. You'll get sick.'

Lucy came back in, walking with a jerky gait. He could see the whites of her eyes and the sweat on her face. She passed a yellow tongue over cracked lips and curled herself into a ball on the bed, where she seemed to sleep immediately. He wasn't sure on those days if either of them ever slept, or woke. He tried to make himself eat the remaining biscuits when he woke, or drink from a sticky can of Coke by the bed, until he came to one time and found it hiving with ants. He tried to make Lucy eat but she shook her head, moaning.

'Lucy. Please.'

'Nooo. Leave me.'

He thought they had a fever. He thought she would die, or they would both die. He gave her aspirin from the medical kit until each silver blister was empty, and he thought: I never should have brought you here. And then, later, in the honest bottom of the night: I never wanted to bring you here.

Days slid into one, until the last.

'Is it Friday?' said Lucy, on waking, however many days it was into the time.

Friday had long been and gone, but he heard it too. The unmistakable rumble of engines. 'Come on.' He threw back the mosquito net.

Lucy stood, still naked. She hadn't been dressed for days, he thought. 'But what – what is it?'

He was at the door already, shuffling his feet into sandals. When he stepped outside he felt weak, as if he might fall. He blinked as he came up the steps and it was a like a stranger appearing in your front room. The dining room was full of soldiers, poking into the fridges, feet on the tables, rifles propped up. They sounded loud and cheerful and their dark skin shone with sweat. They fell silent as he approached, and a man came forward. Shorter than the rest, with badges on his ragged uniform, he gave off a strong stink of bodies.

Rob licked dry lips. 'Hi,' he managed. 'Is something wrong?'

The man looked him up and down. 'American?'

'English. Er, British. I'm on holiday.'

The man stared.

'Um – the staff went away. We've been here all this time. We didn't know what happened. Did something happen?'

He saw the man's gaze move, and followed it; Lucy was at the bottom of the steps. She hugged her arms over her chest. She hadn't put any clothes on and her sunburn patches outlined all the white places on her, all the soft vulnerable flesh. Rob shouldered the weight of the men staring at her.

The leader shifted his gun, black, heavy. Rob had never seen one in real life before. 'The others?'

'The others?'

'Yes. Others. Where?'

'Oh.' He couldn't explain. 'There are no others. They all went.' He could see the man still not moving, and down the steps, Lucy standing frozen, her burnt English skin on display. He tried again. 'You see – there isn't anyone else at all. We're the last.'

THE POLAR BEAR KILLING

Michael Ridpath

Michael Ridpath worked as a credit analyst, but then became a bond trader, managing one of the largest junk bond portfolios in Europe. When his first novel, *Free to Trade*, was accepted for publication, he gave up working in the City to become a full-time writer. He went on to write seven more thrillers set in the worlds of business and finance, before turning his hand to a series featuring an Icelandic detective.

This was going to be the most important day of his life. He knew it. He could *feel* it. This would be the day when he left his mark on the world.

Constable Halldór's fingers tightened on the wheel of his police 4×4 as it hurtled through the fog towards the farm by the river where the polar bear had been sighted. The professional hunters in their souped-up Super Jeep were at least five kilometres away. He would get there first. He would have only a few minutes to make the shot.

The polar bear had been spotted on a beach six hours before by some fishermen who had

236

immediately called the coastguard. Polar bears were not native to Iceland, but once every couple of years one would pop up along the northern coastline, usually having ridden sea ice that had drifted westwards from Greenland. Often they swam the last few miles to shore. By the time they reached Iceland, they were tired and hungry. And dangerous.

The fishermen had only caught a brief glimpse because of the poor visibility. But it had been enough for Halldór to organise a couple of parties to scout for the bear, including the two professional hunters armed with the kind of rifle that could kill a reindeer at a thousand metres. Halldór had been following on behind when he had been alerted by the call from a young girl, a farmer's daughter, who had said she had seen the bear. Her mother was shopping in the village, and her father was out with the other scouts.

The girl was alone with her little brother on the farm, and Halldór was closest to her. In the back of the police car was his .22 rifle. It was much too small a calibre to kill a big bear under normal circumstances. But many years before Halldór had read the story of some hikers in the West Fjords in the 1970s who had come upon a polar bear, carrying only a .22. One of them had waited until the bear had approached really close and shot it through the eye. That had taken real nerve. And marksmanship.

Halldór had nerve. And he was one of the best shots in Iceland. As a policeman in Reykjavík he had applied twice for the Viking Squad, the Icelandic SWAT team, and been turned down each time. The problem wasn't his ability to handle firearms, but his physical fitness. And now, aged forty-nine, and after seven years driving his car round and round the village of Raufarhöfn in north-east Iceland, his girth had grown even greater. But he still knew how to shoot. And he still had nerve.

After a lull of several years, there had been a spate of polar bear invasions from the sea. Each time the bears had been shot, and there had been an outcry from urban do-gooders, people like his daughter Gudrún, for a national polar bear policy. Anaesthetic darts had been stockpiled, and experts flown in from Denmark. But even then, when the next polar bear had shown up, it too had had to be shot before it harmed any of the sightseers who had driven out to gawk at it. And so the new polar bear policy had been determined: shoot on sight. It was too expensive and too dangerous to do anything else.

The road sloped downward, and the police car emerged from the fog into a shallow valley with a fast river tumbling down its middle. A cluster of prosperous farm buildings with white concrete walls and red corrugated metal roofs appeared. The farmer made a little money from sheep and quite a lot from leasing salmon fishing rights on the river.

Halldór scanned the fields and pasture surrounding the farm. A flock of sheep were scattering in all directions: something had spooked them. And then he saw it. A dirty white bear loping along towards the farmhouse. And in front of it a little girl standing still staring at it.

Jesus!

Halldór leaned on his horn, swerved off the road and on to the grass and accelerated towards the girl. The bear stopped to look at the new arrival. The girl, too, turned towards him.

He pulled up between the girl and the bear, which was only about a hundred metres away. He lowered the window. 'Jump in, Anna!'

The girl opened the passenger door and climbed in.

'What do you think you were doing?' Halldór said.

'I wanted to speak to the polar bear,' she said.

'Those animals are dangerous!' Halldór said. 'He's come a long way and he's hungry.'

'He's not dangerous. Egill told me about polar bears. They are friendly. They help people.'

Egill was the old man who lived in the run-down farm barely visible at the base of the cloud on the slope on the other side of the river. He was about eighty and had long ago lost his marbles. 'They are not friendly, Anna, they attack people, believe me. Now where is your brother?'

'Back in the farmhouse,' said the little girl.

'Good.' Halldór looked at the bear, which was staring at the vehicle. 'OK, sit tight, Anna.'

Slowly he climbed out of the car and went around to the back to take out his rifle. The bear watched, but the girl couldn't see him. Once the gun was loaded Halldór made his way around the car, rested his elbows on the bonnet and aimed at the bear.

It was smaller than he had imagined it would be, and thinner: he could see its ribs. But it was still a magnificent animal.

It was also a hundred metres away, and had turned its rump towards Halldór.

A .22 bullet in the arse would do nothing to a polar bear apart from make it really angry.

'You're not going to shoot it!' shouted the girl.

'This is a dart gun,' said Halldór. 'I'm going to put it to sleep.'

'It's not a dart gun,' the girl said. 'My dad has a gun like that he uses to shoot foxes. I'm not going to let you kill the lovely bear.'

What happened next would be etched in Halldór's brain for the little time that remained of his life.

The girl jumped out of the car and ran towards the bear, shouting, 'Look out, polar bear!'

The bear turned, and after a second's thought ambled towards the girl.

Halldór's instinct was to run after the girl and pull her back. But if he did that, the bear would escape, run off into the mist. Sure it would be shot eventually, by one of the professional hunters. But not by him.

The girl stopped, suddenly aware that a very large animal with teeth and claws was approaching her. She was only a few metres from the police car, there was still time for her to turn and run, there was even time for Halldór to drag her back, but she froze.

Halldór took careful aim. The bear was coming directly towards him, its eyes two round black holes staring straight ahead.

At last the girl screamed and turned. The bear was nearly on her, only twenty metres away.

Halldór took his time. He could make this shot ten times out of ten as long as he kept his nerve. He inhaled, then exhaled slowly and squeezed the trigger. The bear dropped to the ground, as the bullet tore through its eye and into its brain.

The two young men, a German and an Icelander, breathed heavily as they climbed the hill. The sky was a pale blue, and there was no sign of the thick low cloud that had settled over the area for the previous five days.

The Icelander paused, and raised the binoculars that were hanging around his neck to scan the ponds and marshes of the Melrakkaslét-tarnes, the fox plain, that stretched out to the north of the village. 'Nothing.'

'She must have drowned,' said the German in English.

The bear that had been shot four days before was not yet fully grown, and the theory was that its mother might have landed as well. But now that the weather had cleared up and it was possible to see more than a couple of hundred metres, that was looking increasingly unlikely.

'I'm afraid you have wasted your trip, Martin,' the Icelander said, turning back up the hill.

'Yeah,' said Martin. 'It would have been cool actually to see a polar bear. And to stop those bastards shooting it.'

'Here it is,' said the Icelander, whose name was Alex. 'The "Arctic Henge".'

On the crest of the hill above them lay a giant stone circle, recently built in the manner of Stonehenge, with four tall stone gates at each

241

point of the compass rising to a point. The low sun painted geometric shadows down the eastern slope of the hill.

'Cool,' said Martin again. It was his favourite English word. 'You say it acts like some kind of sundial?'

'Apparently.'

They walked around the site, trying to figure out what it all meant. Alex thought that the layout was based on an ancient Icelandic poem, but he was confused about what signified what, and Martin's questions were just confusing him more.

'Well, let's ask that guy,' Martin said.

'What guy?'

Martin pointed to a black-clad leg sticking out from behind one of the stone pillars of a gate.

As the two men approached the gate, more of the figure came into view.

'*Mein Gott*!'

It was a man. He was wearing a black police uniform. He was slumped against the stone pillar. And where his right eye should have been there was a bloody mess.

It was a long journey from Reykjavík to Raufar-höfn. Detective Sergeant Magnús Ragnarsson flew half the distance to Akureyri, and then took one of the local police cars for the remaining three-hour drive. Raufarhöfn was in the far north east of the country, and the road there hugged the north coast to a point only a couple of miles south of the Arctic Circle. To his left the sea was a ruffled greyish blue, to his right the land was a

242

ruffled brownish green. Farms were few and far between. The landscape was wet, dotted with ponds, marshes, lakes and rivers. It was a fine day: the sun shone a weak yellow in the pale blue sky on to the eerie remoteness of the Melrakkasléttarnes.

Raufarhöfn was a sad village. It had been a boom town in the 1960s, when herring had been harvested from the surrounding seas, but with the disappearance of the herring the town had shrunk, leaving abandoned fish-processing plants and houses. The Arctic Henge guarded the town from its little citadel to the north, oddly modern like a frame from a fantasy computer game, especially when compared to the rundown twentieth-century decay of the village itself.

Magnus was reinforcements. The investigation of the murder of the local policeman, Halldór Sigurðsson, was being led by Detective Inspector Ólafur from Akureyri. Magnus's colleague Vigdís had joined the inspector immediately the body was discovered, with two members of the forensic unit from Reykjavík. She had been there two days when it had been decided that Ólafur needed some extra help.

The police station was easy to find, as was Vigdís, the only black detective in Iceland. To Magnus she was familiar, reminding him of the black police officers in Boston, where he had served in the police department for ten years before being transferred to Reykjavík. But Vigdís had never met her American father, a serviceman at the Keflavík airbase, and refused to speak English. She was an Icelander and was determined to let her fellow countrymen know it, however sceptical they were. She was also a very good detective.

The police station was small; it had accommodated only one officer, Halldór, but was now the centre of a murder enquiry. A selection of odd chairs were crammed around two desks and there were a couple of uniformed policemen and a detective that Magnus didn't know sitting at them. But Ólafur, the inspector in charge of the investigation, was out.

Vigdís was clearly pleased to see him. 'You made it!'

'This is not an easy place to get to.'

'At least the weather's not too bad this time of year,' she said. 'The town can be completely cut off in winter.'

'So, what's been going on? Any suspects?'

'I'll brief you,' said Vigdís. 'Do you want to take a walk? See the sights of Raufarhöfn?'

'Sure, why not?' said Magnus. 'I've been cooped up in the car for hours.'

So they left the police station and strolled through the village towards the harbour. There are a number of small fishing villages dotted around Iceland's coastline. Some of them are quaint. Some of them aren't. Despite a church and the odd brightly painted house, and a cluster of fishing boats bobbing about in the harbour, Raufarhöfn wasn't.

But the wind had died down, the sun was on their faces, and it was almost warm.

By the time I got here, they had already made

244

arrests, said Vigdís. The two guys who found the body: Alex Einarsson, 22, an Icelander and Martin Fiedler, 25 a German citizen. They are both animal-rights activists, Alex in Iceland alone, but Martin Fiedler has travelled all over Europe. He received a six-month prison sentence in England a few years ago during a protest at an animal laboratory.

They both came to Raufarhöfn as soon as they read about the shooting of the polar bear on a website called animalblood.com. The theory was that there might be another adult bear some-where around. There were search parties comb-ing the area looking. They found nothing, but because the visibility was so bad for three days, they couldn't be sure that there was nothing to find.

Alex and Martin caused real problems, trying to be as disruptive as possible. They irritated the hell out of the locals, including Halldór, the local cop, and the man who shot the polar bear in the first place.

He had become a bit of a local hero. He killed the bear with a single shot through the eye with a .22 bullet, just as the bear was about to attack a little girl. A hero with everyone but Alex and Martin, that is. And one or two other inhabitants who don't believe polar bears should be shot on sight.

Alex and Martin denied they had anything to do with the murder, of course. Neither of them had ever shot a gun before, or at least that is what they claimed. They admitted to hating Halldór, but they acted as if finding his body had been a genuine shock. And we couldn't find the weapon. We searched the area. We checked at the farmhouse where they were staying, but neither of them had had any luggage that looked as if it could hold a rifle. There was no gunshot residue on them of any kind.

We kept them locked up, and then drove them over to the district court in Akureyri to get a warrant to keep them in custody for another week.

Forensics came up with nothing, or very little. They found the bullet that killed Halldór, but not the casing. There were the usual small bits of rubbish you would expect at a tourist site, and they collected it all, but there was nothing interesting. No one had seen anyone going up the hill, apart from our two suspects. Halldór's body was discovered at about six-thirty in the evening. He had last been seen driving out of Raufarhöfn to the north at about four-thirty. He hadn't told anyone where he was going.

Ólafur and I went to Halldór's house. His wife died seven years ago in a car accident in Reykjavík: Halldór was driving. He was a policeman in Kópavogur, I remember him vaguely. Anyway, he wanted a new life and so accepted a transfer to Raufarhöfn. According to the mayor he was mostly popular, although some people thought he could be officious. He made friends in the village. He was an enthusiastic member of any search and rescue mission, and a year after he arrived he had played a big part in the rescue of a farmer who had fallen off a cliff in a snowstorm. He was a keen shot, and would go hunting foxes with a couple of the locals, as well as target shooting on a friend's farm.

He had two children, a daughter at the University of Iceland, and a son who lives in Reykjavík. Only the daughter was at home. Her name is Gudrún. She is small and neat with short blonde hair and glasses: she's twenty years old but looks younger. She has been back a week from Reykjavík. She was completely distraught, she didn't know what to do. A couple of neighbours had come round to help, and she said her grandmother and her brother were due to join her from Reykjavík soon.

She had no idea who might have killed her father. She said there were a couple of people whom she knew didn't like him, and he didn't like them: local troublemakers and one of the fishing captains, but she couldn't believe that any of them disliked him enough to shoot him. She claimed that she had never met Alex or Martin, although she had heard her father swearing about them.

Apparently, Halldór had fallen out with his son, Sveinn. Sveinn is a couple of years older than Gudrún. He was a student at the University of Iceland studying chemistry, but dropped out in his third year. Drugs. He does casual work in bars in Reykjavík, lives somewhere in Breidholt. Gudrún sees him occasionally: she says he is a bit of a mess. She let the drugs thing slip out and then refused to tell us more, she said it wasn't relevant. She was clearly worried she might get her brother into trouble.

I noticed there was a photograph on a bookcase

of Sveinn with his father and sister, and a rifle. They were at a makeshift range in a field. Sveinn was holding the rifle.

Afterwards, I went on to see the little girl, Anna, who had spotted the polar bear. Her farm is about ten kilometres from Raufarhöfn. She was quite upset, both at the death of the polar bear, and about Halldór being shot. She wouldn't speak to me: apparently she hasn't spoken to anyone about what happened the afternoon the polar bear was shot. I tried talking to her, but she seemed scared of me. You know how impatient I get with the way some of these country people deal with me because I'm black, but in her case I could see I must look strange to her, so I didn't push it. Her mother was worried: she wanted to take her to see a psychiatrist, but her father thought it was a waste of time. They mentioned that their neighbour over the river, Egill, had seen the bear being killed.

I decided to talk to him. There was a good chance that the killing of the polar bear was an important factor in Halldór's death, and I wanted to make sure we knew what had actually happened.

Although Egill's farm is only three hundred metres away, it is an eight-kilometre drive up to the bridge and down the other side of the valley. The farm is old and falling apart; the roof of the barn needs fixing. It's clear that Egill doesn't have any of the salmon fishing rights: just a few chickens and some sheep. He's old, God knows how old, one of those ancient farmers with beady blue eyes and a face like a lava field under a

248

white wispy beard. The farmhouse is tiny, but the kitchen has one of those old stoves in the middle and is really warm. And clean.

When I told him I was a detective, he didn't believe me until he had examined my ID very closely, and then chuckled to himself about a 'blue' policewoman; you know how they used to call black people blue in this country? But he was nice enough about it and seemed very happy to talk.

He said he knows Anna well. She enjoys playing down by the river, and he shouts across to her; tells her stories. He knows lots of stories. He makes up little poems that he recites to her; she loves that apparently. Her parents seem to like her relationship with him, but he scarcely ever sees her face to face.

I asked about the polar bear. He went off on a long tangent about how he was born on the island of Grímsey in the north. There is a famous story about how one day all the fires went out on the island. It was in the days before matches and so three islanders had to try to get to the mainland to bring back embers to rekindle them. The sea was iced up, and one of the men got lost and drifted out to sea on an ice floe. The next morning, he came across a mother polar bear trapped on another slab of drift ice. The bear allowed the man to suckle her milk with her cubs, and kept him warm. When the man had regained his strength, she swam over to the mainland, with him on her back. He gathered some embers and then returned on her back to Grímsey, and all the fires on the island could be rekindled. The man gave the bear cow's milk and two slaughtered sheep and the bear swam off.

This was Anna's favourite story. Which was why, when Anna saw the polar bear, she wasn't afraid of it.

Egill didn't realise that the bear was there until he heard the sound of the police car arriving. It was a foggy day, but at that moment the fog lifted and he saw the bear and the girl and the policeman. He still has good eyesight at distance, he says. The bear was a youngster and in bad condition. He saw the girl climb into the police car, and then the policeman take out his rifle. Then the girl jumped out of the car, and started off towards the polar bear.

At this point Egill paused and stared at me. His beady little eyes shone with anger. Halldór did nothing to stop her. According to Egill, he had plenty of time to shout to her, or to drag her back, but he didn't. He just aimed his rifle and shot the bear.

Egill seemed very upset by this. In his view, Halldór need not have shot the bear at all. He could have coaxed the child back into his car and taken her off to the farmhouse. Then he could have called for help and they could have captured the bear and taken it back to Greenland. It was small and weak, so doing this would have been possible.

The next day Egill had gone into town and talked to some people in the café at the petrol station. Everyone seemed to think Halldór was a hero. Egill started trying to explain what he had seen, but no one was listening to him. Except maybe the waitress, Lilja. No one listens to him much any more.

I asked him whether he had any idea who might have killed Halldór. He said he hadn't been away from the farm for a couple of days: he didn't know Halldór had been murdered. But no, he didn't have any ideas.

Someone from the German Embassy in Reykjavík arrived in town, together with a lawyer from Akureyri. The pressure was on to find more evidence against Alex and Martin. We decided to interview everyone in town. The population is only 194 and someone *must* have seen something. But Ólafur asked me to look at the website Alex and Martin had said told them that the polar bear that had been shot might have had a mother.

I checked it out: it was very interesting. You can see the flurry of messages after the first reports of the polar bear being shot. Everyone was angry, and someone with the nickname *Foxgirl* suggested that volunteers come out to Raufarhöfn and disrupt the search for a second bear. Two members said they would go; they turned out to be Alex Einarsson and Martin Fiedler. Martin said he was flying from Düsseldorf to Iceland.

I couldn't figure out who *Foxgirl* was from the website, although it was clearly someone who lived in or near to Raufarhöfn. And *Foxgirl* makes sense when you think of the Melrakkasléttarnes with all its foxes. It made me wonder about Gudrún. Maybe she was *Foxgirl*, or if she wasn't, maybe she knew who was. I spoke to Ólafur about it, and we decided to return to

Halldór's house to ask her more questions.

Gudrún's grandmother and brother had just arrived from Reykjavík. We decided to talk to them before Gudrún, see if we could get more family background. The grandmother didn't tell us much we didn't know already. She was Halldór's mother-in-law. She had good things to say about him, but I got the impression that they had fallen out over his decision to move from Reykjavík to Raufarhöfn. And over Sveinn, his son.

We spoke to Sveinn. He had a shaven head and dirty clothes and seemed strung out. He fiddled with a cigarette the whole time, desperate to light up. Definitely a junkie. He said he had a job in a bar in downtown Reykjavík. When we asked him what we would find when we checked his criminal record, he said he had been done for possession a couple of times, and assault once.

'How were relations between you and your father?' Ólafur asked him.

'Not good,' he said. 'Dad was really angry when I left university. Chemistry just wasn't my thing and he didn't understand that. And I told you I got busted for possession. He assumed I was a pusher. Which I'm not.' He glared at us, daring us to contradict him, but I wasn't convinced. 'I didn't talk to him much after that.'

'Did you talk to Gudrún?' Ólafur asked.

'Yeah. Not often. But every now and then.'

'And how was the relationship between her and her father?' I asked.

'Oh, Gudrún is a good girl,' Sveinn said. 'You can tell that just from looking at her. Works hard, passes exams, has nice clean boyfriends. Dad used to point out to me what a good girl she was.'

'So no major arguments?' I said.

'Not until last week.'

'Last week?'

'Yeah. Gudrún called me. I'd seen the news about how Dad had shot the polar bear and was a big hero. I knew Gudrún would be upset about that; she's a big save the elephant fan. And save the orang-utan. And the chimpanzee. So I was pretty sure I could guess her attitude to her father shooting a polar bear.'

I exchanged glances with Ólafur. Gudrún hadn't told us any of that.

'So they had a fight?' Ólafur asked.

'A massive one. But it wasn't just that Gudrún was upset that he had killed the polar bear. It was *how* he had done it.'

'What do you mean?'

'Gudrún has a friend who works in the petrol station who overheard an old farmer who lives on the other side of the river from where the bear was shot. Apparently Dad let a little girl wander over to the bear so he could shoot it, rather than getting the little girl out of the way and letting the bear escape. Gudrún was horrified that Dad would use a child as bait like that.'

Sveinn broke the cigarette between his fingers and swore. 'But I'm not surprised. If Dad thought he had a chance to be the guy who shot the polar bear, then he would take some big risks. And not just with his own life.'

'Did your father teach you to shoot?' I asked.

Sveinn frowned. 'Yes. But only when I was a kid.'

'Were you any good?'

Sveinn nodded. 'Not bad. Not as good as Dad, though. He was an excellent shot.'

'What about Gudrún?'

'She wasn't a bad shot either, for a girl. Not as good as me.' Sveinn's brows knitted again. 'Hold on. What are you suggesting?'

'We're just asking questions,' Ólafur said.

'No you're not. You are suggesting that Gudrún shot Dad, aren't you? Well, you know what? You're out of your minds. You've met Gudrún. She would never shoot anyone, let alone Dad, no matter how angry she was with him.'

'Just a couple more questions,' said Ólafur.

'No! No way! I'm not answering any more questions.' Sveinn got to his feet and pulled out a packet of cigarettes. 'You two are mental, you are. Bloody useless. All you cops are bloody useless. My dad was bloody useless.' I noticed a tear appear in his eye, but he rushed from the room before it had a chance to escape. He threw open the front door and lit up outside.

We took Gudrún down to the station. She admitted she had had a row with her father. She was angry with him for killing the polar bear, and very angry with him for putting the little girl's life at risk, although he denied it. He said that he couldn't stop her from going up to the bear, and the only way to save the child was to shoot the animal. Gudrún didn't believe him. She said that she did use the nickname *Foxgirl*

254

online, and she had urged concerned people on animalblood.com to come out to Raufarhöfn to stop another polar bear from being shot, although she had been too nervous to actually make contact with Alex and Martin once they were here. And she said that her father had taught her to shoot. But she denied killing him herself.

There was an obvious way to find out. We took the rifle and some spent casings we found at his house, and rushed them to the lab in Reykjavík for analysis. Either it will match the bullet that killed Halldór, or it won't. We persuaded the coastguard, who had had a helicopter up looking for a second bear, to fly a constable to Akureyri with the evidence, and from there he flew on to Reykjavík. We should have an answer back any time soon.

They were sitting on a wall by the harbour. In front of them a fisherman was loading a very large net on to a very small boat. 'So you see, Magnús, I'm afraid you've wasted your time. It looks like you'll be heading back home tomorrow.'

Magnus sat silently, his hands thrust into the pockets of his coat.

'Magnus?' Vigdís said. 'What is it?'

'You said Gudrún denied killing her father,' he said at last. 'How did she seem?'

'Totally distraught. At the end of her rope. She just broke down. She answered our questions quietly, with tears streaming down her cheeks. It was hard to read her: I couldn't tell whether she

255

was upset because of all the pressure of the last few days, or whether she couldn't face what she had done. Inspector Ólafur was sure she was guilty.'

'And what about you, Vigdís? What was your instinct?'

'I told you: I wasn't sure.'

Magnus looked at her steadily. He raised his eyebrows. 'I know you, Vigdís. Not being sure isn't your style.'

'What do you mean?'

'I think your gut feel is that she's innocent and you don't want to admit it.'

'Magnús, that's ridiculous! We are detectives. We deal in evidence.'

'We deal in people,' said Magnus. 'It takes a certain kind of daughter to shoot out the eye of her father. I've met one or two of that kind of woman in America. None in Iceland that I can think of.'

'So are you saying Sveinn shot him? He wasn't even in Raufarhöfn.'

'No.' Magnus was quiet for a minute, staring at the fishing boats. Vigdís let her boss think. 'Do you have any spare spent .22 bullets among the evidence? Doesn't matter which gun they are from.'

'We have a few from the range Halldór used back at the station.'

'Perfect. Let's grab one and then go for a drive.'

It was a rough drive from the bridge to the farm. On one side of the dirt track the salmon river rushed down towards the nearby sea. On the other side the Melrakkasléttarnes stretched northwards through marsh and bog. A tough bleak place to scratch a living.

They parked outside the farmhouse. An Icelandic sheepdog rushed up to them barking and wagging its tail at the same time.

'Bjartur! Quiet!' The old farmer came out to meet them, wearing blue overalls and a peaked cap. Vigdís was right, the skin under his beard was criss-crossed with crevasses and fault lines, but his face broke into a smile of welcome when he recognized Vigdís. 'The blue policewoman! Come in, come in! I have a little coffee, but no cakes, I'm afraid.'

Before they entered the house, Magnus glanced across the river towards the more prosperous farm on the other side. The view was clear and uninterrupted. 'So that's where the polar bear was shot?' he said.

The farmer frowned and nodded. 'Yes. It was a cruel day.'

They sat at a table in the cosy kitchen and Egill poured a small quantity of thick gritty liquid from a thermos into two cups. There wasn't enough for himself. 'I'm sorry, I wasn't expecting visitors.'

Magnus sipped the coffee and tried hard not to grimace.

'Do you know who murdered Halldór yet?' Egill asked Vigdís.

'Not yet,' said Vigdís.

'Yes,' said Magnus. Vigdís glanced at him quickly.

And so did Egill. The bright blue eyes focussed on Magnus under bushy eyebrows.

Magnus produced a clear plastic bag, inside which was a small brass-coloured metal object.

Egill's eyes turned to the bag.

'Did you know, Egill, that our scientists can examine a rifle and determine whether it was the one that fired this bullet? With 100 per cent accuracy.'

Egill shook his head, still concentrating on the bullet.

'We've come to ask you for your rifle,' Magnus said slowly. 'So our scientists can examine it. See if it was the weapon that fired the bullet that killed Halldór. Can you fetch it for me?'

Egill didn't move. He stared at the bullet. Then looked up at Vigdís and Magnus. He sat back in his chair. 'You know I told you about that polar bear in Grímsey. The man the bear saved was supposed to be my great-great grandfather.'

'It might be wrong to shoot polar bears,' Magnus said quietly. 'But it's very wrong to shoot people.'

'That man risked Anna's life just so he could get the credit for killing a bear,' Egill said, his eyes suddenly on fire. 'OK, so he shot the bear through the eye, but that was just because the bear was moving slowly.' He leaned forward. 'If the bear had charged, and it could easily have charged, then it would have been almost impossible to hit it with that accuracy. If he had hit the bear in the chest or the neck, Anna would be dead now. So I couldn't understand when everyone was treating the man like a hero when he had

258

almost killed a child.'

'How did you get him up to the henge?' Magnus asked.

'I told him what I had seen. Said I needed to talk to him, and suggested we meet at the henge by one of the gates there. I made him think I was going to blackmail him. I waited a short distance away from the henge and shot him. Through the eye. He was standing still.'

'I think you had better show me where your rifle is and come with us,' said Magnus.

Egill bent down and patted the dog at his feet behind the ears.

'Sorry, Bjartur, old fellow. I'm going to leave you now. Perhaps Anna will look after you.'

For the first time a tear appeared in the old man's eye.

ENCHANTRESS

Peter Robinson

Peter Robinson was born in England, but moved
to Canada, and now divides his time between
that country and Richmond, North Yorkshire.
His first novel, *Gallows View* (1987), introduced
Detective Chief Inspector Alan Banks, and
launched a long-running series, now success-
fully adapted for television as *DCI Banks*, with
Stephen Tompkinson in the lead role. He has
written many short stories, winning numerous
awards, and his non-series books include *Caed-
mon's Song* and *Before the Poison*.

The train journey passed pleasantly enough,
despite a long delay at Crewe. It was a hot day,
and the compartment smelled of warm uphols-
tery. Occasionally, a puff of acrid steam drifted
in through the open window. As we rattled out of
the station past the backyards and allotments, the
rhythm of the wheels clacking on the lines and
the flashes of sunlight on car windscreens grew
faster and faster. I felt as excited as when I had
been a young boy, and I realised I could hardly
remember the last time I had taken a train.

We passed a canal where two boys sat fishing

with nets against a backdrop of distant cooling towers. At one level crossing, a farmer in a tractor raised his flat cap to us, and two young lovers shared a long goodbye kiss at Nuneaton. As we chugged through the lush green English heartland, I settled back in my seat and alternated between reading Ian Fleming's new novel, *From Russia With Love*, and watching the landscape go by, thinking about where I was going and what had triggered my journey.

A week ago, I had received notice that my oldest friend Roland Stringer had died. It wasn't unexpected; Roland had been suffering from cancer for almost two years, and many would call his death a blessing. He had always been the more successful of the two of us. While I slaved away trying to communicate the joys of Beethoven, Schubert and Tchaikovsky to children who wanted to listen only to Cliff Richard, Tommy Steele and Elvis Presley, Roland was out there in the fields, fishing boats and factory yards collecting folk songs, writing about them, and generally making a name for himself in the world of musicology. It was folk music that had brought us together, as university students in the early Twenties, and it was folk music that was to bring us together again now, after his death.

Roland had asked in his will that I be made his literary executor, should I so wish, and his son Cecil had offered his father's house in Highgate, now empty, as a place to stay while I worked. At first I was uncertain about taking on such a task, but the summer holidays had just begun, and I had no plans, nothing stretching ahead of me but empty, futile days, dragging into weeks, so I decided to go. The news that a small but adequate sum had been set aside for my expenses and remuneration certainly helped to sway my decision.

The outskirts of London snapped me out of my reverie: rundown housing estates, factories stacked with pallets, a small church, a school, a football ground. Finally, we arrived amid the smoke, bustle and clamour of Euston station, and I made my way to the taxi rank.

I was overwhelmed by the apparent chaos in Roland's study. The high-ceilinged room was filled with teetering piles of papers, reels of tape and boxes of wax cylinders. However, I soon began to discern a pattern in Roland's work, and after a few days, what had seemed impenetrable chaos became more manageable. Fortunately, Roland had transcribed all the songs and variants he had collected into large bound notebooks, listing their corresponding tape or cylinder number; I was therefore able to match the notebooks to the recorded versions far more easily than I had thought I would.

After I settled down to work, I soon found out that Roland had not only been collecting songs and writing about them, but he had also been setting down his experiences on the road and making notes on the characters he had met. To Roland, the folk song was a living, growing entity. There was no end to it, never any one final version. Go to the next fishing village, the next farm, the next back-to-back terrace house, and

262

you would find a variant, an extra verse or two that a singer had added, perhaps, or a name substitution, subtle alterations in the narrative. It would be fascinating to explore his work, I couldn't deny it, and if my name appeared with his on any opus, magnum or other, that I could mould from the raw material of his research, then so much the better.

As I made my way through Roland's life's work, I found variants of such familiar songs as 'Bruton Town', 'The Wind that Shakes the Barley' and 'Famous Flower of Serving Men' alongside songs I had never heard before. And then one day I came across something I hadn't expected.

Roland had discovered several variants of a Child ballad known as 'Little Musgrave and Lady Barnard' or 'Matty Groves'. Most changes were minor, of course, but one version I came across made the hairs on the back of my neck stand up.

He had listed the title as 'Mattie Greaves', and the song mentioned a place called Swainsdale Manor, the family seat of the Bewlays, one of the area's most prominent families. I knew this place, and the people who had lived there. My Aunt Gwynneth had been in service to Lord and Lady Bewlay before the Great War, and my mother and I lived in nearby Eastvale. I had spent many an idyllic summer's day as a young lad within its majestic walled grounds.

On checking Roland's notes, I found that he had collected the song from Jack Metcalfe, landlord of the Black Heifer, in the village of Lyndgarth, in 1928. The manor, as I remembered, was only half a mile or so from the village. The song itself specified no date for the events it recounted. All Roland's notes said were: 'Jack Metcalfe. Bit of character. The jovial host. Likes to tell stories. Clearly has grudge against gentry. Seems something of a laughing stock locally, but at least left interesting variant of Child ballad 81.'

The Bewlays were an old family, and generations of them had lived in Swainsdale Manor. How could I know whether Jack Metcalfe's variant referred to the Lord and Lady Bewlay I had known? I say *known*, but, of course, as the mere relation of a lowly serving girl, I was hardly privy to the family's friendship and patronage. But there was more, far more, than a casual relationship. What came back to me most of all, and what still shook me to the core, was that I remembered Lady Bewlay. Her first name was Isabella, and Isabella just happened to be the name of the lady in the song. One summer, almost forty-five years ago, I had fallen in love with Lady Isabella Bewlay.

Of course, it was an adolescent infatuation, and perhaps one of the first examples of my setting my heart on someone I could never possibly have, which, in turn, may be one reason why I never married. The only women I ever wanted were like Lady Isabella: far beyond my reach. I was fourteen years old, and had just started to feel excited and awkward in the presence of girls. We were living in Eastvale when Mother first took me to Swainsdale manor to visit Aunt

Gwynneth on her afternoon off. It was the beginning of the Great War, and my father was already away fighting in France.

I won't say it was an opportunity I jumped at. What fourteen-year-old boy wouldn't prefer playing cricket with his mates, fishing out on the Leas, or swimming in the river by Hindswell Woods if the weather was warm enough? But I went along dutifully, as my mother was still a sad and lonely figure in the wake of my father's departure, and I soon found myself fascinated by another way of life – a paradise, it seemed to me, beyond the high garden walls – and I was enchanted by the beautiful young woman I met there. Without a doubt, she was 'the fairest among them all'.

We got off the bus at the village green and walked the half mile or so of winding country lanes to the manor. Then I got my first glimpse of the place. I had never seen anywhere so magnificent, so opulent, so regal as Swainsdale Manor, but then I had lived a somewhat sheltered life. It was built of local limestone with a portico and marble pillars at the front, like some sort of Greek temple. It had a classical symmetry about it that I admired, and as one approached it down the long drive, it almost resembled a face.

I am not sure how many rooms there were, for we never ventured far beyond the kitchen and my aunt's small bed-sitting room. All I remember is a broad staircase and a profusion of dim wainscoted corridors, varnished wood gleaming in the candlelight, paintings of local landscapes in ornate gilt frames, brass-handled doors leading off to bedrooms or salons.

The grounds were extensive, with woods, a pond, a folly, and even an old well, covered with a wooden lid for safety. With Lady Bewlay's permission, Mother let me go off and explore by myself, and mostly I pretended to be Robin Hood in the woods while she and Aunt Gwynneth sat on a blanket on the grass, ate cake and drank tea, and gossiped in the shade of the great copper beech.

Lord and Lady Bewlay were quite young. I remember hearing that he was thirty and she only seventeen when they had a married a year or two before my aunt went to work there. The young lord's parents had been drowned in a tragic boating accident off the Isle of Wight shortly after the wedding, and consequently he had inherited the land and title at an early age. Though he would always say hello to me, ask me how I was doing at school, I remember him mostly as a remote and distracted figure, never quite there.

But Lady Isabella. What a contrast! She was life itself – so young, so full of energy, so gay, with a smile that would light up the darkest corners of any sad soul and dazzle the very angels. And her laugh. It was the kind of music that made you want to make it your mission in life to make her laugh all the time. But there also seemed, to my romantic soul, a deep sadness and loneliness about her, too, as if she had lost something important to her, or had not yet found something she craved. Of course, it is only with the benefit of hindsight that I can indulge in such fanciful ramblings.

When I first saw her, she was leaning against one of the columns, her skin pale as the marble, wearing a long summer dress, her blonde hair cascading over her shoulders. With her girlish figure, cornflower blue eyes and unblemished complexion, she looked for all the world like some sad medieval princess waiting for her prince to come and rescue her. Whether she needed rescuing, I had no idea. While I was perfectly capable of being smitten by such a beauty, I was far from any understanding of the ways of married life, or of the grown-up world in general. Now that I think of it, perhaps she did need rescuing, and no doubt I believed that I was the one to do it.

In most versions of the Child ballad, Lady Barnard sees Little Musgrave in church and persuades him to spend the night with her at her bower. Her page overhears this and runs to tell his lord, betraying her. As the two lovers lie in the afterglow, Lord Barnard enters and challenges Musgrave to a duel, giving him the best sword. Musgrave strikes first and wounds the lord, then Lord Barnard strikes and kills Musgrave. He asks his wife what she thinks of her lover now, and she avows that she loves Musgrave best, even though he is dead. At this, Lord Barnard kills her, then he has the two of them thrown in a grave together, with his lady on the top.

In the version Roland collected from Jack Metcalfe, however, Lord Bewlay goes off to war, and Lady Isabella takes up with a young lad called Greaves, another name I knew from that period. The lord is killed in battle, and one night a ghostly, disfigured creature turns up at the manor for vengeance, slaughters the young lovers and throws them in a grave.

Why, I wondered, would Jack Metcalfe alter the narrative details of a ballad that dated back to the seventeenth century? It also seemed to me that he was mixing the supernatural and the revenge ballad with the domestic tragedy. And why hadn't I heard anything about this before? I could recall hearing no stories or rumours of such a lurid nature. Surely, if anything like that had happened, I would have heard?

Though perhaps not. We left Yorkshire for Dorset in the late summer of 1916, and we lived on a remote farm with my grandparents for some years after that. Communications being what they were back then, I never heard another word of Lord Bewlay or Lady Isabella. I was miserable for a time, pining for my lost love, but life went on, and in the end I suppose I accepted my inevitable bachelorhood much as I accepted most other things in life, without much of a struggle. I pursued my music, my school teaching career, such as it was, and I had a rather unmemorable war as part of the Army Transport Corps, where I saw a great deal of the world, but very little in the way of action.

I thought of her often over the years and wondered what had become of her, always stopping just short of trying to find out. I know that I was merely an adolescent boy, and she was a young woman, a fantasy, an unattainable dream, but somehow, I had never experienced such depth of feeling for any woman other than my own mother before or since. I have never known how to talk to women, to be at ease with them.

When I closed my eyes in that Highgate study after reading Roland's transcription, I could picture her as clearly as if she stood before me. I had the sudden realisation that I had lived my life in a fantasy – the needle of the gramophone stuck in adolescence – all to a soundtrack of old folk ballads and Romantic composers. This surely must be fate, I told myself. Now that I had got this far, now that the past had reached out and grabbed me by my lapels, I couldn't get free. The old song says that as love grows older, it grows colder and fades away like the morning dew. But my love had never been consummated, had never been given the chance to grow old or cold. Now that I had 'found' Isabella again, the old feelings came back with a vividness that startled me.

The song left too many vexing questions in my mind, and I felt the need for answers Obviously, I had to go back to Swainsdale, to Lyndgarth, and do some digging around.

Some summers live forever in the memory, and for me it is 1916, the summer of my sixteenth birthday.

Lord Bewlay came and went, much involved in military matters, though in what capacity I had no idea, as I never saw him wearing a uniform until later. As I was older now, I was allowed to wander further afield, and sometimes I even went as far as the village, especially when Harry Langthwaite, a school friend of mine, was at home.

One day when Harry and I were playing cricket on the village green, I twisted my ankle. Harry helped me hobble to Dr Greaves' surgery. The doctor was new to the village, and through various circumstances, I would like to think he became my friend. He was much younger than I would have expected a doctor to be, so there was naturally much speculation as to why he was not in France.

Harry told me he had overheard his mother and father talking about that very subject, and it seemed that Dr Greaves had served at a field hospital and had been wounded. He was now unfit for active duty. He didn't look unfit to me, but I have since learned that many of the wounds inflicted by war are invisible to the naked eye. With so many doctors and teachers away fighting, it was a godsend to the village to find him, and his credentials were quickly accepted. Luckily, my ankle was not seriously injured, and the application of an elastic bandage and a little less running around for the next few days proved the perfect cure.

Tragedy struck that July. We got news that my father had been killed in the Battle of the Somme. I felt numb at first, unable to cry, unable to comfort my mother. I couldn't believe that he was dead, that we would never again go fishing together, or that Mother and I would never again sit around the fire on a winter's night and listen to him sing 'The Trees they Grow so High' or 'The Banks of Green Willow'. It seemed so *wrong*, so *unfair*, and I remember feeling angry all the time.

Until, that is, a week or two later, when Lady Isabella first asked me if I would do a small favour for her.

My heart leapt into my throat. Grief-stricken as I still was over my father, a chance to be of service to Lady Isabella was all I had wished for these past two years, and now she was asking for my help. Perhaps she needed to be rescued, I thought, like the sad princess I had first imagined her to be.

She put her finger to her lips, leaned forward and laid it against mine. An electric thrill rippled through me. I was in heaven. Perfect bliss. Her finger tasted of lavender water, and to feel its exquisite softness against the sensitive surface of my lips was almost more than I could bear. It was to be our secret, she said, when she handed me an envelope and asked if I would deliver it to Dr Greaves. I think I might have asked her if someone was ill, but all I really remember is her smile and her wave as I set off on my mission. I knew that Aunt Gwynneth had what my mother referred to as the 'falling sickness', and perhaps I thought that Lady Isabella was doing her a kindness in sending for the doctor. Whatever the reason, I ran and skipped all the way to Lyndgarth, feeling as if I were dancing on air.

I found Dr Greaves alone in his surgery and handed him the note. He asked me to wait while he read it, wrote a hurried reply, gave me sixpence and asked me if I would mind delivering the letter to Lady Isabella. I thought it a little odd that he wasn't dashing off to help Aunt Gwynneth right away, but I didn't dwell on it for long. I ran back. Whatever I was doing, I was doing for Lady Isabella, and if it made her happy, then I was happy, too.

It did. Her eyes sparkled as she read the note.

And so it went. On at least two more occasions that summer, I delivered a note to Dr Greaves from Lady Isabella. He would give me a reply and a sixpence. Sometimes we would linger in his surgery, and he would show me his instruments and tell me what they were used for. He let me listen to my heart through his stethoscope. It was beating fast. He had a skeleton in the corner, I remember, and he used it for a hat stand, which I thought very funny. I told him about my father, and he rested his hand on my shoulder and told me how sorry he was, that the war had taken so many good men. I could tell that his sympathy for me was genuine. He said nothing about his own experiences in France, but the little muscles at the corners of his jaw tensed and twitched, as if he were struggling to hold back words and emotions.

Then, one day in August, around the time Lord Bewlay turned up in his officer's uniform, yet another disaster struck. There would be no more need for servants at Swainsdale Manor for some time, Lord Bewlay said. He had to leave for France the following morning. Much of the manor would be closed down until the war was over, and Lady Isabella would manage with only

Peggy, her personal maid, in the few remaining rooms.

I thought how terrible it would be for Isabella to be so isolated, so alone. She was such a vivacious creature that I worried she would wilt and fade without company. And, of course, I would have no reason to see her any more.

And so, almost as abruptly as we had arrived, we were exiled from Eden.

The journey to Lyndgarth was relaxing enough, despite my agitated state of mind. Again, the soothing clickety-clack of the train and the warmth of the day worked their magic on me; the landscape seemed bathed in honey, everything golden, so still and sweet and slow. But despite it all, I was aware of a certain tension in my chest. After all, I was going back to a place I had not visited in many years, and I was hoping to find out something about the roots of a folk song that mentioned the brutal deaths of people I had known and loved.

I changed trains at York, and we headed west on an obscure branch line. Soon, we passed through Eastvale, on the far side of the river, the brownish water foaming like beer pulled from the cask as it fell over the terraced falls. I saw the steep walls of the ancient castle for the first time in over forty years and remembered how I used to play there with my father when I was a boy, scrambling up and down the ruined battlements with ease. It was a scene that hadn't changed much in centuries past, and it probably wouldn't change much in centuries to come.

From there, we headed out into the Yorkshire countryside, the hills rising more steeply on each side, crisscrossed with drystone walls, humped with limestone outcrops, white dots of sheep grazing on the high slopes. It had been a wet spring in the north, and the greens of the meadows and hillsides were dark and rich, dotted here and there with clumps of wildflowers, white, yellow and purple. Finally, we came to Lyndgarth.

I walked the short distance to the village green. Some local children were playing cricket with makeshift stumps, just as Harry and I had done on the day I twisted my ankle, and nearby, a young couple sat enjoying a picnic on a checked tablecloth, the way Mother and Aunt Gwynneth used to do at Swainsdale Manor. For a few moments, the illusion continued, and I thought that I had stepped back in time. I went straight to the Black Heifer, one of the two pubs that stood beside the green, separated by a general store and a post office.

I had no idea whether Jack Metcalfe was still alive. I hadn't known him at all, except by his name over the door. Even if he was no longer there, I thought, the odds were that I would find *somebody* who remembered the old days.

Jack Metcalfe had died in 1942, I discovered, but his son Jimmy was now landlord of the Black Heifer, and he frowned with remembrance as he pulled me a pint. Jimmy said he was too young to remember so far back, as he had been born in 1920 and was only a child at the time. He did remember that his father had a passion for folk music, though, and that he had a bee in his bonnet about the Bewlays. Jack Metcalfe had been caught poaching once on Lord Bewlay's land and had had to plead for forgiveness. That had rankled with his proud nature, and with his professed allegiance to the Russian Revolution, and he had borne a grudge ever since.

Jimmy knew nothing of what had become of Lady Isabella or Dr Greaves; they were not a part of his childhood. The only other information he had for me was that Lord Bewlay had been living at Swainsdale Manor since the end of the Great War with his French bride, but they kept themselves very much to themselves.

He then pointed me in the direction of one of his regulars, Ted Sharp, who looked as if he had been sitting in the same chair over by the window since time immemorial. He had known Jack, and he would talk to anyone, Jimmy said, so long as the drinks kept coming. I thanked Jimmy, picked up my glass and walked over to introduce myself.

Ted Sharp had a pipe clamped firmly between his teeth, and at first I thought he was going to ignore me completely when I asked if I might join him. Then I noticed his lips move around the pipe and distinctly heard the words, 'Gin and tonic. Double. No fruit,' which I took as my cue and duly returned with the required beverage. Ted took the pipe out of his mouth, sipped the gin, smacked his lips and fixed me with his ancient eyes. 'Go on, then, lad,' he said. 'Cat got your tongue?'

Now that I was here, I didn't really know how or where to begin. Somehow, it all seemed faintly ridiculous – an old folk song, a youthful love, the growing sense that things were not as they had seemed. It was a struggle to get out the words, but I managed to ask Ted if he had known the Bewlays up at the Manor.

Ted snorted. 'Now what would an old farmhand like me be doing hobnobbing with the gentry?'

'But you must have seen them around?'

'They didn't mingle. Not with the likes of us.'

'I understand that your friend Jack Metcalfe didn't like them, that he wrote a song about them?'

Ted gave what I assumed to be a low-pitched cackle. 'Too much imagination, old Jack.' He pointed the stem of his pipe to his head. 'Too much imagination and not enough gumption.'

'You mean he imagined things?'

'Let me put it this way. If you sent old Jack out to buy a pot of striped paint, he'd go to t'shop and ask for one.'

'So he was gullible?'

'Aye. You could say that. He imagined he'd see some sort of ghost or monster coming out of the gates of Swainsdale Manor around the time they disappeared. I ask you!'

'Disappeared? Who disappeared?'

Ted knocked back the rest of his drink and banged the glass on the table. I got the message. 'Same again?'

'Since tha's asking.'

I came back with another double gin and tonic.

'You mentioned a disappearance.'

'Aye. Did a bunk with Lord Bewlay's wife, didn't he?'

'Who did?'

'T'young doctor. Matthew Greaves.'

So it was true, the terrible fear that had been growing in me. Even though I had begun to suspect as much ever since I first heard Jack Metcalfe's song and started thinking about the past, it still hit me like a punch in the stomach.

'What's up lad, tha's shaking like a newly shorn sheep?'

'Nothing,' I said. 'When did this happen?'

'In t'war. Great War, like.'

'They disappeared, just like that?'

'Aye.'

'Was there a police investigation?'

'Came around asking questions, didn't they? But there was nothing for 'em to investigate.'

'What was Jack Metcalfe doing out there?'

'Ha! Poaching, like as not, knowing old Jack.'

'And where was Lord Bewlay?'

'Away at war, weren't he? Everyone thought he was a goner.'

'But he wasn't?'

'He came back.'

'When?'

'After it were all over. Nineteen or twenty. Thereabouts. Had a lovely French bride with him.'

I tried to picture the Manor, Lady Isabella in her flowing dress, the handsome, distant Lord Bewlay, but the image shattered into fragments that blew away on the wind. 'What happened?'

'Nowt. They went to live at t'Manor. Lord Bewlay had been wounded on the Somme, see, and he'd stayed in France to recover. I think he'd had a bit of surgery over there, too. Scars on his face. One of his eyes drooping. Sloppy French work.'

'Are they still at the Manor?'

'He is,' said Ted. 'She died a few years back, and he's become a bit of a hermit. Not that he wasn't before, like, but you never see him at all these days. Has all his groceries and whatnot delivered. There's some as says he's not much longer for this world, hisself.'

Ted banged his empty glass on the table again, but I had enough information to be going on with. I thanked him for talking to me, ignored his grumbling as he counted out his small change on the table, and went up to my room.

I cannot say that I slept at all well that night. Perhaps it was the unfamiliar bed, though I suspect it was more likely the disturbing tale I had heard from Ted Sharp. I was also restless because I couldn't wait for the morning. After breakfast, at a decent hour, I intended to present myself at Swainsdale Manor and find out whether Lord Bewlay himself would talk to me. After all the bits and pieces I had picked up from Jack's wild imaginings, and from Jimmy and Ted, I found I needed more than ever to know what had happened to Isabella and Matthew, where they had gone, what had become of them, and what role I had played. Lord Bewlay might just be willing to tell me.

I rushed my breakfast and regretted it all the way along the winding lanes to the manor. It was another day of sunshine and blue skies, reminiscent of the summers I spent there as a young lad. I remembered dancing along that very same lane on my first mission to Dr Greaves for Lady Isabella, full to bursting with my absurd happiness, my foolish devotion. I was on another kind of mission now. A mission for the truth, no matter what pain it might bring.

I slowed down in amazement as I approached the manor walls. They were overgrown with climbing plants, the stones cracked and crumbling. The rusted gates stood open, one of them hanging on a single hinge. Weeds grew between the paving stones of the path. The beautiful gardens resembled a jungle, some of the trees were clearly dead due to neglect, and the pond was covered over with scum and slime, the water stagnant, smelling like a blocked drain. The folly was in ruins.

But the house itself was still intact, the Greek columns, portico, classical symmetry, though it, too, showed signs of neglect: missing slates, moth-eaten curtains in the upstairs windows, a front door badly in need of a fresh coat of paint.

As I stood there trying to take it all in, the door creaked open, and a hunched figure stood there pointing a shotgun at me. I held out my hands and said, 'Don't! Please. I mean no harm. I'm George Lomax. My aunt worked here. I used to play here when I was a boy.'

He paused and squinted at me. I could see what

Ted Sharp meant about the scars and drooping eye.

'Are you my Nemesis?' he asked.

'No,' I answered. 'I've just come to ask you some questions.'

After staring at me for some moments, he grunted, cracked open the shotgun and rested it over the crook of his arm, beckoning me to follow him inside. We entered what I guessed had once been a grand receiving room, now almost bereft of furniture, its surfaces covered in dust, cobwebs in the ornate cornices of the ceiling threatening to invade the crystal chandelier. He fixed me with his good eye. 'I remember you now,' he said. 'Weren't you that young lad who made doe eyes at *la belle dame*?'

I think I probably blushed. *'La belle dame*?' I echoed weakly.

'Don't you know your poetry?'

'I...'

'Keats. *La Belle Dame sans Merci*. That's what I called her. Isabella. "Alone and palely loitering." That's what you were doing. "I saw pale kings and princes, too, / Pale warriors, death-pale were they all; / They cried – *La Belle Dame sans Merci* / Thee hath in thrall!".'

By the sound of his laughter and the gleam in his eye, I thought he was mad, but he seemed to regain his composure, put down the shotgun and sat wearily in a deep armchair. I sat opposite him. 'Are you all right, Lord Bewlay?' I asked.

'I'm tired and ill,' he said, tapping his chest. 'And empty. An old man. It's a long time since I've spoken with anyone. A long time since

280

anyone's called me by my name.'

I explained to him about the odd chain of events that led to my coming here. He listened, nodding occasionally. 'It was all so long ago,' he said, after a deep sigh. 'I didn't deserve her.'

'Isabella?'

His lip curled. 'Marianne.' Then he said nothing for a while. A clock ticked in the silence. It told the wrong time, I noticed. 'It's true that I was wounded,' he said finally. 'Twice. Such irony. The second time, a French family found me in a ditch and took me in, even though it could have cost them their lives.'

'They nursed you back to health?'

'Yes. And that was when I fell in love. Fell in love for the very first time in my life.'

I was stunned at this comment. Here was the man who had been married to Lady Isabella, with whom a life together would have been beyond my wildest dreams, and he was telling me that it meant nothing to him, that he had never truly loved her. 'But why did you marry her if that's what you felt?' I cried.

'Do you think it was my choice? We were a good match, or so everyone said. My parents. Her parents. That was before I knew she was an inconstant, cruel, heartless woman.' His eyes gleamed dangerously again. 'Isabella was the very devil incarnate. *La Belle Dame sans Merci*.'

I could hardly bear to hear my old love spoken of in this way, but I knew that losing my temper would gain me nothing. I swallowed my anger and went on. 'What happened to her?'

He stared at me for a long time, then seemed to

281

come to some sort of decision. 'It's a relief, in a way,' he said. 'To tell you. And yet another irony. I feel that I've come full circle.'

'Where are Lady Isabella and Matthew Greaves?'

'Oh, they're dead,' he said softly. 'They've been dead for a long time. Since October, 1916, as a matter of fact. The first time I was wounded.' He pointed to his drooping eye. 'When I got this.'

'What happened?'

'One of the servants from the manor enlisted in my regiment. He was friendly with Peggy, the lady's maid, and she told him that my wife Isabella had been running around with the local doctor, Matthew Greaves, that they had become more and more brazen since I'd gone away, and that the whole village was talking.'

'But you didn't love Isabella! You didn't care about her!'

'La Belle Dame was a witch, and witches enchant. She had her ways. It's true I didn't love her, but I couldn't get enough of her, and there I was in a trench in France, up to my eyeballs in mud, and there she was, in my warm clean bed with the young doctor. I couldn't bear it. Can you understand that?'

'I think I can understand jealousy.'

'Yes. Jealousy. Perhaps even more than that. Obsession. I don't know. I wasn't thinking clearly, and that's how I got wounded the first time. Thoughts of my wife's infidelity were eating away at me, and I was careless. You can't afford to be careless in battle. But the wound wasn't actually as bad as it looked. The worst part was lying there with my dead comrades in the mud, crying, playing dead among the scattered limbs, waiting for the shooting to stop. That was when I decided. If I survived all this, by hook or by crook, I would kill the both of them.

'Then I had an idea. One of the dead men, a corporal, was so badly shot-up as to be unrecognisable. We were about the same build, so right there, in the mud, I exchanged uniform and identity tag with him. After that it was easy. I was bandaged up and sent back to a hospital in England as Corporal Saunders, and everyone assumed Lieutenant Bewlay was dead. It was easy enough to sneak out of the hospital and come up here while I was convalescing. I found them at it. Would you believe it? When I walked in, they were actually doing it in *my* bed, making the beast with two backs.'

I tried to keep the image from my mind, but I couldn't. I saw Lady Isabella with Dr Greaves, naked, thrashing on white bed sheets. I gritted my teeth. 'What did you do?'

Lord Bewlay laughed. 'Do you know, I don't think they even recognised me. They probably thought I was a burglar at first. Or a ghost. I still had bandages on my face. Greaves went for one of the swords on the wall and came at me. I dodged him and went for the other. I'd had quite a bit more experience with the things than he had, so I was able to kill him quite easily.'

'And Isabella?'

'I wasn't going to kill her, witch though she was. I thought I was a gentleman, you see, that I

283

would draw the line at killing a woman and take whatever punishment was meted out to me.'

'What changed your mind?'

Lord Bewlay paused, then said, 'She cradled his body in her arms and kissed his lips. Kissed him as a lover would, you understand. The next thing I knew, she was dead, my sword thrust right through her breast and stuck in the floor-boards.'

'My God.' I felt a chill all down my spine. *'Isabella.'*

'I cleaned up behind me, put the bodies in the well, sealed it up, returned to the hospital, then went back to France to carry on with the war. That would have been November, 1916. I didn't care whether I lived or died. But dammit if I didn't get wounded again. I decided this was the opportunity to put an end to Corporal Saunders once and for all, but I wasn't certain how to bring back Lieutenant Bewlay. In the end, it didn't matter. I passed out in a ditch from loss of blood. I woke up in a bed in a French farmhouse with Marianne gazing down on me, and my life was transformed from that moment. When I opened my eyes, I truly thought I was in heaven. I stayed there for two years, and when I wandered back home after the war was over, I simply told everyone I had lost my identity and my memory, which both came back slowly, with the right treatment. Nobody even asked about my identification. Perhaps they hadn't found Corporal Saunders' body. Anyway, there were no repercussions. I got a hero's welcome. The rest you know.'

'Did no one ever wonder what had happened to your wife and Dr Greaves?'

'Everyone assumed they had run off together, gone to Canada or Australia or some such far-flung outpost.'

'What about Jack's song?'

'Metcalfe must have seen me coming from the manor that night, around the time they disappeared. He couldn't have known who he'd seen, or what I'd done, but he had imagination enough to make something of it. I probably made a rather terrifying figure in the moonlight. He knew about Greaves and Isabella – everyone did by then – and when there was no sign of them in the following days, I suppose it fit with one of the old songs he had in his mind. Some avenging demon, or some such rubbish. In an odd sort of way, he got it right, didn't he? I mean, my wife and this Greaves did have an affair, and I did kill them both. Metcalfe was no doubt also struck by the similarity in the names Greaves and Groves, and the idea of some nobody bedding the lord's wife appealed to his warped sense of humour. But for the few who ever had to listen to it in the Black Heifer, it was just another folk song. As far as anyone knew, I hadn't been in England since August, 1916. Corporal Saunders had been here, of course, but nobody knew that, or cared tuppence about him. After a decent interval, I was able to bring Marianne over, and we had many happy years together here. Sadly, we were not blessed with issue, but that was a small price to pay for all the happiness we had.' He paused, then looked me in the eye again. 'So what are you going to do now you know the truth? Tell the police?'

I shook my head, feeling well and truly as if someone had scooped out my insides and replaced them with jelly. 'I don't know,' I said. 'There doesn't seem much point, does there? But *Isabella...*'

'Isabella was an enchantress and a whore. She certainly worked her spell on you. I know all about the messages.'

It had taken me close to forty-five years to see the significance of what I had done that summer, and even then the realisation had come only indirectly, through names linked in a variant of a folk song. But whether I had been aware of it or not, I had played my part, however small, in the tragedy that had unfolded at Swainsdale Manor, in the deaths of the woman I had loved and the damaged young man who had been kind and understanding towards me.

'I don't think you'll be seeing or hearing from me again,' I said, and got up to leave. My feet felt heavy, my legs bound in irons, my heart like molten lead. I walked out of the room and out of the manor, back into the garden, where I stood for a moment leaning on one of the marble columns the way Isabella had done that first time I saw her.

I walked around the pond to the edge of the woods and looked for the circle of wood that covered the old well. It was no longer there, or at least I couldn't see it. When I found the spot where I remembered the well had been, I stamped with my foot and thought I sensed a hollowness beneath.

There were no garden implements nearby, so I grabbed at the sods and pulled them up one by one with my bare hands, slowly revealing the cover. I grasped the metal ring and tugged with all my might. It was heavy and had been stuck in place for a long time. The sweat broke out on my brow, under my arms, trickled down my back. My heart pounded. And still I pulled. Finally, it budged. An inch. Two inches. More. Then it came away, and with both hands I was able to lift it up.

The well wasn't very deep, and it had dried up over the years. The sun was still bright, and a beam of light illuminated the bottom. Even though Lord Bewlay had told me what I would find there, I gasped when I saw the latticework of entangled bones.

I stood there for I don't know how long before I heard the sound of the shotgun blast from the house. Frightened birds flew from their shade among the leafy branches.

I made to go back, but I could only stand rooted to the spot by the well, staring at the bones, the sweat drying on my skin. What could I do? I knew it was partly my fault for stirring up such old feelings, and I knew that Lord Bewlay was right about Isabella. She had used a vulnerable young boy callously to aid her in deceiving and betraying her husband. But knowing that didn't stop me from feeling a great weight of sadness and loss descend as I remembered the beautiful young woman so full of life and vitality, her smiles, her laughter, and the touch of her finger against my lips.

I looked at the bones again. I couldn't tell whether Isabella was on the top, but I hoped so.

'A grave, a grave,' Lord Bewlay cried, 'to put these lovers in.

'But lay my lady on the upper hand, she was the chiefest of her kin.'

NIGHT NURSE

Cath Staincliffe

Cath Staincliffe is the author of the Sal Kilkenny private eye stories and creator and scriptwriter of *Blue Murder*, ITV's detective drama starring Caroline Quentin as DCI Janine Lewis. She writes the Scott & Bailcy books, based on the ITV1 police series. Her stand-alone titles, starting with *The Kindest Thing*, often focus on topical moral dilemmas. She has also written for radio.

Joan's research was always impeccable. After all, it wouldn't do to be going off half-cocked; not when someone's life was on the line.

She trusted her instincts, mind. Instincts were underrated these days. Talked of like so much mumbo-jumbo, on a par with homeopathy and crystal healing. Whereas Joan knew, over twenty-eight years of working with the sick and the halt and the lame, that people's instincts were usually spot on.

For example, those close to death could feel it coming, their family too, though they might not admit it. But there was a collective reaction. For some a drawing back in preparation for letting go. For others, those with issues – a buzz-word Joan loathed but was bandied around by everyone these days. Issues, as far as Joan was concerned, meant offspring or the unsavoury by-products of medical conditions; issues were new sets of stamps or copies of magazines. Joan preferred the term unfinished business or scores to settle, troubled waters – for those people there was a frantic often unseemly last bid to get closer.

Instinct was normal and natural, we're animals after all, so much blood and bone and hair and we've survived by our instincts for thousands of years. It was when you ignored your instinct that the trouble started. Like the time she'd been offered a lift home by one of the junior registrars. A filthy night, rain like stair rods and a mix of coal dust and sewage scenting the air. Her, soaked to the skin. But there was something about him, more than the curl of his smile and the hard brightness in his eyes, something like a smell coming off him that made Joan's flesh crawl and her stomach turn over. She'd said, 'No, thank you very much,' and walked instead. Her skin white as tripe by the time she got back and had peeled off her clothes. Nine years later, a consultant by then, he'd been charged with sexual assault, found guilty and struck off.

As a rule, her antennae started twitching at visiting time. 2 to 4 p.m. and 6 to 8. That was when she first observed the couple at play, as it were. He'd have come up from Emergency, fast-tracked for surgery or booked in after a GP referral and outpatient tests.

Body language told her most of the story, the tableau of tension: the lowered gaze and anxious glances, fretful hands, the bitter twist of his mouth, the clenched knuckles.

Joan added sound to this, tending to one of the other patients behind the curtains, always amazed at how out-of-sight really was out-of-mind. It wasn't strictly necessary to make out the actual words because the rhythm and tone, the cadence and the silences offered enough to add weight to her suspicion. Variations on a symphony she'd grown up hearing, could have scored herself, choreographed, sung the theme tune. Nevertheless, something verbal was always a helpful contribution to the evidence. The put-downs, the insults, the veiled threats: *Why on earth did you park there? Good God, woman, I didn't mean that book.* The stone cold cruelty: *Christ, you're so bloody dim, they won't operate until I've seen the anaesthetist.* The humourless laugh more like a bark and the wife's answering giggle or half sob, breathy, fearful or unnaturally calm. Her whispered attempts to placate: *I'm sorry. Yes, of course, love.*

The one before last had been Pakistani, they talked English but not to each other, so Joan couldn't make out what they were saying though everything else fit and her intuition had proved correct.

But Joan didn't rely solely on her instincts.

And she was cautious; if there was any doubt about it, what she thought of as her diagnosis, then she stayed her hand and kept the peace. The monitoring phase continued as long as was necessary. Getting the lay of the land. She always made a further check and for that she'd developed a couple of little tricks that worked every time.

Joan would chat to the husband, who was charm personified to all but his other half. Simple enough to become his favourite nurse and glean a little personal information. *Heather? That's a lovely name, your age is she? Just thinking of afterwards, the rehab, if she'll be able to cope. Younger? Two years. No impairments? Grand – should be fine.*

Then the star sign ruse. Perusing the horoscopes when the wife next visited. *'Money in the air from a surprising source.' Oooh, I like that one. What's yours, Heather? No, let me guess – Taurus?* And when the reply came, whether it was, *Yes! Taurus,* or, *No, Pisces/Capricorn/Libra,* Joan would widen her eyes and laugh aloud, *Same as me! I'm the tenth.* No one could resist giving their own date, least they hadn't yet, and Joan would read out that day's horoscope and then get back to work.

Armed with both name and date of birth she would wait until, in the depth of a night shift, she could check the wife's admission records.

She had been wrong once. A painfully shy young woman married to a much older man. The husband had actually slapped his wife's face when he thought no one was looking. The young woman had gone beet red and blinked back tears. Joan had checked her out but found nothing, no A&E visits, no pattern of accidents and falls. It didn't mean it wasn't happening but Joan held her fire that time. Checks and balances. She had to be ninety-nine percent certain.

The latest one – Heather, had been in and out like a yo-yo. The last two admissions for broken bones.

A 20-bed ward, five four-bed bays. Male cardio-surgical. Men whose hearts were bursting, leaking, obstructed, engorged. Men whose hearts were broken and among them, here and there, men whose hearts were rotten to the core.

Joan did a revolving pattern of earlies, lates and nights. Nights were when she undertook her missions. She'd missed one candidate when a run of norovirus had buggered up staffing levels and shoved her back onto days. That man had left after his double bypass to return to the marital home.

Unlike the rest.

This last one was only her sixth, in fifteen years, so it wasn't like she was running amok, dishing out treatment willy-nilly. The post-op period was ideal, the immune system weakened by the procedure, and the vagaries of individual recuperation subject to wide variation which provided ample camouflage. With almost thirty years' experience to draw on Joan had a battery of weapons at her disposal: drugs withheld or increased, fluid introduced into the respiratory system, air into the blood, vital signs misreported, alarm systems disconnected and reactivated at the appropriate times. A jot of adrenaline or a tot of insulin, a blast of morphine, a tube pinched, a pillow judiciously applied.

Of course it was a shock for the wife left

behind: the risks associated with surgery were never really believed, better to focus on the big, positive percentages. And at first the women were at sea, like they'd had their legs kicked out from underneath them – metaphorically this time.

It had been the same with Joan's mother, at a loss without him there. Frozen. Uncertain how to act, how to be, without her lord and master, his nibs. A crude beginning for Joan, shoving him down the cellar steps as he swayed at the top, about to go fetch another pint of homebrew. Satisfied that the crack to his skull would be the death of him, if left unattended, and with her mother off on a church outing, Joan went to the market on Grey Mare Lane. She took her time, browsing, chatting, cup of tea and a barm cake in Bea's Cosy Caff. Came back and discovered him unresponsive, no pulse (she was in her first year of nurse training) and dutifully rang the ambulance.

For her mum, as for the later women, the relief, the sweet, dizzying sense of escape, of freedom, only came later. As they learned to be at home in their own skin, in their own homes. When they could feel carpet beneath the soles of their feet, or grass or sand, in place of eggshells. When they could sleep without each sense attuned to the possibility of attack: the hand at the neck, the fist in the face, the obscenities showering down in a spray of spittle signalling start of play.

There was a period of transition, a need for rehabilitation and Joan considered it her responsibility to help with this. Using her role as carer to offer balm and comfort: *It's never easy but perhaps you'd like to come along for a cuppa one day, there's a couple of us meet at the café in the garden centre.* Or a trip to the theatre, or an afternoon shopping. *Not Selfridges's, mind, not on my wage.* As new found friend edging them slowly back into the big, wide world, recommending book groups and local history societies, volunteering and WEA classes, helping run a fund-raising raffle for the women's refuge. Never prying, never needing to know but always a good listener.

Joan had fretted about how to support the Pakistani widow, had called round for tea a couple of times but then the woman had explained that she was going to Birmingham, where her brother's family would take her in. She seemed excited at the prospect.

The widows blossomed in time, the chill and terror of their marriage replaced by the comfort of female friendships and the delights of small and selfish pleasures. Gradually Joan took a back seat as they found their feet. Over the years her reward had been to hear those simple words: *New lease of life; A teenager again; I don't miss him at all, if I'm honest; Feel like a new woman.*

Today they'd a fresh admission. Cardiac arrest at home, still on a ventilator. Ashen colour. Judging by the wife's face he'd been using her as a punch bag when his ticker gave out. Bruises fresh and ripe as plums. 'He knocked into me when he fell,' the wife said, to anyone who'd listen. 'I should have got out of the way.' An apologetic titter after every comment, eyes stark as a headlit rabbit.

Joan checked her rota. Smiled. And went to say hello.

CATCH-13

Andrew Taylor

Andrew Taylor is the author of a series of books about William Dougal, as well as the Lydmouth mysteries, the Roth Trilogy – which was adapted for television as *Fallen Angel*, with Charles Dance – and a number of historical crime novels, including *The American Boy*, *Bleeding Heart Square* and, most recently, *A Scent of Death*. His other books include *The Barred Window*, novelisations and books for young people. Among other awards, he has received the CWA Diamond Dagger.

'It don't smell right,' Winston said, scratching his nose.

'Don't be stupid,' I told him, as kindly as I could. 'It's just like the guy said. No windows. No cameras. And look – see the pipe? On the left there.'

Winston stared through the van's windscreen. The drainpipe was just beyond the back door, held to the wall by a series of clamps. The man had told us that we'd find the spare key wedged in the brickwork at the back of the pipe just above the third clamp.

Winston sniffed. 'I don't know.'

'Well, I do,' I snapped. 'I know he gave us a hundred quid, and after we've walked in and out that door there's another four hundred to come. I also know I'll lose my flat as well as the car and the van if I can't pay the rent again.'

Before he could answer, I opened the door and got out. As I knew from bitter experience, Winston is someone who needs telling what to do. Before the recession, before everything went wrong and when I still had the business, he used to work for me. He did deliveries in this same van that used to belong to me and now belonged to him. He was always getting lost, or delivering the wrong box of organic veg, or no box at all.

I walked quickly towards the back of the workshop. It was on the edge of a small industrial estate on the wrong side of Slough, not that I necessarily mean to imply Slough has a right side. The estate had plenty of security at night, the man had said, but nothing in the day.

The workshop was a small, single-storey building with double doors at the front. The key was behind the pipe, just where the man said. Winston scrambled out of the van and joined me by the back door. He'd turned up the collar of his coat and pulled his woolly hat over his forehead. He looked like a burglar.

I pushed the key into the lock and turned it. The door swung open. I stepped inside, pulling Winston after me, and closed the door. Now we were actually doing it, my hands were shaking and I was finding it hard to think straight.

We were in a little room at the back with a

298

paint-spattered sink. Beyond it was the half-open door of a little toilet and another doorway with a curtain half-drawn across it.

'He said it was a joke,' Winston said behind me. 'No one pays five hundred quid for a fucking *joke*.'

I told him to shut up and pushed past the curtain. But Winston was right, of course. There was something a little fishy about this. Maybe the guy was using us for a theft. Or maybe it was revenge or something. Not our problem, as long as we kept our eyes open. What counted was the five hundred quid.

Winston whistled. 'Jesus. What a tip.'

'It's normal,' I said. 'It's the creative ambience.'

The studio was maybe twenty feet square with windows covered with steel shutters. Grey November light filtered down from two long skylights. The room was littered with junk – tables, easels, stuff dangling from the ceiling, brushes, jars, tins, fag ends – and everywhere the spatters of paint.

'Is that it?' Winston's voice sounded uncertain. 'That thing there?'

He pointed at what looked like an old plant-stand, Edwardian maybe, in front of the double doors. Where you'd expect to see an aspidistra there was a transparent box about the size of one of those biscuit tins that my auntie still gives me at Christmas.

I went over to it, tripping over a dismembered bicycle on the way. The box was made of perspex. It rested on a thin stone base. I stared at what was inside.

Winston peered over my shoulder. 'Oh my God,' he whispered. 'I mean, that's sick.'

'It's art,' I said. 'So it's the concept that matters. That's all. Think Damien Hirst. Or Tracey Emin.'

'Who?'

'It doesn't matter.' Explaining modern art to Winston would be like outlining the principles of evolutionary science to a chicken: it was simply better not to start. I lifted the box, which was surprisingly heavy. 'We need a bag or something.'

'This do?' He grabbed a canvas-and-leather backpack hanging on a hook by the door. He lifted the top flap. 'It's empty.'

At that precise moment everything went wrong. Someone tried the handle on the door. They rattled it. There was the sound of a key sliding into the lock.

I'll say this for Winston: he kept his head. Still holding the backpack, he pushed me towards the doorway at the back. I had the box in the crook of my arm. We belted through the little room and out of the back door. I pulled it shut behind us. We sprinted across the concrete apron to the van.

We lost five seconds while Winston fumbled for the key. Would you believe it, he'd locked the door? Then at last we were inside. The engine fired. The workshop's back door was still shut. Winston accelerated away from the kerb. Rubber squealed as he pulled out in front of a lorry.

'Don't drive like a maniac,' I hissed. 'For God's sake, try and act normally.'

He had the sense to take the side entrance out

of the estate, so we wouldn't pass the front of the workshop. I stuffed the box into the backpack that Winston had nicked, and pushed it down on the floor by my feet.

Neither of us spoke until we reached the motorway, with me checking the rear-view mirror every thirty seconds for flashing blue lights. Traffic was heavy and we made slow progress. The rendezvous was at a service station – not the one where we had met the man but the next one to the west. We were going to be late.

Winston turned on the radio and tapped his fingers on the wheel in time to some musical drivel. I opened my mouth to tell him to turn it off and then closed it as I remembered that he was no longer my employee and that it wasn't my van or even my radio any more. Instead I opened the backpack and examined the box.

It contained only one thing: the mummified corpse of a small fish. It had decayed so far that it had reached the point where it was almost inoffensive, like a vaguely fish-shaped scrap of dirty leather. Probably it stank but the perspex had an airtight seal and I couldn't actually see any maggots so perhaps they'd all died off as well.

In fact, I realized as I examined the thing more closely, there was more than one fish in there. The other one was on the upper surface of the stone base itself. The corpse was actually resting on part of it. At first I thought the second fish was painted or inked on the stone, a skeletal shadow in faded orange. Then I saw I was wrong. It was actually embedded into the stone.

It was a fossil.

Conceptual art isn't so hard once you get the hang of it. This was obviously telling us that there was more than one way of being dead.

'Yuk,' said Winston, glancing at the box. 'Lush bag, though.' He stretched out a hand and touched it. 'Can I have it?'

'But we've got to put the box in something.'

'No prob,' he said. 'There's a black plastic sack in the glove compartment.'

The glove compartment had silted up since I'd owned the van. It was full of the debris of Winston's life, empty cigarette packets, copper coins and broken pencils. I found the black sack under my old *A-Z*, which now had half its pages missing. A blob of chewing gum had attached itself to the plastic but I eventually got the bag open.

When I transferred the box I saw underneath the base for the first time. There was writing, perhaps a signature, incised into the grey stone. It looked like 'G. Ring'.

It took us nearly an hour to reach the service station. I hated leaving the shelter of the van and I hated carrying that plastic sack across the car park. I knew there'd be cameras and security men everywhere. I felt as though I had a neon sign on my back saying 'THIEF'.

Winston nudged me. 'He's there.'

He sounded as relieved as I felt. The man was sitting in the café just to the left of the door. He was a big guy with grey hair and a close-cropped beard flecked with reddish hairs. He looked like a semi-retired Viking in a leather jacket. His English was excellent but it probably wasn't his first language.

He had been chatty enough this morning, which was the only other time we'd met him. Winston had taken me out for a coffee to cheer me up after they repossessed my car. The man had been at the next table. He'd eavesdropped on us talking about money, or rather the lack of it. Then he'd sidled over and bought us another coffee. While we drank it, he oozed charm over us and made his proposition.

But on this occasion he didn't waste time talking or oozing charm – he just nodded, waved us to chairs and almost snatched the black sack. He opened it and examined the box without taking it out.

'Good,' he said. 'Very good. And this is for you.' He put a white envelope on the table and stood up, the box under his arm. 'Goodbye.'

Winston stared after him. 'He's in a hurry.'

I opened the envelope and found a wad of twenty-pound notes. I gave one of them to Winston. 'Let's celebrate, shall we?' I still found myself telling Winston what to do. Someone had to. 'I'll have a small latte and one of those chocolate muffins. Can I borrow your phone?'

While Winston was queuing at the counter, I went on-line and Googled 'G. Ring artist'. And there he was, the top result: Gerhardt Ring, born Munich in 1959, a performance artist.

Performance? What performance?

I soon found out. The more I found the worse it got. Ring specialised in creating sequences of stills from videos he had shot. Just the one set of prints – and then he destroyed the original video.

The guy had an international reputation. He was a visiting lecturer at the Royal College of Art. Tate Modern had put on a retrospective of his work last year. The Museum of Modern Art in New York had paid $1.3 million for his most recent piece, 'Catch-12', one of a series. A Tokyo gallery had bought 'Catch-11'. 'Catch-10' was in Sidney. The BBC had devoted a *Culture Show* special to him.

Oh Christ.

Winston came back with the coffees and I told him how we'd been set up. Soon the whole world would be able to see us making prats of ourselves for as long as art galleries existed.

'Catch?' he said, frowning. 'What's all that about then?'

'Because it's what you do with fish. You catch the bloody things.' I took a deep breath and explained, 'Ring made the box we nicked for him, right? But for him that's just the start. Each of the "Catch" pieces is based on a video of someone like us stealing it, the same box. Someone who doesn't know it's not a real theft. See?'

While we were talking, the phone was downloading a photograph of Gerhardt Ring. I glanced down. It was our man, all right, though the photo had been taken a few years ago. The beard was longer and wilder, and above it was a mass of red hair.

'He's German,' I said. 'And he's a red head. Herr Ring. Red Herr Ring. Red Herring. Get it? It's a pun! And I bet the fossil's a herring, too, and the rotting fish on top of it. Ha bloody ha.'

'Is that a joke?' Winston said. 'Don't seem

very funny to me. But maybe that's the Germans for you. My gran says—'

'Shut up about your gran. Can't you see? He's actually telling us that the box is a diversion, a distraction. The real thing's the video. Or rather the stills he gets from the video and sells for millions ... In other words, he's getting a shed-load of money out of making fools of us.'

The coffee didn't taste good and I couldn't face the muffin.

'Come on,' I said. 'I want to go home. While I still have one.'

'Can I have the muffin if you're not going to eat it?'

We walked in silence to the van. It started to rain, which suited my mood. We sat side by side, looking at the water streaming down the wind-screen while Winston ate the rest of the muffin.

'Look on the bright side,' he said when he'd finished. 'At least we got five hundred quid. Bird in the hand, eh?' He leant over the back of the seat. 'And this bag. Nice – it's Italian, you know. Lovely bit of work. Milan, probably. You could say it's a sort of bonus.'

His face changed.

'What is it?' I said.

'There's something in the side pocket.' He drew out a small, shiny object. 'Will you look at that – a video cam. Nice bit of kit. Look – he cut a little hole in the bag and mounted it so the lens goes there.' He fiddled with the buttons. 'We can sell it on eBay. But it's a shame about the hole in the bag. That's vandalism, that is. Hang on, though – look at this.'

Winston angled the video cam so we could both see the back. Miniature people flickered on the tiny screen.

'That's me,' I said bitterly. 'And that's you. And that's the part when someone tried to get in at the front.'

But Winston was smiling. 'So that's all right then.'

'What do you mean?'

'He'll be back, won't he? That Herring bloke. All we have to do is come here tomorrow, have another cup of coffee and wait.' Winston dropped the video cam in the Italian leather-and-canvas backpack. 'This is what he really needs. It's worth one point three million dollars to him. Maybe more.' He was still smiling. 'One red herring. Catch-13.'

THE WRONG MAN

Charles Todd

Charles Todd is the writing name of an American mother and son duo, Caroline and Charles Todd, who are best known for their historical mysteries. Their first Inspector Rutledge novel, *A Test of Wills*, appeared in 1996. In addition to the Rutledge books, they have written a series featuring Bess Crawford, and two stand-alone titles.

Summer, 1920
The church was full that Tuesday morning. Alexander Fletcher had been well liked. He'd sent three sons to war, lost all three, and was never bitter about it, saying he believed strongly in King and Country and had done his best to serve both. His money, what there was of it, he'd left to the fund for the church roof.

The hymns had been sung, the rector was just finishing his eulogy, and the organist was waiting for the signal for the Recessional.

A hollow rapping began, tentative at first, and then much louder, growing more frantic with each blow. The rector stopped in mid-praise, and all eyes swung toward the coffin, watching in horror as it began to wobble. The organist, taking the silence for his signal, began to play again. The undertakers, Messrs Lassiter and Sons, rushed forward to fumble with the locks as the pounding reached crescendo. The lid, released, seemed to spring open of its own accord, and as it did the dead man rose to a sitting position and looked wildly around.

Pandemonium broke out. The parishioners stood as one body and began to scream.

The man in the coffin, realizing where he was, tried to leap out of his prison and succeeded in sending it flying. Unhurt, he stumbled up the aisle, his bare feet slapping on the stone paving, and he disappeared through the church door before anyone else could move. He was never seen again.

Afterward, the only thing everyone could agree on was that the revived corpse was not Sandy Fletcher. Where Sandy had got to, no one knew, least of all Mr Lassiter or his sons.

Inspector Ian Rutledge was sent to the village of Merrow because he was already in Oxford. The undertakers had been adamant that the local constable was not up to the task of finding either Sandy or whoever had put a live man in his place. Their firm was being accused of a reckless disregard for the dead and they were having none of it.

It was late that Tuesday evening when Rutledge drove into Merrow. But there was a lamp burning in the rectory, and he decided to stop there before finding lodgings for the night.

The rector answered his knock almost at once, glasses in hand. 'Am I needed somewhere?'

Rutledge gave his name, and the rector led him to the study where he'd been working.

'We were beyond words, all of us. Unable to do anything but stare, it happened so quickly. And then we realized it wasn't Mr Fletcher after all. I shudder to think what would have happened if the coffin had been buried. Half an hour was all that stood between that poor soul and eternity. The doctor suggested later that the man had been drugged, awaking before he should have. It's the only explanation.'

'And the undertakers had no idea when or how the switch was made.'

'None at all. They're reliable men, the Lassiters. They've been in business here for three generations. This will ruin them if the police can't find out what happened.'

'Describe the fleeing man.'

'I don't think any of us could, it all happened so quickly. Dark hair, medium height, slim build. Bringing back the image in my mind, I could remember that much. Young or old, I couldn't tell you.'

'Did Mr Fletcher have enemies? Or the Lassiters for that matter?'

'Not that anyone knows. The constable has asked.'

'Was there a funeral shortly before Fletcher's?'

'You're thinking the bodies were switched? Or put one on top of another? Monday we held services for Maddie Hamilton, and the coffin was open. Her express wish. I was there when the lid was put in place. I ask you, who would wish to bury a man alive?'

'Perhaps someone wanted him to wake up and find himself unable to do anything about it. A crueler death than most.'

Rutledge thanked the rector and left. Just off the market square he found an inn. The sleepy night clerk gave him a room on the front, and from his window he could see the church tower's clock. It had gone one.

Hamish was busy in the back of his mind, a voice Rutledge had carried with him from the battlefield, a daily reminder of the Great War, even though he knew very well that Corporal Hamish MacLeod was dead and buried in France. Shell shock, Dr Fleming had said. A wound with no treatment, no exorcism. He strove to live with what had happened in France, reminding himself that if the blind and the burned and the maimed could find a way to cope, so must he. But his service revolver was oiled and loaded in a trunk in his flat, if a time came when he couldn't bear it any longer.

Sleep eluded him, Hamish's Scottish voice a reflection of his own thoughts as he struggled with the image of being buried alive. In 1916, a shell landing by his trench had entombed his company in heavy black earth smelling of dead bodies. He had been the only survivor.

Hamish was saying, 'It must ha' been a man, ye ken. To remove one corpse and put a drugged man in his place.'

'Or a woman and whoever helped her.'

'Aye, the laudanum.'

310

'A hot drink before bedtime? Perhaps intended to kill him, perhaps hoping it wouldn't until he was in the ground.'

'Where did yon false corpse go, then? Without his shoes or a halfpenny in his pocket?'

A good question. Rutledge quietly let himself out of the inn and walked down the moonlit street to the churchyard. It fronted the High Street, while the church itself was set back behind a stand of yews. He circled the apse to reach the far side, and realized that beyond the churchyard wall was a pasture. Two horses, one silver in the moonlight and one dark, grazed quietly in the summer night.

Before the stunned mourners had regained their wits, the victim could have come out the west door and run for the cover of the high summer grass. No one would have looked for him there – and it explained why no one in the village had seen him fleeing. He could have lain there until he'd caught his breath and considered what to do.

On this same side of the church a mound of earth marked where Mr Fletcher was to await the Last Trump. Rutledge walked over to it and stared down into the black pit that was the grave.

Only it wasn't a completely black pit. Something lay at the bottom, and it was pale.

He ran back to the inn, retrieved his torch from the motorcar, and came back to shine it into the grave. Now he could see that the thing in the pit was a man.

He rather thought that Sandy Fletcher had finally turned up.

But when he'd summoned the constable and the constable had awakened Mr Lassiter and his sons, the corpse that they brought up out of the grave was a stranger. And still relatively warm. He was missing his shoes.

'Anyone recognize him?' Rutledge asked. 'Is he the man who was in the coffin at the funeral?' But they shook their heads.

'Doesn't look like what I remember seeing,' the constable said. *'His* hair is a ginger colour.'

Mr Lassiter said, 'I think you're right. I'd have said the dead – the resurrected man – was dark.'

One of the sons leaned forward. 'We're missing one corpse, one live body, and now we have a *third* man in an empty grave. This'll be the ruin of us.'

'How did he die?' the other son asked. 'Can you tell?'

'He was stabbed from the look of it,' Rutledge said. 'Only once, but it was enough.' He'd been squatting by the corpse, looking for identification, and he got to his feet. 'All right, let's get this body to the doctor.'

'But who is he?' the constable asked.

'I'd be willing to wager that this man is the one who put our live body into the coffin in Mr Fletcher's place. And he was killed for his trouble. Turn about.'

There had been nothing in the corpse's pockets except for a key, a handkerchief and a few pounds.

It wasn't until the next morning in Dr Blake's surgery that he saw the victim in the full light of day. Middle height, ginger hair, a heavy scar across his back, another down his left arm, and a third on his thigh.

'Cavalry?' Rutledge asked. 'He must have served in the war.'

'It's the knife between his ribs that killed him. Know him?'

'No. Do you?'

Blake shook his head. 'I attend the villagers and most of the outlying farms. He's not one of ours.' He pulled up the sheet again. 'There'll have to be an inquest.'

Rutledge went next to the firm of Lassiter and Sons, on Oak Street, not far from the inn. Mr Lassiter was busy polishing the brass fixtures of his hearse. He looked up as Rutledge came through and said, 'Any news?'

'Nothing. Does your firm serve only Merrow?'

Lassiter smiled wryly. 'Since the war we've taken on Lakehurst as well. The undertaker there never came back, and his father's dead of a broken heart.'

'Then someone from Lakehurst would know where to find Lassiter and Sons. Do you sleep on the premises?'

'We have a house down Primrose Lane. But surely someone would have seen any intruder coming here with a drugged body over his shoulder!'

Rutledge looked beyond the shed. 'There's an orchard on the far side of your garden. Is it part of the farm that backs up to the churchyard?'

'Yes, that's Mr Denholm's place. Closest thing we have to a squire, Mr Denholm is.'

'Then the intruder could have come that way,

unseen by anyone.'

'I don't think it's likely. Mr Denholm discourages trespassers.'

'This would have been sometime after midnight, when Denholm was asleep.'

'Still...' He brushed at a speck on the shining black body of the hearse.

'Do people generally lock their doors in Merrow – or Lakehurst?' Rutledge held a key out for Lassiter to examine. 'This was in the dead man's pocket.'

He peered at it. 'That looks very like the key to my back room. I keep it locked, you see. It's where we take the bodies. I don't want the village lads daring each other to step in and have a look. But if it's mine, what's become of the fob and chain?' He walked across to the door, tried the key in the lock, and it turned. 'Now how did the dead man come by that? And where's the rest of it?'

'A good question. Was the chain in the grave under the body?'

'No. My son had a good look around.'

He hurried to the small room that was his office. 'Look here – *that's* my extra key.' He held it up for Rutledge to see. 'Lassiter' was burned into the wooden fob. 'Where did yours come from?'

'Have you had any workmen in over the past several weeks?'

Lassiter frowned. 'Well, yes, Saturday the drains backed up. Simmons from Lakehurst came over on Monday...' He broke off. 'I let him have the extra key. We were burying Miss

314

Hamilton that morning. You don't think ... I've known Simmons for twenty years.'

But of course copies could be made. Rutledge thanked him, drove the five miles to Lakehurst and went in search of the plumber. Mr Simmons was out, according to his assistant, a gangly twenty-year-old.

Rutledge put the key down on the counter. 'Where could I get a copy made of this?'

The man stared at it. 'The ironmongers, I should think.'

'Is that where you had a copy made for one of your mates? It's the key to the rear door of the undertaker's firm.'

Flushing, the assistant said, 'I did no such thing.'

'But you know who ... er ... borrowed it. Don't you?'

He bit his lip. 'Mr Simmons put it right here Monday evening, when he'd come back from the Lassiters'. I saw it, then I went into the back room, and when I came out again, it was gone. I searched for it, but it was time to close. Then on Tuesday morning, I opened that drawer yonder, and there it was. I thought Mr Simmons had found it and put it away. He took it back to the undertaker's, finished his work, and left it there, the way he'd been told to do.'

'Who was in the shop that morning?'

Frowning, the assistant said, 'A few people. Mrs Perkins was here, as I remember. Mr Denholm's son about the drains in the dairy. And Harry Watkins, from the pub.'

'Describe Denholm's son. And Watkins.'

'Denholm is thin, dark hair. Watkins is heavy set with ginger hair. What does it matter?'

'Watkins was in the cavalry in the war?'

'No. That would be Mrs Perkins's son, Freddy. The lads are always begging him to show his scars. Come to think of it, he's got ginger hair. Like his grandfather.'

'Is there any hard feeling between Freddy Perkins and Denholm's son?'

'I doubt they've spoken three words to each other.'

'Any chance that Freddy Perkins came in to see his mother? While you were out of the room?'

'It's possible. But he's a day clerk at the hotel.'

Rutledge asked for directions to Mrs Perkins' house, and he found her in.

She couldn't understand at first why someone from Scotland Yard had come to her door. He simplified his morning by asking if he could speak to her son, who might have witnessed some trouble the day before in Merrow.

'I heard a frightful story about goings on in the church that morning. At a funeral! Is that why you're here? But Freddy couldn't have been in Merrow. He works at The Green Man Hotel.'

'How does he spend his evenings?'

'At home. Where else would he be?' Her tone was testy. 'He only walks out with Miss Carlson at the weekend. She stays with her grandmother during the week.'

'Where does her grandmother live?'

'At The Hall, in Larchwood. It's a village the far side of Merrow. Miss Carlson comes home at

316

the weekend to visit her mother. That's when her cousin Gerald looks after Mrs Carlson. Sometimes it falls to Freddy to take her there or bring her back.'

'Describe this cousin for me.'

'I've never met Mr Mowbray. He lives in Oxford and comes to the hall on the Friday, then travels back on Sunday.'

'Where is your son now?'

'At the hotel, of course.'

'Did he join you for dinner last night?'

'No, he was meeting someone, he said. He'd be late coming in. He was late the night before, come to think of it. But I saw him Tuesday morning at the plumber's.'

'And was he here at breakfast today?'

'He takes his breakfast at the hotel. It's more convenient, he says, and it isn't necessary to wake me.' She rose and went to the table by the window. 'Here's a photograph of my son with Miss Carlson.' The hand holding the frame was gnarled with rheumatism.

Rutledge looked down. Here indeed was the dead man. But this was not the time to break the news to his mother. He studied the two smiling young faces for a moment, then passed the photograph back to Mrs Perkins. 'Do you take anything?' he asked her. 'For your hands?'

'A little laudanum, when the weather is damp, and I can't sleep for the hurting.'

When Rutledge went to The Green Man, he found that Freddy had asked to leave early the evening before and hadn't returned.

He drove then to Larchwood and saw the hall

on the outskirts of the village. It was tall, brick, and set well back from the road behind formal gates. The house name was affixed to one of the brick pillars.

At the handsome portico, he lifted the knocker. A young woman opened the door to him. 'Miss Carlson? Inspector Rutledge, Scotland Yard. I'd like a few minutes of your time, if you please. I'm looking for a Frederick Perkins. I thought perhaps you'd seen him recently.'

'Freddy? Is anything wrong?' she asked anxiously. 'He brought me back to Larchwood Sunday afternoon. I don't expect to see him again until Friday evening, in Lakehurst.'

'I've just come from The Green Man. He wasn't at work this morning. I was told that he sometimes visits you here at the hall.'

She cast a glance over her shoulder as an elderly woman's voice called to her. 'It's something to do with Mr Perkins, Grandmamma.' To Rutledge she said, 'He never comes during the week. Is his mother ill? Is that why he wasn't at the hotel?'

'And your cousin Gerald? Does he come to the hall during the week?'

Colour rose up in her cheeks, making her eyes appear brighter. 'He stayed over on Monday. He ... he wanted to ask me to marry him.'

'Then he was still here on Sunday, when Mr Perkins brought you to the hall?'

'Yes. Freddy didn't stay. I think he must have realized why Gerald had waited for me.'

'Cousin Gerald went back to Oxford on Monday evening?'

'I expect so. I told him I'd think about my

answer. He ... he's a barrister in Oxford. Only a junior in chambers at present, but very highly regarded.'

'And your grandmother believes you'd be wise to accept him?'

The blush deepened. 'I don't see that it's any concern of yours,' she said, lifting her chin.

'Can you tell me where I can reach your cousin?'

Reluctantly Miss Carlson gave him the address, and Rutledge drove directly to Oxford. He'd gone to university there, and he liked the city. The noise and bustle of the streets, the timelessness of the colleges.

It was his duty to call on his opposite number first, but he needed only to speak to the chambers where Gerald Mowbray practised as a barrister. If he was there, then Rutledge could cross him off the list.

But he was not. No one had seen him since the previous Friday when he left to travel to the hall. Nor had the man sent round to his house Monday evening found anyone at home.

Rutledge thanked the clerk and left.

There was a connection between these two men. Was it Miss Carlson? Hamish pointed out that more than one man had killed for jealousy. 'And ye ken, Perkins was verra' clever – he didna' want the body to be found in Merrow. The police would be searching Oxford when yon barrister was reported missing.'

It was after dinner when Rutledge knocked at the door of the hall once more.

Miss Carlson was not happy to see him on the

319

doorstep again.

'Mrs Perkins told me you were walking out with her son.' Rutledge went directly to the point. 'Yet you're considering your cousin's proposal. Was Freddy Perkins jealous, do you think?'

'Freddy? We've known each other all our lives. We enjoy each other's company. It's Gerald I'm to marry. Besides, they'd never met before Sunday last.'

'Did they appear to like each other?'

'It was the oddest thing. Of course Freddy and Gerald knew about each other. How could they not? But when Freddy saw Gerald standing here in the drawing room, he stopped short and simply stared. Gerald looked as if he'd seen a ghost. And then they shook hands and talked for a few minutes. I thought perhaps I'd imagined it. Still, I asked Gerald later if anything was wrong, and he said there wasn't. He'd just been surprised that Freddy had ginger hair. He said I hadn't mentioned it before.'

It was a lame excuse for Gerald's reaction. But Miss Carlson appeared to accept it.

Hamish spoke in Rutledge's head. 'The war.'

'Did either man serve in France? Is it possible they knew each other there?'

'They were in France, yes, but I told you, they hadn't met until Sunday evening.'

Rutledge believed they had.

He had to travel back to Oxford to find a telephone, and there he put in a call to the War Office.

It was three hours later when his friend had the

320

information Rutledge needed.

'You're wrong. Perkins was a sapper, not cavalry. When his own officer was killed at Ypres, he served briefly under Mowbray. A matter of hours, to be precise.' He went on, adding the details.

'Are you quite sure about this?'

'Have I ever failed you?' The voice on the other end of the line retorted.

It was Thursday morning that Alexander Fletcher turned up. Someone reported crows behaving oddly in a far corner of the Denholm orchard. When the constable went to investigate, he found that in the night foxes or dogs had uncovered a shallow grave, and the crows had been attracted to Mr Fletcher's remains.

If Fletcher was accounted for, and Perkins as well, where was Mowbray?

He was, in fact, in his chambers in Oxford's Beaumont Street. Or so Rutledge discovered when he got there. Mr Mowbray, he was told, had been recovering from an intestinal complaint.

Rutledge didn't wait to be announced. He walked into the small room where his quarry was untying the pink ribbon around a set of instructions to counsel, and said, 'Gerald Mowbray? My name is Rutledge, Scotland Yard. I've come to ask what you can tell me about the death of Frederick Perkins.'

Mowbray smiled. 'I don't know anyone of that name.' He set the ribbon to one side and shoved the papers into a drawer.

'You recognized him when he stepped into Mrs

321

Carlson's drawing room on Sunday evening. A sapper. Like yourself. According to the War Office, you sent a young lieutenant into the tunnel when the fuse you laid failed to fire the charges. But it hadn't failed, had it? You'd measured it wrong, and Lieutenant Perkins was buried when the tunnel collapsed.' Mowbray opened his mouth, about to deny the accusation, but Rutledge lifted a hand. 'No. It's in the official record, I'm afraid. So is the fact that Lieutenant Perkins was in hospital for weeks afterward, recovering from wounds incurred while investigating a faulty charge.'

'Miss Carlson told me that Perkins was in the cavalry.'

'He preferred to let everyone think he was because of the scars across his body, where falling timbers had pinned him. I don't think he wanted to remember how he got them. Besides, you lived in Canterbury before the war. He never expected to find you in Oxford, much less proposing to Miss Carlson.'

'Do you know how many men there are by the name of Perkins? I—'

'Why did you meet again on Monday evening, before you went back to Oxford?'

'Did we?'

'You must have done. Did you look him up at The Green Man after you left Miss Carlson? To be sure? Only, Perkins managed to drug you and leave you to be buried alive – as he nearly was. Or at the very least, badly frightened to find yourself in a coffin. You were furious, and so you killed Perkins, and threw him into the grave intended for you. Mr Fletcher's grave. A key to the Lassiters' back room where the corpses were kept was in Perkins' pocket when he died. I think we'll find the ironmonger made it for him. A bit of luck, that key. It offered him a brilliant way of disposing of you.'

'I only went to see him because I'd thought he was the man who ruined my sister. A man named Perkins.'

'Perhaps that's what you thought in France. When you deliberately sent him in to check the fuse. But he was the wrong Perkins. The wrong man. Still, you knew when you went to the hotel which Perkins *this* was.'

'I can assure you, none of this is true. Miss Carlson will tell you I'd never seen this man before.'

'In fact, she realized that you did recognize each other. Your grandmother wants her to marry you. You were a better prospect for a Carlson than a lowly clerk. But she loved the lowly clerk, and when you're on trial for his murder she won't lie to protect you. She'll seal your doom.'

Mowbray rose. 'You have no proof of any of this farce. I can tell you from my professional experience that it won't fly.'

'I'm sure your grandmother has a photograph of you I can show to the staff at the hotel dining room.' Still, Mowbray was right, it would be a difficult case to prove. And so Rutledge took a leap into possibility. 'And the horses. A white one and a dark one were in the Denholm pasture Wednesday night. Yours and Perkins'? Before you took his back to its stable? You'd hidden the

323

saddles well. I didn't see them at first. Were you about to fill in the grave, when I walked into the churchyard and interrupted you? I have only to ask Mr Denholm if the mounts were his. Or Miss Carlson, who will know what you ride.'

And it worked.

Frowning, Mowbray said, 'He attacked me. It was self-defence. When he saw his attempt to kill me had failed, he came at me. We struggled. He drew a knife. And when we both went down, it ended up in his chest. There was nothing I could do. I heard someone coming – and I panicked. I threw his body into the grave.'

'But there were no signs of a struggle on Perkins' body. Your own face and hands are not bruised. A jury will wonder why you didn't go to the police after he'd drugged you – instead of deciding on revenge.'

'The police? I didn't want my head of chambers to hear about my humiliating experience. Foolish of me – but there you are.'

'Here we are, indeed. The inquest will most certainly find cause to bind you over for trial. Let's see what a jury makes of it. Gerald Mowbray, I'm arresting you for the murder of Frederick Perkins.'

THREESCORE AND TEN

Margaret Yorke

Margaret Yorke was a former Chair of the CWA who was a recipient of the CWA Cartier Diamond Dagger. After writing a number of romantic novels, she turned to crime fiction, with five books featuring Patrick Grant as an amateur detective. *No Medals for the Major* marked a turning point, and she established a reputation as an outstanding author of novels of psychological suspense. She died in 2012.

On the morning of her husband's seventieth birthday, a Thursday in September, Ellen Parsons rose as usual at seven o'clock. She went quietly into the bathroom, careful as she moved about not to disturb Maurice, who still slept, a straggle of grey hair falling across his pale, domed forehead.

After she had washed and cleaned her teeth, inserting her dentures, three stark molars on a pink plate, Ellen, in her woollen dressing-gown, went down to the kitchen and put on the kettle. While it boiled she laid the table in the dining room: blue-and-white Cornish crockery, honey and butter, on a linen cloth.

This was the last meal at which she would sit across the table from Maurice, and she hummed under her breath as she finished her early routine. When the kettle boiled, she made the tea and carried the tray upstairs, setting it on the table between their twin beds. After it had had time to stand, she poured out two cups, with two lumps of sugar in Maurice's. But nothing sweetened him.

'Tea, Maurice,' she said and took her own into the bathroom, where she dressed out of his sight.

Maurice did not reply, but she knew he would now sit up, yawn, showing his bare gums, belch, and drink his tea in gulps. She would return to the bedroom to do her hair in time to pour his second cup. When he was ready to rise, she would be downstairs cooking the bacon and egg he was able to eat daily without putting on weight.

She had decided to kill him one Sunday morning a year ago in church, hearing the words from Ecclesiastes: 'To every thing there is a season, and a time to every purpose under the heaven: a time to be born and a time to die...'

I have not lived yet, Ellen had thought.

Her mind ranged back over the years of her marriage to when she first met Maurice. Her father, a widower, had died after a long illness through which she had devotedly nursed him. Maurice, then junior partner in the firm of solicitors acting for her father, had called at the house to advise her. He had said she should decide nothing in haste and counselled her to keep the house for the present.

Ellen, weary from the strain of her father's illness, was glad to agree. She set about the neglected garden and washed curtains and paintwork indoors. Maurice watched both her and the house revive under this treatment. One day he brought her some violets – another time, a book of poetry. She looked forward to his visits; he had a sweet smile.

Soon she exchanged one form of bondage for another. She and Maurice, after their marriage, continued to live in the large old house on the edge of the village, and here they were still. Their only child, a daughter they named Priscilla, was born. Priscilla, against her father's wishes, had married a young farmer and the couple had at once emigrated to Australia. Priscilla wrote happy letters every fortnight and sent snapshots of her four children. She urged Ellen to come out for a visit and see her grandchildren, but Maurice wouldn't go himself and absolutely refused to permit Ellen to go without him.

Maurice required his life to be organised smoothly. The smile that had once charmed Ellen was seen rarely after marriage. He insisted that meals be punctual to the second. A small girl should be seen and not heard. Arguments were not allowed. And only Maurice's opinions might be expressed.

He controlled the money Ellen inherited from her father, allowing her small amounts for her personal needs. During their short engagement Ellen had anticipated long talks with him such as she had enjoyed with her father, and discussions about books they might both enjoy – Dickens and Trollope – but Maurice read only legal tomes and the biographies of the eminent. He enjoyed silence.

Priscilla, as a child, was allowed no parties, and her friends were not encouraged to visit the house, though Ellen was able to welcome them while Maurice was at the office. Later, as Priscilla grew older, if any dared to enter the house while he was there, they were subjected to such an interrogation about their lives and views that few risked a second encounter. It was not surprising that Priscilla escaped as soon as she could. The only guests Maurice invited were business acquaintances he took to his study for brandy. Once a year his partners and their wives came to dinner.

Ellen's fragile links with other people grew weaker after Maurice retired. If she invited anyone to tea he would sit scowling and looking at his watch, finally leaving the room with some remark like, 'See that dinner's on time, Ellen,' and thereby humiliating her.

But now all this would end. The resentment that had simmered for so long had at last boiled over. The house was hers and all the money – both what she had inherited and what Maurice had made – would be hers too.

The days of our age are threescore years and ten...

Ellen had read the words, many times. Maurice had now ended his seventieth year: she had made her plans and at last the time had come to carry them out.

The post that morning brought nothing from

Priscilla. She had never yet forgotten her father's birthday: something must be on the way. What a pity Maurice would not now receive the card, Ellen thought, buttering her toast.

She gave him her own present when he had finished *The Times* leader, a thick woollen dressing-gown. She had bought it with Ben, the jobbing gardener, in mind, for Maurice would never wear it. Maurice thanked her without enthusiasm, saying he would have preferred camel colour to maroon. Ellen knew that cheerful Ben would like the maroon better.

Breakfast over, Maurice went to his study and Ellen set about her chores. After she had made the beds and tidied round, she went into the garden and cut three large marrows: they would get hard and woody if left on the plants and Maurice had pointed them out to her the day before. She carried them into the house and down the flight of stairs leading to the cellar. The door was locked and bolted. Taking the key from a hook beside the door, Ellen unlocked it and laid the marrows on a stone ledge inside. Strings of onions already hung on the walls but otherwise the cellar was quite bare. It was dark, lit only by a tiny window high on one wall.

The marrows deposited, Ellen left the cellar. She closed the door, which opened outwards, but did not lock it.

Now it was time to prepare for her weekly shopping expedition. Every Thursday she made the trip into town, her one outing in the car, for Maurice decreed that once a week was sufficient. She backed the car out of the garage until the corner of the rear bumper and the exhaust pipe were exactly opposite the cellar window which, seen from outside the house, was a narrow slit a few inches above the ground, the glass protected by chicken wire which was now rotten with age. There was a blackened area, caused by exhaust fumes, on the brickwork around the window for the car was always reversed into this position.

But today Ellen reversed too far and broke the window. She smiled as she switched off the engine and uttered a shriek.

Maurice had heard the crash. He came storming out of the house to inspect the damage. The corner of the bumper had gone straight through the rotten wire and the glass; Ellen had practised the manoeuvre until she could have done it blindfold. She stood wringing her hands and apologising meekly while being scolded. If Maurice had not heard the impact, she would have found him to confess, for, as she knew he would, he immediately went to discover what had happened in the cellar, into which most of the glass had fallen. She followed him.

Automatically he reached for the key and found it missing from the hook.

'You've been down here this morning, Ellen,' he accused.

'Yes, Maurice, I brought those three marrows in. You told me to cut them.'

'You didn't lock the door. How many times must I tell you everything?' he exclaimed, opening the door and striding angrily inside.

Ellen had never seen the point of locking the cellar, but now she was glad it was one of

Maurice's rules. In an instant she had slammed the heavy, close-fitting door behind him, turned the key, and thrust the bolt across.

For a moment she leaned against it, panting, her heart pounding. It had been easy! She had spent hours devising the perfect scheme, thinking of first one plan and then another. Now she could truthfully say, when she was questioned, that she had forgotten to lock the cellar door after taking in the marrows and had returned to do it. How could she have known Maurice was in there?

She hurried up the stairs before he had time to begin beating upon the door. In a few minutes she had started the engine of the car, reversed it still closer to the wall so that the exhaust was tight against the broken cellar window, and left it to run, leaving the choke well out. Maurice always insisted she warm the car up thoroughly before driving away. The rich mixture filling the cellar with fumes would make Maurice unconscious very quickly. A mere five minutes in a closed garage with a large car could prove fatal, she had discovered during her research in the public library, and Maurice was due for a much longer diet of fumes from their medium-sized vehicle.

She left the car and walked away, for there were sounds coming from the cellar, shouts and cries, and she could not stay to listen. There was nothing Maurice could stand on to reach the window far above his head. He would go to the door, but he would not be able to break it open.

Ellen went into the house and fetched a bottle

of water. She returned to the car, not hurrying, opened the bonnet and topped up the windscreen washer, concentrating on the task, ignoring the cellar.

There was no sound now apart from the car's engine, which was beginning to run unevenly as it warmed up. She pushed in the choke and, the windscreen washer dealt with, she closed the garage. Maurice would never allow it to be left open when the car was out for fear of passing thieves, although it was behind the house and couldn't be seen from the road. Then she went into the house. She could scarcely hear the car now, its engine purred so sweetly.

She went to her sewing-box and took from it the wad of leaflets about travelling to Australia hidden there for weeks under her tapestry. How would she go? By boat, she thought: a large and luxurious liner which would call at exotic ports on the way, and first-class, of course. No one came to the door while she turned the pages of the brochures. The only regular callers were the milkman and the postman, and on Tuesdays the cleaning woman. Few door-to-door salesmen bothered to come to the isolated house at the end of the village. Occasionally she rose to listen to the car. It still ran, not stalling. At last she decided she had waited long enough and she went out to it.

It had got rather hot and the temperature of the water showed high on the gauge. Ellen moved the car forward. She laid a sheet of slate that normally covered the kitchen drain against the broken windowpane to keep the fumes inside.

No sound came from the cellar.

Then she drove to town and did her shopping.

When she returned more than an hour later, Ellen removed the slate and replaced it over the drain. She backed the car up to the window again and left the engine running while she unloaded her shopping. Finally she opened the garage doors and drove the car inside.

It was now time to prepare lunch, and for once it would not matter if the meal was late. How wasteful, she reflected, peeling Maurice's usual two medium-sized potatoes and slicing runner beans fresh from the garden. She had made his favourite pudding, crème caramel, the day before: a birthday treat. She put the grill on for the chops.

Soon she would have to start looking for him. She could spend some time searching the house and garden and then go into the village to inquire if anyone had seen him. She needn't think about the cellar until later, much later. Perhaps she need not think of it at all, until she told the police he was missing. That was the part she dreaded: finding him. But by then he would have been dead for a long time: most certainly by now he had been dead for hours. He would not have suffered for long, but his hands might be torn and bruised if he had clawed at the cellar door.

She dished up the meal and put it in the slow oven. Then she went upstairs to wash and do her hair before calling him, as she always did.

She didn't see the sleepy wasp among the bristles of her tortoiseshell hairbrush as she raised it to her head. She felt only the sharp, searing stab of the sting above her temple.

Ellen grew giddy almost at once. Three years ago she had been stung on her arm, fainted, and recovered only because Maurice had been there, seen her cyanosed face, and called the doctor instantly.

This time, he could not save her.